A Reckless Memory

CROCUS VALLEY, BOOK 1

MARIE JOHNSTON

LE PUBLISHING

I fled minutes before my wedding when I learned my fiancé had been paid to marry me. Ten years, too many crappy exes, and one drunken decision later, I'm now his boss.

A night out with a friend turned into shots and duping an old ex of mine into taking a job at my budding horse rescue.

The last time Ansen Barron saw me, I was fishtailing away from our wedding with his dog. When he arrives, I expect him to reverse right back down my driveway after he learns I'm his boss.

I don't expect to find a jaded man in the place of the easygoing guy I was once engaged to. I also don't expect my heart to race when he's around.

Or for him to treat me like I always meant more to him than a payday.

I don't regret hiring him. He's the best man for the job, and he's trying to prove he's changed, one melting kiss at a time.

But no matter how hot we are together, I can't forget I once thought he was the best man for me and maybe it's safer for my heart if he stays a reckless memory.

For my readers. I couldn't do this without you.

For new release updates, chapter sneak peeks, and exclusive quarterly short stories, sign up for Marie's newsletter.

One

AGGIE

I hitched up the hem of the sleek white skirt on my bridal gown and admired the white, sparkly cowboy boots on my feet. My sophisticated sister-in-law, Meg, winced every time she got a glimpse of the boots under my dress, but I wasn't a heels-and-skirt gal like her. I could jump on a horse and ride into the sunset—after I married the man of my dreams. The heels Meg helped me pick out were sitting by the mirror, but I was saving my toes for dancing.

From the corner of my eye, I saw Tex's tail thump, his gaze riveted on the swirling material. "Tex, stay."

The one-year-old Australian shepherd whined and went back to trying to free the salmon treat from his red Kong toy. My soon-to-be husband's precocious puppy was being restricted from all the guests. We were keeping him in the house lest he try to herd half the population of Buffalo Gully while they mingled in the backyard.

"Can't we put him in the garage?" Meg whined, fussing

with my wild curls. She'd moussed and sprayed them into submission. With her standing behind me, it was hard not to compare us. Me, the scrawny cowgirl. Meg, the classy lawyer who married my oldest brother. Even all lotioned up, my skin didn't shine like Meg's. Her glossy mahogany hair probably wound itself into the twist behind her head. Her nails pinching my scalp around the base of my bun were pretty razors.

"He'll be fine." I gave Tex a stern look before switching my attention to the mirror and my plain nails.

Meg let out a final huff and peered at my face. "Are you sure you don't want a touch of foundation to cover the freckles?"

Sutton Grant, a future sister-in-law, scooted behind me and put her hands on my shoulders, rubbing them. Her wheat-blonde hair was pulled to the top of her head like a messy crown that matched the vibe of my outdoor wedding. I'd rather be more casual like her.

"She wouldn't be Aggie without freckles." She grinned at me in the glass. "You look great."

"Freckles make it harder for men to take women seriously," Meg said in her imperious tone. She reminded me of Mama, and I soaked up a lot of what she said, but having Sutton stand up with me at my wedding gave me breathing room I didn't know I needed when Meg was around.

I compromised with Meg when she helped me plan the wedding. She'd been beside herself when Daddy insisted— ordered—the wedding be on the ranch. I mollified her by choosing the fitted dress with a high neck and sleeves that covered the majority of the freckles sprinkled over my shoulders. Mama would've loved this dress. She'd have gushed about it right before she repeated all her dire warnings about making sure I wasn't anchored to anyone, much less one man.

It was the man that mattered. And we were going to be partners. Ansen Barron. Horse trainer. Country boy. Hot cowboy. My fiancé. Ansen had been hired to break and saddle train Daddy's Arabians a year and a half ago. When I saw him swing down from a horse only Mama had been able to ride before she abandoned us, I was lost. It took him a while to notice me, but I blamed my four older brothers for that.

"Almost time," Sutton whispered. Delicious nerves fluttered in my stomach.

Meg stepped away and scrolled through her phone. She dropped to sit primly on the edge of the upholstered chair in my bedroom. I studied her moves. I'd have to be careful sitting in this dress. The dresses she and Sutton wore were a similar style to my wedding gown but in a dusty blue. I hadn't cared but had defaulted to Meg's knowledge. The color reminded me of the sky on a hazy fall morning.

I feathered my hands over my hair. No longer frizzy or wild. I almost didn't recognize myself. I couldn't wait until Ansen saw me.

"I'm nervous," I admitted. "Today doesn't feel real."

"You're telling me," Meg said on a gusty breath. "I told Alcott the other day it was like you were just in high school. Because you were. You're barely drinking age." She rarely called my brother Cody like the rest of us, and she was almost ten years older than me, so I would always seem like a baby to her.

"Twenty-one and twenty-three isn't bad," I said. "We're adults, and we'll have our own place. Our own business."

Meg made a grunt that managed to sound ladylike.

I went to my jewelry box and dug out the silver horseshoe earrings my youngest brother, Eliot, gave me for Christmas. My 4-H ribbons lined the wall behind the dresser. Meg thought they were childish, but I liked the proof of my accomplishments. Back at the mirror, I tipped my head to put the earrings on. I'd have to remember to take them out before the wedding night. My ears got angry red if I wore jewelry too long, and once Ansen put his hands on me, I didn't think about anything but him.

"Make sure you build far from the ranch," Meg muttered and turned her attention back to her phone. Knowing what my brother saw in her was easy—she was gorgeous, intelligent, and classy. Not the usual woman you met in a small town in the middle of nowhere, in eastern Montana, where there were more cattle than people. He'd met her at college in Missoula.

I squinted into the mirror. Tex had wiggled along the floor to chew on the leg of the dresser. "No, Tex." He stopped, and I went to get him a treat from the top of my dresser.

"That dog would gnaw the foundation from the house given the chance." Sutton dropped to her knees next to Tex, heedless of getting wrinkles in her dress or slobber by-products on the material.

"Sutton, your dress," Meg hissed.

Sutton ignored Meg's abject horror. I handed Sutton the bag of treats to reload the toy, hoping we could keep Tex distracted until after the majority of people were gone.

"Such a good boy," she crooned as she redirected his attention away from the wood. She emptied the treat bag into the toy.

If we were going to make it through this ceremony without the sounds of barking filling the house, we'd need more goodies and another chew toy—or five. Tex was a smart dog, but all the strangers overwhelmed his youthful senses. "I have to grab another bag."

Sensing I was leaving, Tex crossed to me, and I sank my fingers into his thick coat. Sutton brushed strands of white and brown fur off her dress. Meg was unsuccessfully smothering her horrified expression that we even let the dog in the room.

"I can find some," Sutton offered.

"I had to hide them in the top of the hallway closet, or he'd sniff them out. I'll go." I could walk off some nervous energy.

"You can turn up the AC while you're getting them," Meg said, her attention back on her phone. "You're going to walk out of here looking like last year's beets if I don't drop the temperature."

I didn't turn that red when I was warm. "I'll try. Daddy might let me get away with tampering with the AC on my wedding day."

We were oil rich, thanks to the wells scattering our land, and the ranch did okay. As if Daddy would tell anyone otherwise. He didn't believe in spending money unless it was on prime horseflesh and training those horses to bring in even more money.

"Are you sure?" Sutton rubbed at a drool spot on her skirt with her finger. She was almost done with vet school, and animal body fluids didn't faze her. "I don't want the groom to see you before it's time."

"He's probably out chatting with the guests." Ansen could work a crowd as well as he could our Arabians.

I started for the door, but Tex was hot on my heels, ready to go where I went. He was Ansen's dog, but with Ansen working all day in the ring and me finding my way without getting in my brothers' way, I spent more time with the dog. "Tex, stay."

Sutton called him back into the bedroom, and the thought of treats and some scratches was enough to redirect his attention.

I walked out, running my hands over the bookshelf that

held my mother's books as I went. Like my brothers, I was named after one of her favorite female authors.

Agatha Christie Knight. Aggie for short. Aggie Barron in less than an hour.

Tomorrow, after I woke up in my husband's arms, I'd come to my room and pack the rest of my things, including my mother's much-loved copy of Agatha Christie's *Murder on the Orient Express*. They were all I had of her. I had briefly entertained tucking a book into my bouquet so I'd feel like she was with me on my special day, but I didn't want them to get damaged.

Stepping on the balls of my feet to keep my boots from thudding across the hand-scraped wood flooring, I padded across the expansive living room no one but Daddy used. I almost expected to find him sitting in his leather Chesterfield, gazing out the window at our acres and acres of land, pastures filled with cattle or dotted with oil wells, sipping on his whiskey neat and smoking one of his Foundation cigars. But the room was empty.

Through the large picture windows filling one side of the room, I could see the yard. Rows of chairs were neatly arranged, and people roamed around, forming small, intimate groups. The ceremony didn't start for twenty minutes. Cody was the master organizer, but I couldn't pick him out in the huddle of my other brothers.

On the other side of the house, I turned down another hallway that housed Daddy's bedroom and two more rooms that had been converted to offices. He'd probably start renovations to make my room another office as soon as the cake was cut today.

Voices drifted from the office Cody used to crunch numbers for the ranch. Cody was probably doing some quick paperwork. He was as much of a workaholic as his wife. Who would he be talking to though? I crept closer, not wanting to interrupt what seemed like a heated conversation, but the thermostat was outside the office door.

"I don't know where you're coming up with this wild story." Ansen's deep tone rumbled right down to my bare toes. I would've smiled, but there was a thread of panic in his voice.

"Show me the balance in your account," Cody said, his calm a facade. My normally uptight brother's voice was downright menacing. "I know you can't afford the truck you're driving on a horse trainer's wages, and I've researched where you came from. Your father ranches dirt." There was a loaded pause. "Is Barns paying you more after you say 'I do'?"

My brothers all called our daddy Barns—Barnaby Knight. I frowned, the nerves in my stomach morphing into a low-grade burn. Daddy, money, and my fiancé. Cody's tone set off alarm bells.

"I don't have to show you a damn thing," Ansen said, his slight drawl more pronounced. That only happened when he was angry.

A wash of cold cascaded over my head, filtering down to my chest and abdomen. What extra money was Daddy paying Ansen? Why after we got married?

"You know I have to go to Aggie with this before she walks down the aisle," Cody said.

I drew in a sharp breath. I didn't know what was going on, but I was sure as heck going to find out. I stepped into the doorway. "Tell me what?"

Ansen spun his head in my direction, and the look in his eyes skewered me. Fear.

"Tell me what, Ansen?" I couldn't take my gaze off of him. I could be surrounded by the entire town in puppet costumes, but I wouldn't have noticed. My attention was fixed on the most handsome man I'd ever seen. His shoulders were wide—and strong enough to pick me up and toss me over one. The wind-swept, rich-brown hair pushed off his forehead didn't have its usual cowboy hat indentation, and without the hat, I could stare into the bay-colored depths of his eyes. His lanky but muscular frame was outfitted in a classic black tux, which he'd argued about with Meg, and a crisp white shirt. The look was topped off with a brand-new pair of shiny black boots.

My chest ached. He was so damn handsome. The only person I'd met I could be myself around—avid horse girl, dirty ranch kid, and wanton woman in the bedroom.

But he was hiding something. Cody didn't get upset for no reason.

Ansen didn't answer. His Adam's apple worked up and down. I'd never seen him like this. A dark, unruly storm cloud descended over my sunny day.

"Tell. Me. What. Ansen?" My voice trembled. Today was supposed to be the best of my life. A turning point. A way to prove to everyone I was worth something to someone.

"It's nothing but lies." Ansen's voice broke on the last word.

The back of my throat burned. "What is?"

I finally glanced at Cody. His jaw was set, but I didn't miss the regret in his gaze when he looked at me. "I was always suspicious of Barron's interest in you. Then I found swaths of missing money and did some digging."

"You did some digging," I echoed. Because he wondered, like everyone in town, if my family's money was the only reason a handsome charmer like Ansen would be interested in the only daughter of crusty Barnaby Knight. I pretended to be oblivious, but I heard the whispers at the grocery store and during dart nights at the bar.

That Knight girl doesn't pay one ounce of attention to her looks, while Ansen Barron can flirt the halo off an angel.

"Barns is paying him to marry you," Cody announced.

I barked out a laugh. "Come on, Cody. We don't do dowries these days. It's not like Mama's books."

"Cody," Daddy's pack-a-day-roughened growl broke in, and I jumped. For a large, imposing man, he moved quietly. I pressed against the doorframe, but he stayed in the hallway and faced the room, sandwiching me in the middle of the conflict. "Why the hell are you bringing this up?"

My brother straightened the coat of his tux, back to being the unflappable brother. "Aggie deserves to marry a guy who loves her, not one who's being bought by you."

My groom was being paid off? I tried to laugh again, but Ansen's ashen face robbed me of air. *No.*

Horrible realizations clicked into place. The way he suddenly made me feel like the only woman on earth after he'd already been working for Daddy for six months. He'd looked right through me, then, one day, I was all he saw. He'd seamlessly swept me off my feet, and it had felt like a country fairy tale. Instead, I might as well be on an episode of *Yellowstone*. "Ansen?"

"Aggie, listen—"

"For fuck's sake, girl," Daddy broke in. "You want to marry him or not?"

"Not if he's being *paid*." My breathing quickened, and I gripped the skirt of my dress, crushing the unblemished satin. I was probably leaving prints with my sweaty hands, but the sinking sensation in my stomach suggested it might not matter.

Mama's voice rang in my ears. She'd abandoned the ranch and my brothers quit talking to her, but I never did. Months before she died, she was still giving me warnings.

Never let a man influence your future, Aggie. Listen to me. Never give them power over you. They're selfish creatures.

"Aggie . . ." Ansen hooked a hand on his hip. I knew that stance. It was his *how do I pass on bad news* pose. He did the same when he had to tell Daddy a horse that could've brought in tens of thousands of dollars had a personality trait that made it unlikely to succeed in the competition rings.

It was true. All of it. Heat wicked up the back of my neck, and that burn in my stomach cranked up another ten notches. "How much?"

His jaw clenched, and his gaze dropped to the floor. "It doesn't matter. It'll be our money once we're married."

"She's got enough," Daddy grumped, ever bitter that Mama left me the life insurance money that sat untouched in my account instead of splitting it among me and my brothers.

If something happens to me, she'd told me once, *I want you to have it. Money buys freedom, and Barnaby will use his funds to take that freedom away from you.*

My insides were splintering apart. It was amazing I wasn't seeing double. Triple. Like the room wasn't a kaleidoscope. "You want to marry me for how much?"

He didn't answer, his attention still on the floor.

"So it was all a lie?"

His gaze shot up, his jaw set. "No. I'm not a liar."

"Well, you aren't telling the truth!" My world shattered, inside and out. I'd been devastated when Mama left and again when she died, but I wasn't destroyed and betrayed like I was now.

My chest tightened, and my brain circled like wheels in a mud pit. Ansen first asked me out after I told Daddy I was going to move to Bozeman. I wasn't so much interested in college as in getting Daddy to let me be a bigger part of

Knight's Arabians and Cattle Company. I thought he'd compromised since he wanted me to stay at the ranch, but I had Mama's money. I could call his bluff, and I could actually go to school if needed.

Instead, he'd found a way to keep me on Knight land. Ansen had so many convenient plans. "I'm . . . I almost . . . I stayed in Buffalo Gully for you. So we could train horses and build a business together."

"And you'd be close to home," Daddy finished. "I did what I thought was best for you." He glared at Cody, but my brother was unrepentant.

"By selling me off? Like I couldn't get a husband on my own?" Humiliation seared hot in my blood. As soon as I'd seen Ansen, I'd written him off as unattainable. Guys like him with panty-melting grins and bodies built for sin weren't interested in plain girls like me wearing their old 4-H T-shirts, plain Wranglers, and high-quality but well-worn cowboy boots. Then he'd smiled at me, and it was like the wildflowers grew in our pastures just for him to pick and give to me.

Daddy's scornful chuckle shifted something inside me. Something I wasn't sure would ever fit back into place. "Agatha, please. You're needed around here, and school would be a waste of your time and your mama's money. I can teach you anything you need."

Only he hadn't. He'd spent time with my brothers. Made their lives hell and left me to run like a wild pony. As an adult, my brothers didn't think I was capable of doing more than chores on the ranch. I wasn't allowed to break the horses, and when we worked cattle, they put me on Mathilda, my old reliable horse, at the back. I didn't get to do the vaccinations, the records, the branding, or anything where I might get in the way. My plans with Ansen were a way to be a part of something. To give myself control.

I stared at Ansen. His gaze was stuck on the floor, at my feet, in front of the white, sparkly boots I bought just to wear for our first dance together. The girliest thing I'd ever owned.

He finally lifted his gaze to meet mine, and all my hopes and plans withered like a fallen leaf in fall. There would be no cozy little cabin home. No horse-training business run by the two of us. No blueprints for a bigger home on family land that'd house all the kids I'd planned to have. Nothing but humiliation.

I stepped farther into the hallway. Daddy caught my elbow. "Come on now. Don't be dramatic. I wanted you taken care of."

Men will say it's to take care of you. Now I understood what Mama had been telling me and why she'd had to leave. "This is the wrong way to do it."

Without looking at Ansen again, I picked up the skirt of my dress, circled around Daddy, and ran for my bedroom like a fairy-tale princess fleeing a dragon.

"Aggie." Ansen's long strides caught up to me by the time I stormed into my bedroom.

Tex barked at the commotion. Sutton was standing next to him, her eyes wide. Meg's attention was finally off her phone, her expression just as startled as Sutton's.

"Aggie, dammit," Ansen said, his volume louder than I'd ever heard. He never raised his voice at me, unlike Daddy. "We need to talk."

"I've heard enough."

"Yeah, he offered me money, but I thought we'd use it to start our lives."

I spun on him, and he backed up a step. "Then why didn't you tell me?"

That strong jaw of his clenched again. Chasing me had

knocked a hunk of hair out of place and it hung over his forehead, shading his eyes.

Cody appeared in the doorway. I was determined to have a warmer relationship with my husband than my brother and his wife had, but right now the look they shared and the way she stood and cupped Sutton's elbow in silent communication that they should leave filled me with envy. I thought I had at least that level of understanding with Ansen.

I didn't know him at all.

"Because I knew how it'd look," he said.

I flung my arms out and yelled, "Like you're being paid to marry me?" One of my hands hit the shelves behind me and books thudded to the floor, but I had other things to worry about. Like the deceitful bastard in front of me.

"Come on—"

"Don't 'come on' me one more time, slick." My chest was heaving. I lost my fiancé. I hurt so damn bad I wasn't sure if I'd pulled every muscle in my body when I'd fled the office. "If you have one fleck of respect for me, you'll go out there and tell everyone what you did and that the wedding is off, so I don't have to face anyone."

I didn't want to see Daddy's face or hear his voice for a long time. Looking Cody in the eye would only remind me of my humiliation. I had secretly gloated about inviting those who'd whispered about the unlikelihood that someone like Ansen would want me. They could see for themselves he only had eyes for me. But they'd seen his pupils were dollar signs, and I was the only one who hadn't had a clue. My pride had bitten me in the ass faster than a startled rattlesnake.

"I can't—can't we talk for a minute?" He stuffed a hand through his hair, and it all fell over his forehead. The young, carefree guy I thought I'd spend my life with was really a duplicitous charmer who wanted to use me. To trap me so he could reach my family's money. A knot hardened inside of me. Everyone in town was right. They saw what I hadn't.

I couldn't be that naive again. "No matter what, the wedding's not happening. If you have any feelings for me, know that I never want to see you again. I never want to speak to you again."

"It was a lot of money, Aggie. Life-changing money."

"*My* life wasn't changing."

"Goddammit," he said harshly. "You have *everything*. You've always had everything. You grew up with a silver pitchfork in your hand. You don't know what it's like to come from nothing, to struggle every damn day, to watch your family ranch be taken over, to barely earn enough to buy a new pair of jeans, then be offered that much money."

"No. I don't. But I hope I'd have enough heart that I wouldn't use an innocent girl's emotions to get it."

"You're not innocent!" Bitterness dripped off his words. "You mistake nice and young for innocent. You step on people around town as much as the rest of your family. *Thy Knight's will be done.*"

I jerked at his use of the town's common mockery. My anger was like a whip snap. "Stop it."

"What? Is spoiled little Aggie Knight not used to hearing the truth?"

"I'm not spoiled."

"Says the girl with two fucking horses that cost more than a house in town. Says the girl who drives a brand-new Chevy Silverado. Says the girl who has hundreds of thousands in the bank and complained that her daddy wasn't paying for college."

Hurt closed off my throat. He was right, but he was also wrong. I thought he understood, that someone finally understood. Daddy was willing to pay for all four brothers' college if they wanted to go, but he'd never offered the same for me. "I didn't complain about paying for college." Ansen lifted his brow like *really?* "I was hurt."

"You get everything you want, and you think I'm a lying fake because I took some money to date a girl?"

"To marry me."

He flung a hand out. "We would've been fine together."

Fine. Wasn't that what a girl wanted to hear from the man she'd fallen head over boots for?

He hadn't professed his love, and I thought it was a manly thing, that I'd hear those words today. A deep burn ignited in my chest right next to my heart. I was so stupid. "You've never told me you loved me."

His hostility drained away. "Aggie."

I shook my head. "Leave."

"No, we're finally talking like two real people."

"*I've* always been real. *I'm* not the one who lied. You say I've always gotten what I wanted, but you used your charm and looks to get you just as far. No one can say I had that." All the comments from everyone over the years resounded in my head. *Not a beauty like her mother. Doesn't she know what a brush is? Poor thing . . . could use a woman's touch.* "One day, Ansen, I hope you know what it's like to have your entire heart ripped out, to have your passion stripped down and be humiliated in front of witnesses. To lose everything after you already gave up so much because you thought you were going to be happy." I straightened like I had a fence post lining my spine. "Now leave."

A ripping sound at my feet made me look down. My wail was as much about the horror I found as my broken heart. "Mama's books! Tex. *No.*" Tears that had been too shocked and outraged to flow before suddenly came cascading like a June rain down my cheeks. "No."

I dropped to my knees. Tex's tongue lolled out and he

panted, but in his eyes was more concern for me than I had seen in my fiancé's.

"No," I whispered, my vision blurry. I didn't care about Mama's life insurance. These books were like having a piece of her with me, and now they were shredded and full of slobber.

"Oh, shit, Aggie. I'm sorry." Ansen moved like he was going to kneel.

"Go!" I screamed, hugging the broken books to my chest. *Murder on the Orient Express* had taken the worst damage. Mama had read me this book before bed in the months before she walked out.

The low growl from Tex finally got Ansen to back up. Worry lined his face, but he made a frustrated sound. "This isn't over between us." He spun on his heel and walked out.

My breaths shuddered in and out as I cleaned up the mess. I dumped it all on my bed and stared at it. A couple of covers had been separated and chewed. Loose papers with jagged tears. Crooked spines. The books were ruined, like me.

Ansen would likely tell everyone how I'd handled the news. I didn't dare dwell on how many suspected this wedding to be a farce. Daddy would find me and try to talk sense into me. I was being *dramatic*.

If he saw me now, he'd say, *Too much like your damn mother.*

"I need to go." In a flurry, I rushed around my room. I didn't change but grabbed my suitcase and stuffed random clothing inside. Once I latched my luggage closed, riding high on determination, I stared at the destroyed books on my bed. I yanked my ring off and tossed it on the pile too.

When I turned, Tex was right behind me, his head cocked. I sank my fingers into his soft fur one last time and scratched around the leather collar with his name and

Ansen's phone number stitched in. "I'll miss you, Tex. You can chew up his favorite pair of boots for me."

I yanked up my suitcase and left the bedroom. Tex's claws clicked behind me. "Stay," I said over my shoulder, but it was no use. I didn't have any treats to entice him. He could follow me to the pickup, and I'd leave him behind then.

I went through the laundry room that was on my side of the house, hoping no one had yet had time to come looking for me. The space attached the house to the garage, and I snuck through the garage and out the other side, where the pickup Cody bought me for high school graduation sat. I opened the back door, tossed my luggage in, and Tex jumped inside.

"No, Tex. Out."

He tilted his head, and his tail thumped against the seat.

"Tex." Raised male voices turned to shouts behind the house. Panic galloped through my veins. My brothers were yelling, probably at Ansen. They'd never confront Daddy. He was the power, and we were tools to carry out his bidding. I didn't want to get in the middle any more than I was.

I gave Tex one last look. "Out."

He glanced past me, then met my gaze again, his tail wagging. Dogs didn't lie about their feelings. He wanted to come with me, and I needed to leave. Looked like I had myself a new dog. I got behind the wheel, still wearing my wedding dress.

I took off just as Cody rounded the house, his expression shocked, for once not a mask of professional competence. Ansen charged past him like he was going to run down the truck. I floored it. Gravel spit out from the tires and the back end fishtailed. Tex almost lost his balance and fell off the seat, but I held on and kept control. I was nothing if not a country girl. Only now, I'd make sure I was more.

Ansen skidded to a stop in my rearview mirror. He shoved his hands through his hair and his suit coat lifted, the whole stance making him look more handsome than ever. A heartbreaker.

I blinked back tears. No more crying. I had a new future to plan for. What I saw in the mirror was my past.

Two

AGGIE

Ten years later...

I took another shot and thunked the glass on the counter. Fireball burned my throat like it could incinerate the memories pounding at my brain. The din in the bar added to the assault, reminding me who I used to come here with. A man I had steadfastly and resolutely forgotten. Mostly.

I was home for Meg's funeral. A short bout with brain cancer and she was gone, leaving Cody a widower and a single dad to my niece and nephew. Loss didn't fill me as much as I thought it would. She'd put less effort into building a relationship with me once I had left, but I worried for Cody. He was understandably quieter than normal. Somehow he had gotten more uptight with age, and grief had added a rigidity I hadn't expected.

In the last week, I'd tried to spend time with him, but he

politely dismissed me, citing work he needed to catch up on. Meg's parents doted on the kids and practically strong-armed everyone out of the room.

The night out with Sutton was a welcome break even though I was staying with her and her husband, Wilder, my second oldest brother. She understood my conflicted feelings about Meg. Hers were the same. Just like she knew why I wouldn't go home to the ranch if I didn't have to.

"He did not say that," Sutton wheezed. She'd just taken her own shot. It was our second each.

"His exact words were, 'I thought you'd warm up, but you're cold and uncaring, and it doesn't bother you your dog hates me.'"

Sutton snorted and dropped her head into her hands. "I always knew Tex was the goodest boy."

I grinned, but my smile quickly faded as I recalled the familiar words my ex, Lawson, threw at me. *Cold* and *emotionless* had been just the beginning. The description echoed what my boyfriend before him had said. But neither of them had called me a spoiled princess like the other guy—the one I didn't remember. Mostly.

Lawson had pressured me to mend the bridge between me and Daddy. He probably thought I'd soften if I made peace with Daddy. I'd given in a few times and called home. It hadn't gone well. Lawson assumed I was the issue.

I poured another shot, having bought a half-full bottle from the seventy-five-year-old bartender who called me Birdie —my mother's name. "He said I made him feel *unneeded*."

Sutton groaned and slid her glass over. "Men can be so clingy." I filled her glass and pushed it back. She lifted it and studied the amber liquid in the neon bar sign across from us. "Except for your brother," she muttered and downed the liquid.

I followed suit, not knowing what to say.

Between the funeral and my recent breakup, me and the bottle of cinnamon-flavored hell in front of me were destined to have a long night together. My third oldest brother, Austen, had taken leave from the army and was staying with Cody, but he spent a lot of time on the ranch with my youngest brother, Eliot. Wilder was out there too. My irrational fear that I'd get sucked back into the house that had been a posh yet rustic prison was too strong.

The funeral was the second time I'd seen Daddy since I'd left home with Tex. The first time had been memorable, and though I lived only a few hours away now, I didn't think another visit would go better. The few phone conversations we'd had told me enough.

My move was a recent change, and the motivation behind it was one of the reasons Sutton and I were holed up at the local watering hole, surrounded by obnoxious bar signs and pictures of Highland cows.

She pushed her glass to the edge of the counter—a sign she needed a break from downing shots. "So, tell me about your new place. Wilder doesn't say much other than it bugs the shit out of Cody."

Cody had other things to worry about now, but he'd pestered me from the beginning of my move over a year ago. Until Meg got sick, I was interrogated every time he checked in. *Why are you moving for an equal-paying job? Why aren't you paying down the land before you build? You have that trailer house to stay in on the property. You're surely not building when lumber prices are so high? The economy sucks, Aggie. You majored in finance. Run the numbers. A hobby farm, Aggie? While you're working full-time? You know that's not possible.*

He'd gotten Wilder, Austen, and Eliot to address the

same concerns. If I avoided their calls, one of them showed up on my doorstep.

Daddy never left the ranch.

I poured a fourth shot but let it sit. "My place is as bad as the photos I sent, but it's mine."

Sutton rested her head in a hand with her elbow propped on the bar top. Her light hair spilled onto the counter. She was dressed the same as she had been when I first met her—worn Ariat boots, Wrangler jeans, and a T-shirt with an old flannel over it. I'd seen her dressed up, and oddly, she didn't look much different. As gorgeous in a powder-blue bridesmaid dress as she was gloved up and ready to do a bovine rectal exam.

She was the same contemplative woman I had first been introduced to by Wilder, but I was no longer the hick girl she'd first met. I'd like to think I was a real Cinderella transformation, but I just grew up. Tonight, I was dressed much like I had been for the funeral, which was what I wore at work and in my off time. I had my knee-high riding boots on that had never seen a horse, cranberry leggings, and my favorite striped eyelash chenille sweater. My complexion was perfect, and my hair was tamed and in its standard bun.

I looked like what I was—a finance manager and a property owner. The property, however . . .

I liked a challenge.

I pulled out my phone and paged through photos of the defunct hobby farm I'd taken over from the bank. The animals were gone, having been adopted out—or butchered, not that the real estate agent put those details in the description. My new house and shop sat in front of an old red barn, a sagging smaller brown barn, randomly pieced together pens and fence line, and old riding rings that were really diamonds in the rough I didn't have time to polish. "It's in tough shape, but now that the house is built, I can get the barn spruced up and fix some fence."

"How's the new job?"

"Good." It was a corporate job in a blue-collar industry. "The refinery has a good work environment, and my boss is tough but fair. He's not warm and cuddly, and he doesn't expect me to be." So, it was perfect. I'd had enough bosses who thought I should be the maternal voice in the office because I had boobs. I'd just left a boss who passed me over for an asshole.

"Don't . . . " She rolled her lips in and eyed her shot glass. "Don't, uh, *his* relatives live around there?"

"You mean 'he who shall not be named'?" The man I'd almost forgotten about. He was nothing but a reckless memory.

"Yeah, that guy. Wilder couldn't believe you moved near Coal Haven and all the Barrons around there."

He'd told me. So had Cody, Austen, and Eliot. Some days, I expected them to tell me I was putting my socks on wrong.

"It's the safest place." At her perplexed look, I explained. "Ansen"—my throat ached saying his name again after all these years—"didn't talk to his family. He barely had anything to do with his dad and brother. When we were"—I swallowed hard—"together, he'd never even visited North Dakota, and Coal Haven is three hours away from Buffalo Gully."

"What if he's reconciled since then?"

I shook my head. "No, see, there's this brewery not far from the refinery, and it's run by Ansen's cousin. I went there after I interviewed, and she struck up a conversation, telling me all about her family—her dad's my boss."

Sutton screwed her face up. "That's some small-town shit."

"Tell me about it. I had heart palpitations during the whole visit for my interview. But she mentioned Archer and that he was in Coal Haven now and that she hadn't met Archer's brother."

"And Archer is Ansen's older brother?"

I nodded. Should I take the next shot? The night was young, but talking exes was depressing on a good day. Talking about *him* ripped open bandages that had been haphazardly placed and that Lawson had loosened with our final argument. "Just in case, I found the property in Crocus Valley, about twenty minutes from Coal Haven. The position at the refinery was too good to pass up. The benefits are better than what I was getting."

If I had to work in an office, then I wanted to afford a decent retirement. As much as I avoided Daddy, I hated to think about his eventual passing, and I refused to live my life gambling on an inheritance. He'd probably dock mine in half because Mama's life insurance had gone to me.

Inheritance or not, I didn't need guys like Lawson who thought they could swoop in and "take care" of me when I was doing just fine for myself. I was done with guys like Penley, my boyfriend before Lawson, who'd whined about how I made more than he did and felt it emasculated him but was just fine soaking off my income.

Sutton squinted at the next photo. "Whose horses are these?"

"Yeah, that." I swiped through the next few. "My real estate agent knows my background and approached me about pasturing them. They were seized from a neglectful owner, and she's keeping all five in one of her pastures for now, but they need care and training."

"You said yes? You just moved there."

I lifted a shoulder, hesitant to tell someone else about

my plans. Sutton wasn't bossy like my brothers, but I'd had enough opinions in my life. "She's waiting for my answer when I return home. I miss having horses around." Eliot said Daddy had put down Mathilda when Daddy got sick of treating her arthritis, and my other horse was never really mine. She was a project horse that was actually fully trained. She'd been a way to dupe me into thinking I was contributing to the ranch. "I thought maybe . . . it could be a side gig. A nonprofit."

"You're going to start a rescue?" She sounded mixed parts surprised and impressed.

"I dunno. Maybe? I have the facilities, but they need a lot of attention, and I work full-time."

"Can you hire someone?"

"Maybe, but I'd have to vet them, and I'm not sure I have time to go through their records, hire them, then hang around and make sure they're not worse for the animals." I had more reasons not to, like marketing and forming a company for the rescue, but my mind kept circling back to the possibility.

She poked me in the side. "But you've thought about it. You've thought about doing a rescue or even flipping horses."

"You don't like horse traders."

"I know you'd be ethical."

"Don't you dare tell my brothers about this conversation." I playfully scowled at her and swiped through the photos again. The kid of a horse rancher and the finance woman inside me couldn't help themselves. I missed working with animals, horses especially. If I didn't open a full rescue, I could buy problem horses, train them properly, and sell them to good homes.

I wanted to take the horses, so I'd better figure it out.

A slight blur overlaid the pictures. The alcohol was hitting my bloodstream, and I didn't drink often. Sutton never did either, but it'd been *a week*.

I struggled to refocus. "Yeah, I thought of opening a rescue." There. I admitted it. Out loud. The pressure stayed crowded on my shoulders.

"Would you quit and work the rescue full time?"

"I need the benefits." I had some of Mama's money left. I'd gotten my degree with it and supported myself until I landed a decent job. I had enough in reserve to make the idea of opening a rescue by myself almost not crazy. "I could hire someone to get everything started with the rescue, but I can't take much time off since I'm new. They'd have to know what they're doing."

"It sucks you felt like you had to quit your job in Wyoming and move."

"It was an easy decision after they promoted Lawson instead of me." I should've been sorry, too, but an office was an office whether I was in Wyoming or North Dakota. "It's worth it not to go to work and see him frowning at me across the boardroom."

"Ugh, men. And you had to move out of Bozeman because Penley was being a dick."

"Mr. 'Follow Me To Work Until I Threatened Him With A Restraining Order'? Yeah." I downed that fourth shot.

"Men." She shook her head and dropped her hand down to the bar top.

"Hey, Aggie." A guy sidled up next to me, my age, with close-cropped, sandy-blond hair, wearing jeans, a sweater pullover, and a *you want me* grin. I rolled my eyes toward him. His gaze dropped to my legs, stroking down to where my ankles were crossed on the stool's footrest.

"Chad." He'd graduated high school with me. Football player. Farm kid. Asshole.

"Been awhile." Appreciation was ripe in his voice—something I never thought I'd hear from him aimed my way. "How's it going?"

"Shitty. I'm in town for Meg's funeral."

He recoiled slightly, like he hadn't expected me to be blunt. No one ever did, and he should've put two and two together. Meg's death and the return of all five Knight siblings were big news in this small town.

He leaned against the bar between the next stool and me. "Maybe we can get together while you're in town."

I feigned regret. "If only I didn't recall you telling Macey Jones that between my hair and my attitude I remind you of a rabid poodle."

His brows popped up. "Shit, Aggie. That was years ago."

"Being in town is bringing back memories, and I'm done with men who think they can walk all over me and expect me to forget how much they didn't care about me or my feelings." He'd become a target of my resentment, but he was Chad. He probably deserved it.

He drew back and pushed off the counter, his mouth twisted. As he walked away, he snarled, "You're probably still as flat of a lay now as I heard you were then."

"I've learned it makes a difference when the guy knows what he's doing and has a big dick," I called over my shoulder.

Sutton choked on her laugh. I returned my scowl to the bottle of liquor. I wasn't drinking over that bastard.

"You tell 'em, Birdie," the old bartender said.

A flush inched up my face. I didn't have to look in the mirror to know I was turning red. I had lost my virginity to one of the guys on the football team, more as a way to find out what sex was all about, but his lips had flapped more than a pony going for a carrot.

"Men are clueless pricks." Sutton's words seemed laced with more significance than my interaction with Chad, but I was mentally struggling to right myself. It was like Chad hit my horse with a switch and I was galloping at full speed into the past.

"Such fucking pricks," I said, clenching my hands. Releasing them only to grab the bottle, I poured another shot. I wouldn't do a shot over Chad, but there was another guy . . . "And they always get away with it."

Sutton grabbed the bottle from my hand and filled her little glass. "Chad's dating the mayor's daughter and says it's not serious, but she's planning a wedding." A light slur hit her words.

The drink burned my throat, and I could've breathed fire after I swallowed, but the pain tampered the humiliation of Chad's parting comment. "My stalker ex is remarried, but he's sent me two messages in the last five years. I never read them."

"*Nooo*. Who'd marry him?"

I pulled up the account his wife posted all her pictures on. Look who was being the stalker now. My special form of torture was watching guys who'd done me wrong get on with their fabulous lives.

Sutton leaned close to the screen like her vision was also lacking clarity after a few shots.

"Dickwad." Sutton sat back and swayed. "And Lawson? Living high after he screwed you over?"

"I should've known better than to date someone I worked with. It failed once already." Just because I could, I pulled up Lawson's account and gasped. A photo of a brand-new Lexus with a gushing statement about how much he loved his new position. "I was told I had to move offices because the tension between us made other employees uncomfortable, and he got a fucking raise."

"That's so unfair, Aggie. It's just not right." She grabbed the phone and punched something into the app's search bar. Her mouth fell open. "And *him*? Look at her."

I glanced over and wished the Fireball had occluded my vision completely. Filling my screen was Ansen with his favorite black Justin cowboy hat pulled down low and a stunning blonde tucked into his side.

My tongue moved sluggishly like it'd been stung by a bee. "She's a pageant queen."

Not that I'd followed Ansen's life at all. I'd forgotten him. Mostly. Except for the few times I checked on his whereabouts—only to make sure I didn't move close to where he was working. How long I did the checking was another issue, but I counted the number of occurrences. It was less embarrassing.

"Her family's loaded and owns one of the biggest horse ranches in Kansas," I said. "And she leaves cryptic comments about *any day now* and *bling bling*." The fear I'd be nosy and learn they picked June second had kept me far away from her profile. I was already cranky that day—the anniversary of nothing. A day filled with a salty disposition and ice cream.

"Cocksucker."

"The biggest," I said with as much authority as possible, even though my chest tightened. What I said to Chad hadn't been a lie. When a guy knew what he was doing and had the right tool—sex was an *experience*.

I should've been devastated over Lawson, but breaking up with him had been an annoyance. A nuisance. I hadn't minded moving, and I looked forward to settling into my own slice of paradise. A place no guy had a say over. It was how I'd found myself looking up Ansen last year. I had to make sure he was nowhere near North Dakota if I was moving close to his estranged family.

Sutton punched frantically away on my phone. I poured another drink. Was I up to six? The effects were snowballing and I needed to stop, but there wasn't much left in the bottle. Still, I didn't drink enough to handle this amount well.

At the same time, there wasn't nearly enough booze to get me through this trip down memory lane. Good thing Wilder said he'd give us a ride if we needed it.

She suddenly straightened with a gasp, nearly slipping off her stool. "He's not getting married."

"What?" I grabbed for the phone before I could remind myself I didn't care. Headlines filled the search page. She'd gone online to look him up, and Google was not as kind as all the pictures in the social media apps.

Sutton tipped close. "Her profile says she's disappointed about how things turned out, but she didn't elaborate. Her feed's nothing but her friends calling him a piece of shit."

I couldn't spare a moment to be smug. I was reading headlines. "Horse trainer and Gustafson Performance Horses parting ways amid scandal." Squinting until the words cleared, I kept reciting the clickbait. "No longer welcome in the reined-horse competition world. Cruelty suspected—fingers point toward trainer." I frowned, suddenly defensive. "That's just not true. He'd never hurt a horse."

"You don't think he would? It's been a long time."

I shook my head and swayed in my seat just like Sutton had. "No trainer would stand up to Daddy about expanding training windows to work better with each horse's personality and then resort to cruelty." Arguing with Daddy wasn't something many people walked away from unscathed, but

Ansen had kept his job *and* Daddy had wanted him to marry me.

"If he didn't deserve it, I'd almost feel bad for him."

"Almost." My lips twitched, then my indignation returned. "Did you see her last name?"

"Her profile only says Stephanie Jane."

"It's Gustafson. As in, the daughter of the guy he worked for."

"The plot thickens." Sutton cocked a brow like she wasn't going to ask me how I had the dirt because we both knew full well how much I'd cyberstalked him. "He must've figured it almost worked once."

"And it failed him again." I scrolled through more headlines. "He's utterly blacklisted. Maybe there's a ranch in the middle of nowhere with an owner who only has sons who'll hire him. But I doubt it. He'll swagger his way into another job, win over some other unsuspecting woman, and be all the better for it. This is nothing but a blip for him." Just like I was. The ache in my chest was back.

A giggle left Sutton, and she refilled our shot glasses. "Wouldn't it be funny if you hired him? He'd be your bitch."

I snickered. "He'd be like an equine Cinderella." I made my voice high-pitched. "Muck those stalls. Stack those bales. Fix my fence."

"You'd be the one in charge—the one with the money."

We laughed, and her smile slipped.

"What?" I asked.

"I have an idea."

∩∩

There was knocking on my door. I cracked an eye open, groaning as I did so. "Yeah?" I said weakly into my pillow, then smacked my lips together, catching some of the pillowcase in my mouth. My tongue was lined with cotton, and the faint flavor of cinnamon managed to be sour.

"I put water on your nightstand last night," Wilder said on the other side of the guest room door. "I'm going to help Eliot with chores before my shift, but I wanted to make sure you're okay."

"I didn't drink that much," I croaked as I rolled up. The room spun, and I put a hand to my aching head.

"Uh-huh. You hit the Fireball like you were sixteen and at a bonfire." His muffled snicker hurt my head. "If you throw up, you're cleaning it."

I dimly recalled him telling me the same thing as he'd loaded me into the back of his deputy SUV. I'd told him it already smelled like puke in the back seat.

I took a long pull off the bottle of water he'd left me, but my stomach heaved. I glanced down at myself. I was still in my sweater that had soaked up the toaster-oven pizza and alcohol smell from the bar. Somehow, I'd gotten my bra off. I retained half of my ladylike demeanor. Meg would've been both proud and aghast.

I straightened my clothing and tried to keep the water down. "How's Sutton?"

His snort was clear through the door. "Hurting. The uncontrollable laughter from last night isn't to be heard this morning." He paused. "You doing okay?"

"I'm fine." Hungover as hell.

"All right, then. I'm going. Eliot and I are going to stop in and check on Cody this afternoon."

"I'll swing by and see him before I leave town." He'd claim he was doing well and act mildly annoyed at our concern, but that was Cody. "Thank you, Wilder." I shouldn't have needed him to bail me out, and he probably wasn't surprised I'd been acting like I was sixteen. Last night had gotten out of hand.

"You can pay me back by driving Sutton to the bar to get her car when the alcohol's out of both of your systems. Don't make me pull you over. Because I will."

And he'd let me go after a lecture. Different brother, same outcome.

I nodded even though he couldn't see, and it made my temples pound. "Will do."

When he was gone, I forced myself to stay sitting up. I had to check on Sutton and apologize for hitting the bottle too hard last night. No one should get dragged into the depths of my man troubles, especially not a happily married woman.

I thought back to her random comments throughout the night. How happily married was she? Happy enough that Wilder was ready to rescue us. The bartender had called Wilder for us and told him to pick up Birdie and her friend because Sutton kept accidentally hanging up on him.

Uncontrollable laughter. What had we gotten up to?

Dawning realization brought horror with it. Sutton's big idea. The way I'd gleefully latched on to it. How I'd justi-fied it.

Even worse—the shameful humiliation that was going to follow after Ansen read the application two drunken women sent to him around midnight on a Saturday.

I grabbed my phone, ignored how shitty I felt, and scrolled through my email. Breathing out my relief, I squeezed my eyes shut. He didn't reply. Perhaps we didn't send it. But it was also a weekend.

My eyelids flew open.

Shit. We used a new email.

Sutton was quite devious while loaded with Fireball. *How about we use a different name and make the email all official? Ooh, name your rescue, and you'll just go by Christie, Rescue Manager.*

Christie. My middle name.

My stomach twisted until the little water I did drink threatened to come back up with the last two shots from last night. I found the new email account, still logged on, with a notification for a new message. Why did we have to be so technologically proficient when it came to this?

I went to the inbox.

I gasped so loud it echoed off the walls. I threw the blankets off my lap and raced out of the room and down the hall to my brother's bedroom, heedless of how I felt moments ago.

Flying through Sutton's bedroom door, I waved my phone like it was a spotlight and I was looking for a lost and wandering sister-in-law. "Oh my dear god, Sutton. He replied."

Only her wheat-colored hair was visible from under the navy-blue blankets. Her groan mimicked mine from when Wilder woke me up. She squinted out from under the covers. "Who replied, and why is it an emergency?"

"Ansen."

Confusion clouded her eyes, and I got to watch how I must've looked as the fog over the memories of last night cleared away. Her gray eyes widened, and she sat up. She put her hand to her head, but her gaze was on the phone. "What'd he say?"

"I don't know." I held the phone out like I wanted her to take it, but I was clutching it too tightly. A team of draft horses couldn't drag it out of my grip.

"Well . . . *look*." Sutton frowned at her nightshirt like she didn't recall putting it on before she went to bed. Water sat on her nightstand, along with a small bottle of orange juice and a mini muffin.

How nice was it to have someone taking care of you at your lowest? I ignored the beat of longing and looked at my phone. The screen was dark once again. I reached out and tapped it. It flared on, and I steeled myself. He knew it was me. He knew I was fucking with him, and he thought I was pathetic after all these years.

He'd be right. Last night though, I'd had loads of justification.

Taking in a steady breath, I calmed myself. I had nothing to worry about. He thought he was replying to Christie from AKA Horse Rescue. I pulled up his message.

My jaw dropped open. "Oh . . ."

Sutton leaned toward me, an inch away from falling out of bed. "You're killing me, Aggie. What'd he say?"

"He took the job."

We stared at each other. I broke contact and reread his reply. Was it really him? Did I hit up another disgraced horse trainer named Ansen Barron to work at my brand-new horse rescue for ridiculously low pay?

"What do I do?" I whispered. I could tell him it was a joke. But if I opened my side business like I'd been secretly dreaming of for years, I'd need help. There were five horses that had a temporary home and very little care they desperately needed. I could afford the vet bills, meds, and farrier fees, but I didn't have the time. I'd missed a week for the funeral as it was.

Could I help them all by myself? And fix fence? Load the barn full of hay for the approaching winter? Make all the vet, horse chiropractor, and farrier appointments? Train them? Then show them to prospective owners when they were ready to sell?

Would I be able to work with Ansen, to contain the hurt and anger seeing him would bring up?

Would he even stay? He was in a bad place, awful if he

accepted my job offer, but working with me might not be worth it for him.

The damn burn around my heart flared up. I should reply, tell him I hired someone else, and forget it. Forget him like I'd been failing to do since I last saw him.

Sutton's gaze was serious. She'd become my closest friend and knew me better than anyone. Studying my face, I knew she read me as easily as all the messages we'd exchanged over the years. "You have a decision to make."

Three

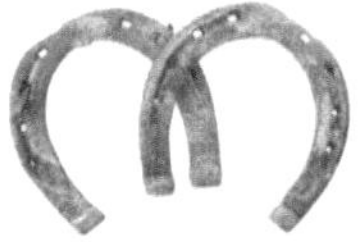

ANSEN

Was Crocus Valley that damn close to Coal Haven, North Dakota?

I blew out a breath. I was stopped on an off-ramp, peering at the directions on my GPS. I closed my eyes. Goddammit. Why didn't I look into the location earlier?

Because I needed a damn job. Because I couldn't get hired anywhere else. Because my name had been smeared worse than shit on a barn door.

A job offer right in my inbox, full of misspellings, from a company that hadn't come up in a search wouldn't have been my first choice—or my twentieth—but I couldn't afford to be picky. Literally.

Was my brother behind this? He lived in Coal Haven with his picture-perfect family. After years of pretending how we'd grown up wasn't good enough, that Dad and I weren't good enough, he was settled into the same life we'd been raised in for a few glorious years, only much farther north and around all the family Dad had once walked away from.

I poked at the GPS screen in my pickup. Was there any way around Coal Haven and the brother I was avoiding? I'd managed to stay out of North Dakota my entire life.

I found an alternate route and pulled back onto the interstate. A call notification blocked out the GPS information. Dad's name scrolled across the screen. Since he was at the age where I wasn't sure he was calling to chat or tell me he was dying, I answered. My feelings about my dad and brother were complicated, not cold. "Hey."

"Ansen." His low growl sparked a pang of homesickness. After fifteen years, I shouldn't be homesick. Dad didn't even live in the same place as when I rode out of Texas. A fact I'd once dreamed of remedying. "Are you on the road again?"

Somehow the man sensed when I was changing locations. If he'd heard about the brouhaha—and he likely had since he'd called more often in the last six months—he didn't mention it. "No, just heading to the store. What's up?"

"Nothing. Just calling to check in. How's everything going?"

I glanced around at the gently rolling hills the interstate cut through. They were a mix of green and brown this time of year. I passed fields filled with dried sunflower heads or golden ones full of hay bales. In between were pastures dotted with black, brown, or white cows—mixed Angus, Simmental, and Charolais cattle. Useless knowledge.

Dad's question should've been, *How long are we going to pretend your life isn't a steaming pile of fresh shit?*

A little longer would be nice, but after months of being shut out of everything I loved in my life, I was tired. "I'm looking for a new job."

"Yeah . . . Heard 'bout all that."

"Don't believe it all." Only some of it. I didn't want to know which part he wouldn't question.

"I know better. You weren't raised like that. Listen, I could talk to—"

"I'm good. It's fine." I didn't know if he was going to mention his boss or my brother, but the answer was no. I wasn't a charity case unless my brother was waiting for me at the end of this drive, but Archer had never mentioned opening a horse rescue in his life.

If he was the one behind this bullshit job offer, I'd leave. I didn't need a handout or a hand up. I didn't do anything wrong, but this was what I got for sticking to my principles for once.

"Okay," he drawled. "I'll let you go. You know you always got a bunk here."

Dad barely had a bunk where he worked. He had a good job and a tidy place to live, but it was fit for a bachelor who just wanted to work cattle and be left alone. I'd get to ride horses, but none of the land would be mine, the horses would have someone else's brand, and I wouldn't be training horses but using them to work cattle.

All in all, not much different than my life had been. Dad shouldn't have to help out a son who was in his thirties.

"I'd better get going. Talk to you later, Dad."

"Take care, Ansen," he said almost wistfully before he hung up.

Guilt chewed at my gut and it wasn't from keeping the details of my life from him. He disconnected because he thought I didn't want to talk. That wasn't the issue. I just didn't know what to say.

I tried to be a good man, and it ruined my career.

Hey, I took a job really close to the town you left and never returned to. I'm almost there.

No, I haven't told Archer I'm within miles of him.

Turning off the interstate farther west of where I'd been stopped earlier, I headed north on a tighter highway with steeper ditches but more cattle and fields. A shit ton of windmills scattered the horizon, some immobile, some with their gigantic blades lazily turning.

There were worse things that could pepper a view, but I wished I could've seen this area unblemished by the occasional oil well and fleet of windmills. I passed a well, its big hammerhead sitting still. Oil wells always brought back memories I'd rather forget.

Was there a period in my life I didn't want to erase from my mind?

I pulled myself into the present. I was close to my destination, and questions I would've normally been insistent on getting answered before I wasted one gallon of gas crowded my brain. Specifics on the accommodations had been sketchy. Same with the low salary offer. And who I was actually working for.

My contact person, Christie, had said the rescue was brand new, that paperwork was being filed as we exchanged emails, but I'd be in charge of the animals rescued. Mostly horses to rehab and train for sale, but the rescue could accommodate other types of animals.

Since it was a new business, I couldn't find information on the owner. Christie's emails said the owner was also new to town but experienced in country living and had raised horses and other farm animals. She'd also mentioned structures around the place would need work.

So worse pay and more duties than what I was used to.

While some pertinent details were vague—like the owners' names—others had been specific enough that I'd accepted the offer and the shit pay it came with.

There'd been nothing but firings and rejections for months.

I'd be back to fixing fence like when I was a teen, breaking my back for Dad's old boss.

Following the directions on my GPS, I didn't have to go into Crocus Valley. The turnoff to AKA Horse Rescue was an unmarked gravel road. At least it wasn't some dark warehouse in the middle of town with a bunch of guys waiting to jump me. So far, the surroundings tracked with the job description.

After driving two miles on gravel, I slowed to inspect road signs. All the green markings I passed were numbered. "Crocus Lane, Crocus Lane," I muttered as I passed each one.

A narrow wooden sign on my left made me skid to a stop and back up. I rolled down the window like I'd see better. Was I getting that fucking old?

Burned into a wooden plank cresting across the top of the road and secured to two vertical posts was Crocus Lane —a long driveway, not really a lane.

The house was a brand-new build. The lawn was covered in green fuzz with straw on the short inclines. Freshly seeded. The structure itself was a sprawling, modern farmhouse with two stories and three garage stalls. Something was vaguely familiar about it, but I'd been seeing all sorts of farm and ranch houses my entire life all over the country. A sizable new shop sat adjacent to the house. Behind the buildings was a different story.

A beige chicken coop that needed new doors had a penned-off portion with several hens running around inside. A large red barn that might've been picturesque at one time now had paint flaking off, but it looked more usable than a second old, brown barn with a dipped roof by a weed-filled riding ring. A small pasture with five grazing quarter horses was next to the better of the two barns. The fence had some shiny wire where it'd been recently repaired, but the rest could stand to be replaced. Another riding ring was behind the barns with its uneven rails. A definite DIY job. The pens lining the big barn were an eyesore, but perhaps they were still functional.

The horses were in the same condition as their surroundings, grazing on any green grass left, and it hit me. These quarter horses were basically given away—or taken away—while just months ago, I'd been working with stock that would earn more in their lives than this property likely sold for.

How the mighty had fallen.

Ironic that the one decent thing I tried to do in my life had turned into a festering pile of crap.

I parked by a red Chevy Silverado. Guess everything was shoving me down memory lane today, but changing jobs and moving to work at a new ranch always had that effect. After getting out, I brushed my hands down my blue-plaid button-down shirt and the best pair of jeans I owned—all freshly washed but slightly wrinkled from the long trip.

I took the three steps up to the cedar porch and crossed to the front door, loving how quiet it was. The strikes of my heels on the wood were the only sounds other than birds and the wind rustling the long prairie grasses outside the seeded area.

Alfalfa fields. One cutting had been done, but the owner could've gotten two in before summer had ended. He'd probably been moving in.

I rang the doorbell. The house was simple but stylish, with the door a dark blue that stood out from the darker earth tones of the siding. A nice place. Not a place that would send out scam postings for my personal information. Barking ignited inside the house, and I stepped away like the dog could barrel out of the door.

No one answered. I knocked.

Nothing. The curtains moved like the dog inside was running from the window to the door. Did I have the right address?

Between the newly built house and shop and the broken-down buildings behind it, this place fit the description. I really should've insisted on a phone call, but Christie had claimed email was fine. I couldn't afford to pass up a job, but the gas money ate a hole in what little I had in savings.

The rescue owner was probably some obnoxious city guy who thought he knew it all. Country or urban, I was used to arrogance and entitlement.

Maybe he was working in the barn. I thought I'd at least meet Christie to get me settled.

I wandered around outside the house, the barking from inside fading. The old red barn had its own majesty. Crooked pens lined the outside of the barn, made out of any wood or metal material the previous owners had found on hand. Feed boxes hung from the rails and probably leaked as much grain as they held.

"Hello?" I called. I'd be gone already if I didn't need this damn job. Too many questions. Nothing close to the responsibility I used to have.

Those days were on pause. My plans to get my own place and start my own business were also stalled. Again. I'd get there, but I had to start back at rock fucking bottom.

I briefly turned my attention back to the horses. At least two mares and two geldings. The fifth was tucked behind the rest like it wanted to stay as far away from a human as possible. From what I could see, they were getting in their winter coats—not as full for this time of year this far north, but their ribs and at least one's sway back told me they needed good nutrition and supplements to finish getting ready for winter.

Where was my contact? "Anyone here?" I didn't shout to keep from startling the already cautious animals.

"Ansen," came a flat reply from a voice that sent a long-forgotten zing through my gut.

A woman emerged from the dark yawn of the open barn door. My heart thudded in slow motion as I took her in.

Did I wake up this morning in an even worse nightmare than when I went to bed? I'd been worried I was walking into a scheme where my personal data was at risk. Or that I would be jumped just for fun. I wasn't ready for my past to bait and trap me.

I stared at the woman who'd haunted my conscience for ten fucking years. A mix of privileged princess and forthright practicality. A girl who'd flown out of my life faster than a Triple Crown winner. Aggie Knight.

Christie.

Christ.

She stood in the opening of the barn, the backdrop dark while the sun shone on her. This wasn't the Aggie I knew. Shadows hung in her eyes like they were permanent, but her clothing was pristine. The precocious, slightly insecure country girl I'd been engaged to was replaced by a cynical, sophisticated woman.

The change resonated inside me as a loss, a faint echo of what I had experienced the day she left.

"Christie?" I asked. "Was that necessary?"

Displeasure, and maybe a little guilt if I wanted to delude myself, rippled across her face. "Didn't think you'd entertain the job offer otherwise."

"What is this?" Why me? My name should be a curse on her tongue. So why the hell was I here?

"Exactly what I said in our emails." She raised her arms up to encompass the land, and I tried—and failed—not to notice how she had an hourglass figure she hadn't possessed before. I didn't know this woman with the cinched red riding coat and knee-high leather boots. The girl who'd shunned all English riding but looked ready for a dressage show. Her jeans were so blue they looked fresh from the factory. This Aggie wasn't wearing a straw cowboy hat, her eyes dancing while she laughed. Her hair was drawn back in a severe bun that couldn't hide the red glints in the light-brown strands.

She dropped her arms. "I wanted to help some horses, but I'm working at the refinery. You were available."

"Were you spying on me?" I pushed the shame to the background of my thoughts. She'd probably read everything and deemed it fitting after what I'd done to her. Still, hiring me didn't make sense. "Are you trying to help me?"

Pink spots dotted her cheeks. "God, no. I was commiserating about shitty exes with Sutton, and we looked all of you up to see how little you've paid for being awful to women. I saw the news. I need a trainer, and you need a job." A sardonic smile curved lips I still saw in my dreams. "Your rate was just right."

My shame reignited, followed by annoyance that was growing close to anger. She wanted to get even. While I could respect her fire, I didn't like being kicked while I was down. "You're a lot like your dad."

Her inhale was sharp, but she maintained her rigid composure. "Maybe I should've stuck around and taken more notes from him." Folding her arms across her impressive chest, she lifted her chin. "You can quit."

She had me by the balls and she was twisting. Aggie was smart. She knew what the accusations of animal cruelty and death had done to my reputation.

I was sick of being hammered for doing the right thing, and when I thought it couldn't get worse, here I was. So, I did what used to work best—took the focus off me. "How many exes exactly?"

"Excuse me?"

God, I'd missed her voice. Her face was as expressive as her tone, and she had a no-bullshit quality to her that I admired. Maybe I was so used to getting smiled at and flirted with that Aggie was refreshing, circumstances notwithstanding. "You said you and Sutton looked up all your exes. How many?"

Her eyes narrowed, and for the first time in so damn long, a thrill lit in my chest. I'd gotten under that icy exterior and it was . . . *fun*.

"None of your business."

We stared at each other. She was a wall of mutinous attitude, and I was . . . I didn't know. I wasn't as worn as I had been. Adrenaline from learning I was deceived into coming here ran through my veins but also trepidation. How long was she going to string me along?

Was she really willing to keep me on and pay me? What if my old employer learned I was here and got a hold of her? Who would she believe? I certainly hadn't given her a reason to trust me.

I really did need a job, or I'd be at Dad's door, asking for a cot to camp out on. Rip the damn bandage off. If she was going to tell me she was just fucking with me for revenge, I had time to get a motel room and point my pickup south in the morning. I had enough money for the thousand-mile drive to Texas. "When and where do I start?"

Surprise lit her eyes and was extinguished by professionalism. "Now, and I'll show you, but we need to pick up some chicken feed before the co-op closes."

The task was so completely normal it sounded weird to my ears. I was picking up chicken feed. From a co-op. In North Dakota. To take my mind off of how different my life was now than when the year began, I asked, "AKA Horse Rescue? What's it stand for?"

Her lips curled on one side. Definitely not a smile. But I couldn't take my eyes off them. Memories from years ago tumbled back. Those lips planting kisses on my chest. Wrapped around my—

"Aggie Knight, asshole."

Aggie

I thought I'd feel vindicated. I'd tricked him into moving to North Dakota—weeks before it got really cold, no less. But instead of righteousness, my pulse fluttered and heat wicked up my neck to my cheeks. It was all I could do not to pat my hair and ensure each strand was in place or to run my hands down my fuller hips.

What did he think of me? I was nothing like the pictures of the girls I'd seen him with—country cool with a good stylist. I had a good stylist, but if I dyed my hair blonde, I'd look like a week-old corpse with a wig. My skin tone didn't play well with blonde. I had my mama's genes and my daddy's taste buds—give me steak and potatoes and my body would pack it away for this winter and next. Add in that I wasn't running around a ranch doing chores twice a day, sitting for most of my eight-hour shift, and I wouldn't fit in the wedding dress Ansen last saw me in.

Instead of being upset, a slow grin spread over the frustrating man's face. "You did all this for me?"

This was the charming Ansen I had to be careful of. He was dangerous to a girl's heart and he ruined other men for her. Other guys were like surviving on crackers for months after having steak fondue and tiramisu for years.

I could go for a good steak fondue after ten years of crackers.

No! Anger ignited in my chest. The blessing of my experience with him was that I saw right through him. He was trying to unbalance me. "No. I did it for me, slick. Daddy sold enough perfectly good horses to the kill pens, and now I have the means to do what I want. Getting back at you is just a bonus. You wasted a year of my life."

His smile died, and goddammit, I hated to see it go.

He rolled his eyes up to the sky. "Fuck me, Ags. It was a long drive, and I didn't plan to rehash the past when I got here." He speared me with his intense sorrel stare. "But it doesn't look like you suffered at all. Brand-new house. New shop." His gaze raked down my body, and I was tempted to peek at myself and make sure his stare didn't incinerate every last stitch. "New look."

I wasn't new. I was Aggie 2.0. Smarter than the original model and more polished. "And you are exactly the same."

He clenched his jaw, and his eyes darkened, close to a wince. "If you're not running me off after an eight-hour drive, where can I put my things?"

"Eight-hour drive? Where were you?"

"South Dakota." He left it at that.

"What happened to Kansas?"

"I thought you knew all that, or I wouldn't be here." Confusion lined his brow. "Wait—why am I here if you know? Aren't you afraid I'll beat your rescues? Shoot a horse if you piss me off?"

The bitterness dripping from his words and the hostility aimed at the situation and not at me would've convinced me I was right if I wasn't already sure. I snorted. "Please. You've always treated horses better than women. Since I'm not planning to crawl into your bed, what happened between you and Miss Rodeo isn't my concern."

"Miss Kansas."

Of course she was. "Don't care. Did you hurt animals?"

"You know I fucking didn't."

"Did you make mistakes that got animals hurt?"

"Only 'cause I trusted the wrong people."

"I know how that goes." We stared at each other for a beat before I gestured behind the barn to the other side of the property. "All right, then. The trailer is your lodging. We can drop your things there when we go to the co-op in Coal Haven."

"You can't get feed on your own?"

"Not when I'm paying you." The pulse of power was heady. Yes, I'd needed this after the way he'd devastated me. Our history was a long time ago, but with him here, I was aware the wound wasn't as healed as it should've been.

One-sided love did that to a person.

The muscles in the corners of his granite jaw flexed. "Right." He glanced around, taking in the run-down condition of the place. I used to think he hid his feelings behind a jovial attitude, but the cheerfulness I knew was gone. A storm raged quietly in his eyes. This job had to be a rusty nail in the heel of his foot for him. "How are your brothers?"

Was he stalling? Was buying chicken feed that far beneath him? But I'd answer. I could stall too. That trailer was going to sour his already dark mood. "Cody's wife passed away a month ago."

"Meg?"

"Yep. Brain tumor."

"Shit. How are his kids doing?"

I shrugged and went to stuff my hands in my pockets, forgetting I was wearing a long coat. I didn't dress like I used to, in an old gray Carhartt jacket. I hadn't needed to for so long, and many of my old clothes no longer fit. I smoothed over my hips instead. "He wouldn't tell me if there were issues."

"In true Alcott Knight form." His bitterness seemed out of place until I remembered Cody was the one who'd confronted him. The memory made this moment, facing Ansen and catching up, surreal.

"Wilder and Sutton finally got married and live in Buffalo Gully." That sadly summed them up. "Austen's still in the army, and Eliot works for Daddy."

"Still raisin' horses?" His twang was subtler since I'd last talked to him. He'd never had a full southern drawl, claiming it was because his dad had been raised not far from here.

"Yes."

"Your daddy?"

"He's sick. Lung cancer." My voice didn't shake. The few times I had called, he hadn't wanted to talk about me. I was a breeding mare to him. I had already mourned what I wished our relationship would've been. "According to Eliot, Daddy's fucking his home nurse, so he can't be that bad off."

"Sounds like Barns."

"Yep."

He nodded. I nodded.

"We can take my pickup." The co-op was closing soon. I meant to go earlier, but I'd had to field some work calls this morning. I'd hoped to run the errand before Ansen arrived. Anticipating a shared ride with him sent a thrum through my veins.

"You work at the refinery full time?"

Was he still stalling? We weren't old friends running through a who's who. Yet here we were. "I work at the refinery outside of Coal Haven. For your uncle," I explained as I walked toward the house, giving him a wide berth. I didn't have to know if he still smelled like horse sweat and soap—a mix that shouldn't work but was apparently designed for my DNA.

He pivoted to face me but didn't follow. "Cameron?"

"Yes," I said over my shoulder, continuing to walk toward the house. "I'm in the finance office."

"You got your degree?" he called out.

"Why wouldn't I?" The challenging tone slipped in before I could stop it.

"Because you hated the thought of college."

I had at one time. I'd only told Daddy I was going to go so he'd give me more responsibilities around the ranch.

I stopped and faced Ansen. Seeing him on my land with my old barn in the backdrop unraveled a secret fantasy that should've stayed locked up. Maybe I should fire him. My gaze strayed to the horses that were now in my care. Too late. "Mama's life insurance didn't come with health benefits or a retirement package."

"You could've gone back for a career you enjoyed."

"I don't mind finance." My pitch rose at the end like I'd been busted in a lie. I was good at my job, and while I wished I wasn't office-bound all day, I actually enjoyed running numbers. I thrived on working in an environment where I was respected. The refinery filled the role.

"Living a life doin' what you hate is a waste."

"I never said I hated it. It's honest. Now load up." I spun, my boots crunching against the dirt path. Whether he followed me or not would seal his fate. I couldn't tolerate insubordination, not after he'd had such a hold on my heart.

The nagging observation that he wasn't the same man I'd left that day haunted me. A haggard man with shadows in his eyes who wore stress like a second outfit wasn't the carefree boy I once loved.

I didn't know this man, and the knowledge sifted through me until I had to admit the Ansen who showed up today was a thousand times more dangerous to me. The only reason I didn't reconsider my plan and offer to reimburse his travel expenses and send him on his way was how he looked at the horses.

His expert gaze had taken them in, and an appreciation he probably wasn't aware he showed shone in his brown eyes. He respected them just for grazing like horses. He read them, could tell they'd been mishandled and neglected, and he was likely already forming a plan in that sexy brain of his.

The animals. They were the reason Ansen could stay.

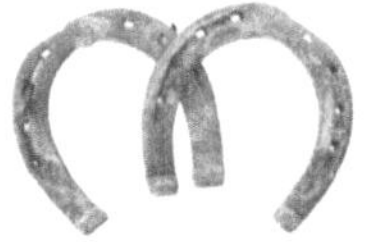

ANSEN

I wasn't ready to go out and about in any North Dakota town. I knew how small the world could be. Circling around Coal Haven earlier had been for nothing. We were in fucking city limits now.

We'd skirted the edges of Crocus Valley on the way to Coal Haven. Crocus Valley had a few businesses lining the highway we'd taken, and the rest of town sloped into a valley and spread out while Coal Haven surrounded both sides of the road. The town was on flatter land, and the seed co-op was on the outskirts. At least we didn't have to drive through it, but it was so small I could see from one end to the other.

The odds of running into a relative rose higher than I first thought. Fuck this day.

I stayed on the edges of the store as Aggie chatted with the older guy behind the counter, who was planted on his stool like he could talk all day. He looked gruff, with bushy eyebrows and salt-and-pepper hair spraying out from under his trucker hat and out of his ears.

He talked like he was Santa the week before Christmas, getting all the information. "Montana, eh?"

I wanted to clear my throat in a wordless plea to move the hell on, but that'd only bring attention to me, and this guy was ferreting out more information about Aggie than the government probably knew.

"Not far from Sidney," she answered with a smile in her voice, the first I'd heard since the efficient, twenty-minute ride here where she outlined the duties she expected from me while I wondered when she'd started using a shampoo or lotion with a subtle hint of coconut in it. It was October, and she smelled like an expensive beach vacation. "My daddy's Barnaby Knight."

"Oh, what the heck. Knight's Arabians?"

I was still trying to catch up with my change in life's direction, and she was winning over the guy working at the seed co-op.

Her grin was serene. "Yes, sir."

He chuckled. "What brought you here?"

While I listened to her tell him about her job at the refinery farther down the highway, I wandered around the entry. Shelves of minerals and supplements lined the walls. The chicken feed we were after was stacked in the corner. The grainy yet subtly metallic smell of the place was something familiar, calming my anxiety. Places like this were my world up until the last few years. The building was a long, flat steel structure with silver grain bins towering behind it. Grain trucks were lined next to the bins, and we'd passed a few leaving as we'd pulled in.

I was still in the world I loved. Nothing but the help, but I should be used to that by now. I just wasn't accustomed to being resigned to it.

The door squeaked open.

"I know where it's at, Mommy!" a little brunette girl yelled as she raced in.

I turned just as she barreled into my knees.

"Whoa there." I chuckled as big brown eyes blinked up at me.

"Hey—you look like my daddy. Mommy!"

Her words froze me in place. This town couldn't be that damn small. My shitty luck couldn't be roaring that strong today.

"This guy looks like Daddy." Her tiny finger pointed toward me, and as a short, blonde woman entered with a toddler on her hip, the girl started jumping up and down.

The new arrival frowned and tilted her head to study me with piercing blue eyes. "Yeah, he does."

She looked familiar. I'd been sent pictures that I'd barely paid attention to. All I'd seen was my brother looking stupidly happy with everything I wanted, and that had been enough to get me to never look at them again.

The door opened again and a tall man stepped through, wearing clothing opposite of the tailored suit I'd last seen him in. The mix of emotions quarreling in my chest were hard to identify, but excitement lost to panic and dismay.

His gaze fell on me, and I barely registered that everyone around us had fallen silent, watching how this weird interaction played out.

"Ansen?" Archer's disbelief rang through the store.

Fuck.

"I, uh, just got to town." My lame answer was the best I could do. I should've prepared for this, but I'd had several other issues to work through and very little time. Goddamn, it'd been a long day.

The little girl ran to Archer and hooked her hand in his. "Do you know him, Daddy?"

Archer wasn't smiling. Hurt mingled with his disbelief. "This is your uncle. Ansen."

The woman who must be Archer's wife, Delaney, looked between the two of us, her mouth open.

Aggie crossed to my side, her expression just as stunned as I felt.

I dropped my gaze to my niece. Was today the day I met all the girls I'd let down? I gave in to the rising delight of meeting the girl who outed me and crouched down. "Hiya. I haven't met you yet."

"Daddy said you like to do your own thing." She was smart.

"Guilty. You must be Emmaline."

She grinned and showed off a missing bottom tooth. "Do you know how old I am?"

I pretended to think. "Almost six years old." I earned another grin from my niece, and I pointed to the toddler. "And he's Vaden. Just turned two."

"Where you been?" she asked.

Kids and their blunt questions. Guilt might as well stay on simmer. "Busy getting in trouble." I straightened and faced my brother. Eyes a few shades darker than mine stared back. "I wasn't sure how this job was going to turn out."

And if it had fallen through, I had planned to leave as stealthily as I arrived.

He either didn't ask questions because Dad had told him about Kansas or because we had a rapt audience. We grew up in a small community and knew better than anyone how quickly rumors spread.

His wife stepped to his side. "Hi, Ansen. I'm Laney. Only Archer calls me Delaney."

I stuck my hand out. "Nice to finally meet you."

"Sure is," she said as if she realized this situation was more uncomfortable for me than anyone else. Her grip was strong, confident, like she didn't have time for shit from anyone. The brusque handshake reminded me of when I was introduced to Aggie.

Emmaline tugged on Archer's hand. "Daddy says you like horses."

"I like them a lot," I answered.

"Hon, let's go wait outside." Laney tugged on Emmaline's other hand until Archer let her go. "Daddy needs to talk to Uncle Ansen."

Uncle Ansen. What a mindfuck. I'd just met my niece, and she was almost six.

"What are you doing here?" Archer asked quietly, his attention swiveling to Aggie. "A job?"

Aggie stepped forward to offer a firm shake. "Aggie Knight. I work for your uncle at the refinery."

He smiled as he clasped her hand and let it go. Some of the tension drained out of the room. "Uncle Cameron?"

He sounded fond of the guy. My mental feet were slipping off a cliff. I was facing my brother, who used to dress impeccably as an adult, in a way we'd never been able to as kids, and he was now full of dust with the bottoms of his jeans frayed *and* he acted fond of relatives our dad wanted nothing to do with. "I thought we weren't talking to him," I murmured.

Archer's grin fell. "He's different than he used to be. You'd know if you called once in a while."

Any more guilt and shame and I'd need some luggage just for antacid. Hell, maybe the guy working the counter knew more about my family than me, and it didn't matter if he overheard.

"I'm in town now. For a while." I ignored the way Aggie arched a reddish-gold brow at me. "She opened a horse rescue, and I'm her new employee."

"You find a job up here just because or . . . " Archer had never been an obtuse guy. Unfortunately.

"Aggie and I go way back, and she heard I needed work." I was her bitch until I got my feet back under me somehow.

The solemnity in his expression told me enough. He'd talked to Dad and heard it all.

If I wasn't so distracted by my brother's reaction, I would've sensed the building storm at my elbow. She let out a sarcastic laugh and swatted the back of her hand across my shoulder. "Yes, we're old *friends*."

Ah, hell.

Archer's alarmed gaze lifted to mine, but again he was smart and didn't say anything as Aggie stalked to the chicken feed and stooped. I almost jumped to help her, the bags were fifty pounds, but she hauled one over her shoulder and marched past me.

"I bought two. Grab the second one when you're done catching up." Her caustic tone hung in the air.

The employee was silent as a field mouse under a circling hawk, watching everything.

I sighed and met Archer's bemused gaze.

"I'm not an expert," he drawled, "but if Delaney talked to me like that, I'd be under the impression she was pissed with me 'bout somethin'."

The absurdity of today and his ill-timed tease made me laugh, the type of laugh that could lead to crying if I were the type to shed tears. I learned as a kid they did no good. Shit happened anyway.

The co-op employee pushed off his stool. "I'll grab that second one for her. You two take your time."

"I got it," I said, going to a bag and pitching it to my shoulder like Aggie had done. "Gotta earn my wages."

Archer followed me out. Aggie was in the cab, her mouth set in a cantankerous line. Laney was standing at the end of another pickup, and the kids were playing in the bed of the truck.

"Dare I ask how you two know each other?" Archer asked only loud enough for me to hear.

I could brush him off, but after the last six months, I was tired of the avoidance game. "We were going to get married."

Archer jolted like my words were a physical shock. "Married?"

"When I was working in Montana. It turned into a thing and didn't happen." I slapped the bag down in the back of the pickup next to hers and closed the tailgate. Half-truths were wearing me out. "I fucked up. Bad."

He nodded like he'd expected that was the case. I hated that he was right. "When? Then or now?"

"Both." I draped my hand across the back of my neck. "When it comes to the women at least. Not the other bullshit."

He studied me for a moment but didn't inquire more about what happened in Kansas. "And she still hired you?"

"What can I say? My reputation precedes me." I was doing it again. Talking around a subject. I pushed a hand through my hair, wishing I'd grabbed my hat from my pickup before we left Aggie's place. "It's her form of revenge. She learned the trouble I got in and realized she could hire me for dirt cheap. I'll do right by the animals."

"You always did. What the hell happened at your old job?"

His unfailing confidence in my morals was humbling. We used to be close when we were kids, and I hadn't felt that sense of comradery with him in a long time until now. I let out another hard breath and rested my hand on the top of the tailgate. "Pissed off the wrong guy—and his daughter."

"You never did your best thinking with your dick."

"Do any of us?"

His warm gaze landed on his wife. "Sometimes it works out."

Irritation or envy bloomed in my gut—I couldn't tell which. "I should get going. It's my first day in town, and I obviously haven't made the best second impression."

I tapped my fingers on the cool metal. So far, the meet and greet with my brother wasn't like the few times when we'd met up after he left home. He wasn't spewing corporate jargon or the amounts of annual revenue he brought in. He looked at me like he was ready to listen, and he joked with me like we were back on the ranch, wasting the days doing jobs kids our age shouldn't have been responsible for.

The speed of finger tapping increased. If I'd been more responsive to his attempts to repair our relationship, I might've saved myself the special hell I'd been living in. "We should talk sometime." I held my breath. This was worse than asking a girl on a date. A refusal served me right.

"I'd say we're about due," he said easily, chasing away the nerves I had from asking. "What's your schedule?"

I let out a scornful breath. "Whatever she says it is."

Archer lifted his ball cap and ran a hand through his dark hair. A few strands of gray hugged his temples, and my throat worked. The last time I'd seen Archer, we'd been in our twenties. He was almost forty. I'd missed over a decade of his life. "The sooner you realize it's better that way, the easier it is."

"I'm not like that."

He glanced at Aggie in the pickup, watching us in the rearview mirror and then at the feed I hauled out. "Sure about that?" He chuckled and smacked me on the arm. "I owe Delaney a girls' night, but we could meet up the weekend after. I'll let you tell me when."

He was walking back to his wife, and I pivoted on a heel

to face him. "Hey, Archer." I waited until he turned. "Dad doesn't know I'm here. Let me tell him."

"And the rest of our family?"

"What family?" I shook my head. Right. All the Barrons but Dad lived in Coal Haven. I'd worry about my immediate relatives first. "Never mind."

"They're good people. And there's a shit ton of 'em. I know it's not what we're used to, but . . . it turns normal pretty damn quick."

Tension crept along my shoulders. Multiple family members wanting to get into my business. Finding out the rumors spread about me. Or worse, the straight-up facts. "Let me get settled first. Then I'll talk to Dad." I owed him that.

"It's good to see you."

The sincerity in his words stuck with me as I crawled into the cab. I buckled myself in. Aggie methodically backed up and calmly maneuvered onto the highway to return to Crocus Valley.

"Spill it," I said. "I know you're dyin' to chew into me."

"I can't imagine what you're talking about." Her hand tightened on the wheel, but my mind kept wanting to replay how she threw around fifty pounds like it was nothing, and she did it all fancied up in her riding coat and dress boots. Suddenly, nothing was sexier. "You mean how your brother didn't recognize my name when you told me that he was working and couldn't come to the wedding? That he and your dad couldn't get time off or risk their jobs? And I was so incensed for them! But in reality, you didn't tell them about me."

"It was better not to." I slouched in the seat and let my legs take up all the space on the passenger side. Her gaze touched my thighs, then back to my face, and her lips flattened. "If you found out before we got married that your daddy was paying me, the backlash would've been epic—"

"It was."

"—and if it worked out, I would've told them like Archer told us—with a message."

"But you knew Archer eloped."

"Like three years after. They were separated for a while in between. We never met her, though. He didn't bring her to see Dad and the dirt pasture he lives in until they reconciled."

She shook her head, her attention on the road. "I can't believe that was your first time meeting your brother's family."

"Not everyone has a close family."

She flinched. "I've hardly talked to Daddy since I left. I've seen him once and called a few times, that's all."

I closed my eyes. Logically, I knew Barns had ruined his relationship with his daughter by trying to treat her like one of his stock, but the responsibility still rested heavily on my shoulders. "You should visit him if he's dying."

"If it goes anything like before, no thanks." She might think she sounded matter-of-fact, but her words were like armor, like she was protecting herself by feigning nonchalance. "He was enraged when he thought I might've gotten engaged to the last guy I was with."

I ground my teeth together. I didn't like hearing about Aggie getting married, and I had no business stepping in. "Is that why you're still single?"

"I'm allergic to getting engaged."

I snorted. "I've developed the same allergy."

The rest of the drive was in silence. There was only so much rehashing of the past we could do. The hurt that I suspected simmered beneath her skin wasn't something I could heal. All I could do was not make it worse.

As for our present, I had nothing to offer, and I was working through my own shit. I had done enough to her. I didn't need to drag her into the muck with me.

She parked in the same spot the truck had been in when I arrived and hopped out. Barking from in the house caught my attention. I glanced at the picture window to see a brown-and-white Australian shepherd pressed between the curtains and the glass.

"Aggie—"

"See you in the morning." She pushed out her door. "Remember the chickens. Oh, can you haul the feed to the coop? There's storage in the front for feeders and bags. Put 'em on the pallet to help keep the mice out. The keys to the trailer are hidden under the bottom step."

She skirted around the front of the vehicle.

I rushed out. "Agatha, is that Tex?"

She stiffened and pivoted on her pert little heel, but her spin ended up being nothing but a tease I greedily took in. "Don't call me Agatha, and yes."

Saying her full name was a sure way to make her stop. I'd needed that small win. "You still have my dog you stole?" The absurdity put me dangerously close to laughing. I hadn't pursued the stolen dog because I knew better than to take on that fight when all of the Knights hated me. I knew she'd be good to Tex.

"I didn't steal him; he refused to leave my side." Her lips quirked like she was holding back a snicker. "I hate to break it to you, but he's become a city dog. That's why he's inside. He'll gallivant all over the county and get run over. He needs to be eased into country life."

I'd gotten him as a puppy. My first dog as a grown-up. A new addition to the family I had fooled myself I was making. A symbol that said I wasn't tricking a woman into marrying me so I could get rich and have my own place. Seeing him now was . . . bizarre. "He's done okay?"

She tipped her head, and I swear the sun broke through a cloud just to shine on her. "Eventually. He got me kicked out of a few apartments, and I had to fork over a lot of money to kennel him during the day while I finished college, but eventually, I rented a house and gave him some of his own space." She cast a wistful glance at the dog watching us. "He could've used a ranch job. Now I have one for him, but he's too old and doesn't have the experience he needs to survive country life. All I can hope is that I can get him used to the animals so he doesn't erratically try to herd them."

I didn't know what about seeing Tex was hitting me in the solar plexus, but I couldn't quit looking at him. It was like she'd taken a piece of me and cared for it all this time.

"Want me to let him out so you can see him?" She picked at her nails as if her question wasn't like a peace offering between us. Tex was neutral ground.

Not trusting my voice, I nodded.

A minute later, Tex was sniffing me from crotch to toe and circling me, his tail a whirlwind. I stuffed my hands in his fur. "Looking good, Tex." Satisfied with what he smelled, he ran to the lawn to do his business. "He's so much more mellow than when he was a puppy."

"I'd like to say it's all my hard work training him, but it's age. I think he has more than a few good years left, though."

Because of her. If he'd been with me, he might've gotten kicked in the head by a horse, trampled because I was busy working or shot by one of the more ornery bosses I'd had. Aggie did right by him, and he hadn't made it easy. I hadn't deserved her then. I'd fooled myself that taking the money wouldn't hurt her. She grew up working hard, but there was a difference between toiling away while the bank account was loaded and working your ass off while the money you did earn turned to ash and blew away in the wind.

She'd taken my dog and gave him a home. My last ex would've tossed him out of a moving vehicle for having the poor luck to be called mine.

The last ten years only showed me I couldn't pick women and that I couldn't afford the good ones.

Aggie

I was curled up in bed, my hair free and trying to frizz after a night of sleep. My knees were propped up, and I draped my arms over them with my phone in my hands.

On my screen, Sutton's freshly scrubbed face was visible. She was in a time zone an hour behind, but she had to get up earlier than me for work. Wilder was already out of the house, and she'd messaged to talk. "So it's done, huh?"

"It's done. He hasn't come back to complain about the trailer."

"Is it that bad?"

"No, just old. I replaced the nasty carpet with cheap shit and bleached everything possible when I lived in it." I had stayed in the trailer while the house was getting built and had left the furnishings I'd moved in there with and filled my house with an updated, cohesive look. More financial waste, according to Cody.

"I'm sure he's lived in worse."

Probably. Unless I recalled the pictures from my drunken night with Sutton. "Except for when he was sleeping in the pageant queen's bed in her rich daddy's house."

"You have a rich daddy, and Ansen stayed in the cabin where the power kept going out."

True. He'd never complained then, either. "He's not what I expected. He's different."

"It's been a long time."

I agreed, but that wasn't the reason. His jaw was set harder, his eyes darker, and he didn't strut around like he was the only cock in the henhouse. If he was a rooster, he'd be missing feathers and leaving hens the hell alone. "I must seem different to him too."

Better? Did he think I looked more polished? More refined like his beauty queen ex?

She arched a blonde brow. "It doesn't matter how he sees you though, right?"

"Of course not. I just know I've changed."

"You were pretty back then too—and now, of course. Don't let Barns make you feel otherwise."

I'd fortified myself against Daddy and his opinions, but he was still my father. "How is Daddy doing?"

She chewed on her lower lip. "I don't think it's going to be long, Aggie."

Sadness sank heavily in my belly. Every time I had tried to talk to him on the phone over the years, he berated me for ruining things with Ansen. If I had a boyfriend at the time, he raged and called the guy he'd never met names. And Lawson had thought to make nice with him? My ex was either optimistic or thought he'd marry into an oil empire. Daddy's empire was complicated and, as I'd learned, came with strings attached. "I can't bring myself to visit him. Or to call anymore."

"Barns made his choice, Aggie. It's not your fault."

My fault was listening to Mama. My brothers understood, but they blamed me at the same time. Ever since I got the life insurance money, there'd been a distance between us

I hadn't been able to cross. Each year, the gap closed more, but I accepted they felt the way they felt.

She squinted at her phone. "Shit, I've gotta finish getting ready. An emergency cropped up."

Since she was a large animal vet, I made our typical joke. "Something prolapsed?"

She rolled her eyes. "Something's always prolapsed."

Once I hung up, I hopped out of bed and ran through the shower. When I opened the bathroom door, Tex was whining.

"Sorry, bud. I'm hurrying." I threw on a sweater dress and a thick pair of leggings. I usually walked Tex before I got ready for work, but with the possibility of an Ansen sighting, I was changing my routine. Temporarily.

Twisting my hair into its standard bun, I saw my phone light up. Ansen's name came up on the screen and a wave of déja vu almost knocked me over. I dropped my arms and stared. I had added his number when I hired him, but I didn't anticipate what seeing his name again would do to me. A flash of that girl who grinned each time he called ran through my head.

Afraid he'd come to the house, I punched the answer button and put it on speaker so I could finish getting ready. "Yeah?"

"Morning."

I had to close my eyes at the sound of his deep voice booming into my bathroom. Lawson had a deep voice, but there was a whiny quality to it that had grated on my nerves the longer we were together. "Everything okay?"

"Fine. Chores are done." Already? "Where do I find the cat food?"

I frowned at my image in the mirror. "What cats?"

"The cat at the trailer, living under the steps . . . with the kittens."

Forgetting my hair, I leaned on the bathroom counter, staring into the phone like I was facing a boardroom. "I don't have cats."

He chuckled, and my belly clenched. "I'm all up in the pussy here, Aggie."

A pulse between my thighs reminded me it liked when he was all up in the pussy. "Kittens?"

"Over a month old, I'd guess. Six of 'em. Mama cat's in good shape. Friendly but skinny. I assumed they were dumped, and you let them stay."

Damn. I should've expected that living in the country. I was still close enough to town to make my property a prime dumping ground. Which was why I hadn't stressed about getting barn cats. They would find me.

But I wasn't ready for them. "The trailer is right off the highway. Those kittens will get smacked in no time once they start moving around."

"I can try to relocate them to the barn. Mama cat might stay if that's where the food is."

"Yeah, that's fine." As long as I didn't imagine a cuddle puddle of kittens tucked in his strong arms. Swoon. "I gotta get to work, but I can bring some cat food home."

"Don't worry about it. I got it."

Because he worked for me. "Um, thanks."

"You got it, boss. Or should I call you Christie?"

I bit the inside of my cheek. I was alone in the bathroom. No one would see me smile. "I like the ring of 'boss.' Listen, I forgot to mention the vet's coming tonight when I get done with work. He works late one night of the week."

"Got it, boss."

My traitorous mouth wanted to tip up again. "Text if you need anything. I'm in meetings all day."

"Sounds amazing," he said dryly. "I'm going to study the horses and come up with a plan."

The spear of jealousy was sharper than expected, and I punched the button to hang up. I stared at myself in the mirror. I looked the same as my first day working a job in my career after college—work that didn't include manure or dirt.

"Health insurance. Dental. Retirement." I smoothed a hand over my bound hair. "Freedom."

Freedom was hiring my lying ex to work my horse rescue, but from where I stood at this moment, it looked a lot like footing the bill for someone else to live my dream.

Which was ironically what he would've done for me with Daddy's money had we gotten married.

Five

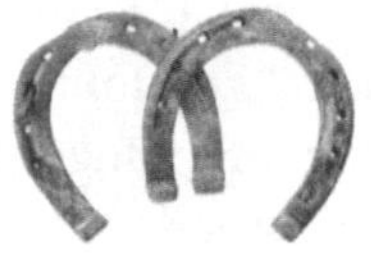

ANSEN

Aggie could've let me deal with the vet, but that wouldn't be her. She liked to be in the thick of it. But when Dr. Jake Burrows hopped out of his red Dodge pickup, I got suspicious. She had told me she hadn't met him before, just talked to him on the phone.

After seeing him, I didn't think there was anyone with hormones who'd want to miss Dr. Jake's visits.

The guy was a couple inches shorter than me but still six feet tall, with a stocky build that lent well to western-cut jeans and cowboy boots. His grin wasn't dental-ad ready, with a slight chip on one front tooth and the type of mildly uneven teeth that wasn't bad enough for braces. He wore a red-and-gray-plaid shirt with a deep-green, puffy vest and managed not to look like he was celebrating Christmas early.

I'd worked with a ton of Dr. Jakes in my time and most of them hadn't been veterinarians. Many of them had been players, but I hadn't cared. They were country guys with ready smiles and casual attitudes that put everyone at ease. I hadn't given them a second thought other than how I worked with them.

I fucking hated Dr. Jake on sight.

Same with the way Aggie smiled and laughed with him as they talked about the rescues. He'd been through all the horses—two geldings and three mares. I'd stood back to watch how the animals dealt with him and how the animals communicated with each other when someone was working with them.

My mental list was long.

"They're filling out real nice and their winter coats are looking better than when Tanya had them."

Aggie noticed my quizzical look. "My real estate agent boarded them before me right after they were seized."

Dr. Jake's grin went to a thousand percent. "I told Tanya to give me some time to find a taker, but she tracked you down." He shook his head and eyed Aggie. "I'll be honest— I wasn't so sure about handing off five cases to a stranger. You seem like you're familiar with horses, at least."

I snorted. Familiar? Aggie used to pester me and Eliot. *That mare's going to foal early. You gotta watch her.*

Daddy worked with him the other day. You're gonna hafta help him unlearn bad habits—I'm talking about the gelding, not Daddy. We've given up on Daddy.

That one won't ever be good around kids. Too high-spirited.

Aggie nodded matter-of-factly. "I had to think about whether I was really going to do this."

"I'm glad to hear it," the vet crooned like he was placating her. "A lot of people love animals and just jump in." Spoken like that was exactly what she'd done.

My teeth were starting to ache from clenching my jaw. I worried Aggie would preen at what his tone said should be a compliment, but her expression was flat. She used to be sensitive to her brothers treating her like she didn't know anything. If she still possessed that skill, maybe she wouldn't end up under Dr. Jake and his croon.

Dr. Jake opened his vest and took a business card out of his shirt pocket and produced a pen from somewhere inside his vest. He scrawled something on the card. "This is my personal cell. Call me if an emergency comes up. Otherwise, you can get ahold of the office to get the chiropractor's referral and schedule their teeth floating. They'll walk you through what all that means." He glanced at me. "You look like you know horses too. Ever worked with equine chiropractors?"

"Once or twice." Or a thousand times. I flourished a grin. "Anything can be Googled, right?"

Dismay passed through his expression before he caught the light tease in my tone. He laughed. "Right. Do you need a farrier's contact?" He was speaking to me. He dug a business card out of his vest.

"Yes, please." Aggie plucked the card I assumed had the farrier's number that was aimed my way and stuffed it into the pocket of the same coat she'd been wearing yesterday. "I don't know anyone around here."

The dress-and-leggings look was new. So were her ankle boots. When we'd dated, I hadn't seen her in anything other than cowboy boots, even when we'd gone out.

"I'll text you. How about that?" His grin should be stomped into the ground. The sorrel mare, Shelby From The Block, would do the job for me. She'd shied away from me and Dr. Jake but was more relaxed around Aggie. After being moved from pasture to pasture after months or years of neglect, I didn't blame her. She startled easily and distrusted anyone with a set of balls.

There were worse traits a horse could have.

"That's fine," Aggie said. "Thanks for coming out."

"I can help you get them caught up." His curious gaze landed on me.

Aggie had introduced me as her new rescue manager, but Dr. Jake had been the same as every vet I'd worked with —get the job done, chat later. In his case, flirt later.

"Yes, Ansen's a horse trainer, so he's an all-in-one package."

Dr. Jake's scrutiny narrowed. "You've worked with rescues before?"

"No, but I'm also not getting them ready to rack up the lifetime earnings, and I don't have owners breathing down my neck about upcoming competitions, so it's a nice change. Aggie will give me and the horses the time we need."

I didn't realize how I meant it until I said it. Her daddy had been one of the worst about rushing training windows. Turnover was income. It was one of the reasons why I wanted my own place. My own business. Time and patience were a couple of the things Aggie and I had talked about when we brainstormed starting our own training business together.

I never thought I'd be her employee.

If I dwelled on it, I'd rage. Or get depressed. Or fuck— just carry on. I couldn't change the past, and in a way, it was a relief to be done running from it.

Aggie's gaze was on me, and I met it fully. I meant what I said. She'd give me the range to do the job these animals needed from me. It was why I had stayed. Even a desperate man had limits.

"All right, then." Dr. Jake gave Aggie one last too-familiar smile. Hers was professional but distant.

Good.

"Call me. Anytime."

I bristled at his smooth tone and glared at his back while

he swaggered to his truck. The horses could probably sense my saltiness toward the flirtatious vet. His invite to call was about more than business.

I'd used the same line before.

I leaned on the railing and watched the horses graze. The ripping of grass and their crunching filled the air. There wasn't much grass left this time of year, and they were limited in their grazing options while I worked with them. I'd be feeding them alfalfa bales, and I'd have to procure more to get them through the winter. Once I was happy with their training, I could turn them out to the larger pasture until they were sold.

After I fixed the sagging and broken fence line. "What do you think?"

She nibbled her bottom lip, and I had to rip my gaze away, reminding myself for the second time in five minutes that I stayed out of professional respect. Sporting an erection would work against my determination. "I think Dr. Jake thinks I'm a silly girl who likes animals and wants to save the world."

"You should be used to that attitude from your brothers."

"Yes." Her sigh was resigned. "So Shelby From The Block doesn't like men, but she's not as cranky tonight as she was this morning when I was out."

"She's already gotten better around me, but I wasn't bustling around like Dr. Jake."

"That's a good sign. And Bruno Mars Bar?"

Horse names didn't surprise me anymore, but some of these made me smile. "Bruno's a mellow gelding, but he's lazy. All of them have been handled, and maybe at one point they were all saddle trained, but all five are project horses."

"Think there was abuse?"

"Negative reinforcement, definitely. Shelby, especially,

and she's got a temper. Bruno's too complacent to argue, so he was probably seen as a good horse. Take Me Home Tomorrow is the youngest of the bunch, and I was worried he'd have the least training, but his memory is the freshest. The other two mares have a bond that makes me think they might have to be sold as a pair."

"Watermelon Sugar Low is going to be called Melon for short. Downtown Girl sounds like a hooker pony."

"You can ride her a long time."

She snorted, and I laughed, startling myself by how long it'd been since I'd done more than smile for an audience.

"The old owner liked to put a spin on musical shit." I pointed at each horse. "Shelby, Bruno, Morrow, Melon, and Downy."

"Agreed." One of the horses huffed while she looked around. "So. Where're the kittens?"

I pushed off the post and led her into the barn, eager to see her reaction to the kittens. They were cute buggers. "Since you wanted to stack hay along the back and have a path to move the skid steer in and out, I made a straw nest in this corner and surrounded it by a couple of old tires I found behind the trailer."

The new food and water dishes I'd bought earlier were sitting on an empty pallet. I squatted by them and peeked behind the tire. A faint mew sounded from the shadows.

"She's nursing." I moved out of the way.

Heedless of the way her leggings would pick up the bits of straw and never let them go, she knelt. On her hands and knees, with her apple ass in the air and me an avid onlooker, she leaned to look behind the tire.

"Who's a good mama?" she cooed.

She was talking to the cat, but my dick thought she was speaking directly to it. Her round butt and that position—I had to blink back memories I had no business reviewing.

They'd been tucked away for my spank bank to use when I was alone and could hate myself later.

"Aw, she's a little tortie. I thought she was a black cat at first, but I see the orange and white flecks. She can't be very old."

"Probably less than a year," I said gruffly, lust pounding at my temples. After my breakup six months ago, I had sworn off women, knowing it wouldn't last, that I'd be stupid and weak in the future. I always was, but I wasn't prepared for it now.

Had to be the self-imposed dry spell.

Her ass wiggled as she dug her phone out of her coat pocket and turned the flashlight on. She didn't shine it directly on them but cast enough light to get details. "Pretty kitties. Oh, you're so pretty."

Somehow, I smiled despite the tightness in my body. She stuffed her phone away and crawled back. She stood up, and I didn't mean to watch her brush herself off, but I tracked every move as if I'd paid four figures for this lap dance.

She straightened and huffed a hunk of hair out of her eyes. I wanted to brush it back, to see a little more of the wild, unrefined girl I knew years ago.

Her gaze flickered when she caught me watching her. "What are you going to call the mama cat?"

"Me? She's yours."

"You found her."

"Tex. Since you're going to claim her anyway."

She smirked. "You wouldn't."

"Maybe a play of a country song. Boot Scootin' Booger."

She laughed. "Gross."

I missed this easiness between us. I hadn't found it since her. "Drunk In A Barn. Body Like A Back Yard. Garth Tortie. Fancy Like Milk."

She waved her hands, laughing. "Stop. Fancy. We'll call her Fancy." She poked a finger into my chest. "*Not* short for Fancy Like Milk."

"And the six kittens?"

She rolled her eyes and drew her hand back. "I'm not prepared to hear your ideas for those."

The horses were linked by music. A little like Aggie and her siblings. "You could do books, like your mama did with you and your brothers."

Her smile fell. "I don't read much anymore."

"Why not?"

"I moved a lot, and Tex was a handful. Didn't accumulate much that he could chew up."

Like the books he'd destroyed the day we broke up. We had a lack of treasured personal belongings in common, but hers was due to puppy collateral damage. Mine was because I didn't form attachments. I'd rather avoid the severing.

I didn't want her to quit talking to me, but our thoughts didn't need to go down that road. "Where's your tack?"

"I . . . have none." She shrugged and stuffed her hands in her coat pockets. The barn was getting cooler with the sun setting and her breath puffed out. "I didn't want to fight Daddy for my saddle. He'd say it was his, and I wasn't using Mama's money to pay him for something that was mine."

Fucking Barns. He was like that. If it was on his land and he'd spent one shiny penny on it, he claimed ownership. I could let it roll off when I worked for him, but growing up like that had to suck.

"You haven't ridden since you left?" I asked.

"No."

"Do you miss it?"

"Do you?"

I clamped my jaw down. I didn't have to answer her. She

was making a point. One thing about Aggie, she didn't push. She hadn't needled me for my secrets. The subject of Archer and my dad, when we'd been planning our guest list, was a perfect example. I fed her a half-truth during our engagement, and she was good with it. The problem was she'd trusted me to tell her more if it was pertinent, and I hadn't.

"I miss riding when it was easy," I said. I used to compete with the horses of my old boss's clients. It had been fun for five minutes before I realized I was as much of a tool to earn other people's money as the horse. I wanted my own place. A house a lot like the one Aggie built . . .

Had she built that house based off our old plans?

And what if she had? I'd entertained her, knowing full well I'd planned to move us to Texas and purchase the only property that had ever felt like home.

A chill stole over my shoulders. Surely it was from the cooler weather and not thoughts of the past. I had on a long-sleeved shirt, but fixing fence and working with the vet had kept me warm. "I miss riding when I'm not dealing with . . . everything else."

Her brows crunched together like she was going to ask me more. Then she nodded. "Same."

She left the barn and started for the house. The more distance between us, the more the cold seeped into my clothing.

"I can give you my card to buy supplies tomorrow," she said. "You have your own tack, I assume?"

"Yes." I'd been away from home for fifteen years, and the closest I'd gotten to my dream ranch was owning my own tack and training supplies. I stopped in the opening of the barn. Watching her walk away was too much of a treat to resist. "You trust me on the loose with your credit card?"

She faced me while walking backward, her gaze solemn.

"My credit card isn't what I'm worried about with you." Then she circled around and continued to the house.

∩∩

Aggie

Sutton: Are your pants on?

I was leaving work when I saw the message from Sutton.

I slid into the pickup but didn't start it so I could reply. The wind was bitter, but inside the cab, I was fine.

I puzzled over Sutton's text. Did she mean to send this to Wilder?

Me: Yes?

Sutton: So he hasn't charmed them off?

I sputtered out a laugh.

Me: Pants have stayed in place. Haven't seen him much this week actually. It hasn't been bad.

He'd also been busy. I caught glimpses of him, all in the name of making sure my new employee was doing what he was supposed to. I spent too many mornings watching him sprinkle flakes of a bale over the fence and slowly let the horses get used to him. He was also Mr. Handyman around the rescue and a shopaholic with my card. The fencing supplies and horse gear were expensive, and a neat stack of receipts was tucked into the door each day.

My reaction to seeing the receipts was like a thrill at getting some secret message from a boy I liked.

Sutton: Wilder has been asking about you. Someone called Cody to make sure Ansen wasn't back working there.

Me: Why?

Sutton: His old boss. I told Wilder about the rescue but not about Ansen.

I didn't specifically ask her to *not* talk to Wilder about me. I would never encourage secrets between the two, but I wasn't sure what Sutton and Wilder talked about these days. My brother got stuck in his head a lot and seemed to be married to his job more than his wife.

Me: He's not my dirty secret.

I groaned. After the way my brothers chased Ansen off, they would have opinions with a capital *O* about me hiring him. And they'd let me know it.

Me: He kind of is. I'll figure out what to do.

Sutton: I won't say anything to Wilder yet. Should be easy enough.

Would she talk to me about Wilder if there were problems? I was his sister, so it could be awkward. Yet, I grew up in the same house as him, with Daddy. I knew we were all fucked up in our own way.

I stared out the window. Cody didn't need to be bothered with this, but as the oldest and with Daddy sick, he hoisted the world on his shoulders and wouldn't let go. If he didn't hear what I was doing from me, he'd be hurt, and he was going through enough right now.

Dialing him, I prepared what I was going to say. He picked up with an "Alcott," telling me he hadn't bothered to check to see who was on the other side.

"Hi, Cody."

His voice warmed slightly. "Aggie, how's the new place? You still sure the builder was decent?"

"Everything's still attached." I tolerated his questions because he'd raised me when Daddy wouldn't. It was nice to know someone cared. Cody looked out for me in his own way. "Listen, before we get too far, I want to talk to you about something."

"Everything okay?"

"It's fine. Really. And keep that in mind while I talk. I opened a horse rescue." I left out the drunken part of my final decision, or he'd never take me seriously.

His breath hissed in—or out. I couldn't tell. "You have a full-time job already."

"I found someone to work the rescue."

"Fuck's sake, for how much?"

"Fuck's sake," I mimicked, "I'm thirty-one, and it's none of your business."

"Please tell me it's a woman and you didn't hire some guy to live and work on your property."

"Not a woman." Ansen was all man.

"Did you at least check his references?"

"That's what I'm calling you about. And it's only out of respect that I'm telling you, but you sometimes forget I can make my own decisions, and I don't need your approval." I wanted it, but that was different. I would probably skate backward on my progress with Cody after he heard who I hired, but I'd rather tell him than have him find out elsewhere. He'd been through a lot since Meg got sick.

"Fuck." I hadn't heard Cody swear this much in years. He was still grieving and probably wasn't acknowledging it. "It's not a coincidence I was called about a former horse trainer, and now you're telling me you hired someone with that hitch in your voice?"

"No." He had to be talking about Ansen. Irritation at Ansen's recent former employer spiked hot in my blood. Why had they gone that far back in Ansen's employment history? "No coincidence."

I was met with silence. I hated adding stress to my brother.

"I'm not after him, Cody, I swear." I didn't sound like the thirty-one-year-old I boasted about being. I sounded like a teenager caught drinking. "He's affordable." I winced at the way I phrased it. "It's not personal. It was a business decision."

"Did you do any background checks? It's been a long time. Hell, you didn't even have to go far. *You're* the research a lot of employers should be doing on him. He took bribe money to marry you." Hearing it out loud still stung. "Of course he's fucking affordable. He can't get hired anywhere, and when he does, his past comes out and he's let go. Didn't you check into him at all? Do you know what they're saying he did?"

"Of course, I know. You know the animal stuff is bullshit."

"Then why is it all over the Kansas City news?"

"I don't know. I didn't ask him the story."

"Aggie."

"Cody."

We sat in a quiet standoff for several seconds. I wasn't defending my actions, or I'd look even more impulsive, and telling Cody I was confident I could trust Ansen around animals wasn't what he wanted to hear. He was right. I had no proof other than a strong gut feeling and trust that I shouldn't have for a guy who betrayed me.

Finally, he said, "I knew you weren't over him." He spoke my fear out loud.

I bit the inside of my cheek. I'd gotten on with my life. I'd done a lot since I was that twenty-one-year-old bride. I was over Ansen. I had to be. "I'm not looking for a relationship. He's been here a week, and other than working with the vet and a few check-ins, we don't see or talk to each other. He's been really good with the animals. Except for keeping all the damn chicken eggs after he does chores."

Cody coughed a disbelieving laugh, and I wished I could've seen the two seconds he lost his composure. The brother, during the funeral, had been laced with titanium and just as expressive.

"If you saw what I was paying him, you would see better how this is screwing him over." My gut flopped. The man working with the horses should be compensated fairly, but I'd never be able to afford Ansen otherwise. "He really does know what he's doing."

"He probably never made a lot training or competing with other people's horses."

Guilt I'd been trying to ignore welled higher in my belly. After reading more of what was said online about him, I could tie on a cape and call myself a hero for giving him a job. I didn't know what happened, but I knew there was a whole side of the story that didn't get aired, and what had been told wasn't the truth. Except for him breaking that girl's heart. I could believe that.

"Why else do you think he was trying to use women to get money?" Cody's words gouged an old wound. He never did think Ansen would marry me for any reason other than cold, hard cash. No one did. The worst reality check was having to convince myself they were right.

"I'm not looking to start anything with him. After Lawson, I don't care to find another guy who thinks he knows better than me. A man who wants me to do all the changing. Is it so wrong to want a little retribution over what happened?"

"That's what this is really about? Ten years later?" Cody sighed and I could picture him behind his giant oak desk in his big, boring office with his head in his hand. "No, Aggie. It's not wrong, but I think you forget how messy things can become when we're dealing with humans. We can't just throw a headstall on them and lead them around."

The mess Cody referred to was the biggest reason why I was keeping my distance from Ansen. We could keep stuffing receipts in the door, and we could message each other. I didn't need to go to the trailer or be outside when he was. Enough about Ansen. Cody was informed. Now I wanted to talk to him as a brother. "How are the kids?"

"Fine." His grumble was unmistakable.

"Your in-laws still being pushy?"

"They want the kids over Christmas break, and Meg's mom dropped a subtle hint about looking for schools in Helena for the spring semester."

Instant anger sparked inside me. Meg's parents were pushy know-it-alls. After I'd met them for the first time, I could see why Meg was an ice princess. "The kids are just fine with you."

"I work a lot, and then there's Barns—"

"Cody, the kids need you. They need their grandparents to be their grandparents. They don't need surrogate parents when they still have you."

"Thanks, Aggie," he said softly. "But I do have a lot of work and the kids are . . . a change might be good for them."

Our roles flipped, however briefly. It was my turn to champion what I thought was best for Cody and less time with the kids wasn't it. "You guys come out here whenever you want. The house is big enough."

"Ansen is in the trailer?"

"Across the property," I assured him. Living in all my old things. A righteous idea during a night out with Sutton was a little sadder in the sober light of day. He didn't arrive with a trailer of belongings and the back of his pickup box had likely had his personal tack. What did the man own other than that and the vehicle? "Maybe Thanksgiving?"

"I think you should come here for at least Thanksgiving. Barns isn't doing well."

Tears poked hot jabs in the backs of my eyes. I should've called Daddy Barns like my brother. Then maybe I wouldn't keep hoping he'd turn into a father figure. "You know what he's like—"

"Suck it up for one last time. Not for him, Aggie. For you. Trust me. I regret not talking to Mama."

My throat grew thick. I was the one who talked to Mama. I didn't know what to think about a world without Daddy. Not having him interfere in my life was different than not having him at all. Could I tolerate one more visit where he didn't see me? "I'll think about it. Come out for Christmas, then. Tell your in-laws the kids have plans to sled in my pastures."

"Their grandparents might storm Buffalo Gully if we don't go to Helena for Christmas." His tone was the lightest I'd heard in a couple of months. "I'll think about it."

As soon as he said that, I knew I'd go back for Thanksgiving. Maybe I did need to say goodbye to Daddy, so I didn't hate myself for avoiding him once he was gone. But Cody also needed support, and I might need space from my employee.

Shelby was even letting Ansen brush her now. The others were more curious about him than scared. Each day I witnessed Ansen working with them, earning their trust, I marveled over how he was the right person for them. And then I remembered how at one time, I'd thought the same about him for me.

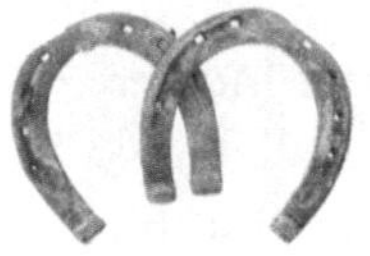

Six

ANSEN

The Purple Petal Bar and Grill was good-sized for a small town like Crocus Valley. Archer said they get a lot of tourist traffic in the summer and that between the coal mine, the refinery, and the coal gasification plant, there were hundreds of workers flowing through the small communities in the area. I could see the whole bar and grill from where I sat with my brother. The bar section was in the center, with high tables and a central counter surrounded by stools. He'd invited me to a place called Rattler's in Coal Haven, and from Aggie's property, it was a less than twenty-minute drive, but the likelihood of meeting other Barrons there was too high.

I glanced at the mostly unfamiliar faces. I'd been in town two weeks now, but I hadn't done much business in Crocus Valley other than buying some supplies. Dr. Jake was at the bar watching a high school football game. He didn't see me, and I preferred it that way.

I did another scan, searching for faces around my age and a little older. "Do we have any relatives in here?"

"I didn't see anyone, but the town is probably quiet tonight. Coal Haven's football team is playing at New Salem. Crocus Valley is at Richardton."

Which was why he'd suggested we meet tonight. Each town would be cleared out for the away games. "Thanks."

"I know how weird it is to meet a bunch of family you don't know."

"It's weird meeting the family I do know." The confession came out raw.

"How long would it have taken you to call if we hadn't run into each other the day Delaney wanted to make getting goat feed a family event?"

His tone seemed carefully neutral, like he didn't want to scare me off, so I answered honestly. "I don't know. Maybe never."

He nodded like he thought the same. "What really brought you here? Dad and I read all we could, but it sounds like a bunch of horseshit."

"Horseshit is more useful than what I went through." I blew out a breath. I wasn't ready to talk about it. The unfairness of it all only hung in front of me, wrapped like a gift that said, *You deserve it.* I'd given my jobs my all. The people in my life had barely gotten scraps. Aggie's words before she left me rang in my head.

One day, Ansen, I hope you know what it's like to have your entire heart ripped out, to have your passion stripped down and be humiliated in front of witnesses. To lose everything after you already gave up so much because you thought you were going to be happy.

She'd gotten her wish. "I was engaged to Aggie. Her father paid me."

Archer cocked his head like he couldn't have heard correctly.

"Yes," I said so he'd know I meant it.

The server swung by and we ordered. Then I was faced with my perplexed brother. "Her daddy liked me, and he wanted her to stay on the ranch."

"How much?"

"Two million."

He let out a low whistle. "Shit, that'd be hard to say no to. Were you already dating her?"

I shook my head, knowing how bad it made me look. "Back then, I had more sense about dating the boss's daughter. She seemed like a cool chick. A girl I could race through pastures with and then go out dancing with, but naw, I wasn't gonna date her. My job was more important."

"When you said you fucked it up bad, I didn't think . . . And here I thought I got myself into a mess with Delaney." He took a drink of his water. Neither of us were big drinkers. For a while, Dad lost himself in a bottle. Enough that Archer and I were social drinkers only. That the two of us refrained when we were together was a little of the solidarity we had growing up.

"What happened with you and Delaney? You were some big shot land broker and then you said you bought some land in Coal Haven with your wife."

He waved it off like his former career had been nothing when he'd made millions a year. "She called me on my city-slicker bullshit. I wanted her, so I listened. I guess you and I needed to be called on our shit."

"I'm not sure if I should be touched or not," I said wryly.

"Well, if I wanted to do any touching, I had to look at what I really wanted from life. And I guess that's where you're at."

"I'm not dating Aggie. She's not interested, and this job is . . . " I had no fucking clue. A saving grace? A stepping-stone? A time killer? All of the above? "North Dakota's not my home."

"I never thought it would be mine either, but I can't imagine being anywhere else." He stirred the ice around in his glass with his straw. "So . . . the job with Aggie? How'd that come about after what happened?"

"Her way to get revenge. She saw I was in a bad way, and I happen to have basement rates for the moment."

"But you and her—"

"Are history. Nothing more." I only watched her walk Tex every damn morning. She kept him on a leash so he wouldn't run and spook the horses—or so he couldn't come greet me, forcing her to get closer than a hundred yards away.

I stayed far from the house when she was home. It'd been hard enough to think about how my world had crumbled around me. I didn't need to see evidence of the good woman I'd missed out on. Especially when she'd take Tex by the horses in the evening to get him used to the bigger animals and to get them accustomed to him. Same with the cats. He was good around the chickens. The barn blocked most of my view, but I caught enough.

"Did you tell Dad you're here yet?"

Sheepish, I pushed my hand through my hair. "I will. I'll call tomorrow."

"He's worried about you."

"He's always worried." Yet I felt like talking to him. Just to ask him how he was doing.

"So. Miss Kansas?"

More of my past I wasn't proud of. "I didn't want the same things she wanted, and I knew she was getting more serious than I was, but . . . I had a good thing going." My brother's jaw tightened. What could I say? Complacent or complicit—the outcome had been the same. "When I finally pulled the plug, she exploded. Accused me of using her, stringing her along, even cheating on her—which was *bullshit*. She spewed all kinds of lies to her dad."

"The dad who was your boss."

"You got it." Telling the story felt like a third-party recount. I was numb by now. The Knights had run me off, then I drifted from here to there, and finally, the blowout. I was the common denominator. Karma, delayed retribution, hell, I didn't know. I must've deserved it.

"The allegations?"

I lifted my hands. "He could've fired me for the breakup. I'd have walked. Instead, I thought we could be professional, but he made work hell. Then the horses I handled developed bruises and behavioral issues, and I'd get blamed. I found another job and quit, and he's been tracking my employers down and telling them lies. I can't do a damn thing but leave quietly every time I get fired. It's my word against his, and his is a lot more powerful than some trainer out of a dirt patch in Texas. It's been months, and the man still has a hornet up his ass."

"All because you broke up with his daughter?" Archer's disbelief matched mine. Made no damn sense, but it didn't have to when emotions were involved, and Stephanie was nothing if not emotional. What I had thought was a harmless personality trait, like flying off the hinges when she was mildly inconvenienced, turned damaging enough when it was more than a venti blended frap getting screwed up. Made sense since she'd honed the trait with her dad.

"It was like Aggie all over again, only no money exchanged hands. They acted like I did nothing but try to worm my way into the family and steal everything they had." Once I'd seen what Stephanie's intentions were—

happily ever after and running her dad's business together, I'd bailed. Hard. The thought made me nauseous. Even worse was wondering if, deep down, that was what I'd been doing.

"Dad said you were winning."

"The horses were."

He cocked a brow, and I couldn't lie to myself. I might've brushed off his admiration before, but now it was a balm to frayed nerves. I'd competed with excellent horses, but I also knew what I was doing.

Our meal arrived just as Aggie walked through the door. The noise of the restaurant died away, and the only thing I saw was her. From where I was seated, I got a closer view than I normally did from the barn every morning.

I clocked her path after she smiled at the hostess and threaded through the tables toward the bar. She wasn't wearing her riding coat but a long, fluffy wrap over a deep-green, long-sleeved shirt and black leggings. On her feet were ankle boots, giving her calves a sexy curve I'd never paid attention to on any woman before.

Archer's gaze narrowed on me, and he discreetly peeked over his shoulder.

I ignored his "You sure about everything you said earlier?" look and finally took a bite of the burger, looking around as if I hadn't been staring at Aggie and only Aggie. The food turned to dust in my mouth as soon as I saw Dr. Jake notice her arrival.

His grin was presumptuous, and he grabbed his drink to saunter over to the tall table she slid behind. She stiffened when he arrived at her table, but he planted his butt into a seat across from her anyway.

"That bastard."

Archer turned to look again. "Who? Dr. Jake?"

"He wants to fuck her."

"I can see that." The humor in my brother's voice was infuriating. This was serious. Dr. Jake was a walking, talking billboard for country-boy players. Aggie deserved more than a cowboy flirt.

"What if she wants to fuck him too?" Archer's innocent question filled me with a righteous rage I had no business feeling.

"Is he a decent guy? I'm not asking about his job—what's he like with women?" I knew the answer without knowing Dr. Jake. Aggie hadn't been a girl swayed by cocky confidence and empty promises, but what if she bought into it? What if they formed a real connection and he changed his ways for her? I should be hopeful for the outcome, but it was the worst one yet.

"He's been divorced twice. Heard he likes to add extra services onto some house calls."

Yep. Aggie was new in town, beautiful, and single. And he made house calls.

There wasn't a reflective surface in sight where I could see her reaction. The line of her back was relaxed again, her shoulders no longer bunched. Not a good sign for me. Was she happy? Did her eyes light up like they used to when I'd surprise her in her daddy's stables and we'd go for a lazy morning ride?

I'd been chasing that look ever since. The sight of a woman who was truly excited to see me. *Me*. Not what I could do for the business or how I looked taking her around town. Someone who saw the bumpkin who had a talent for horses.

Dr. Jake beckoned the server over like he was swooping in as the hero to her neglected table.

He'd better not try to order her some fancy drink. She used to be able to throw back the shots with her brothers and was one of the few who didn't bug the crap out of me for not drinking a lot.

Jake's laughter carried across the restaurant. Hers was mixed in, and her shoulders shook.

I understood why breeding studs could be assholes around the same mare. I mean, I'd known it, but now I sympathized.

"Something botherin' you?" Archer asked slyly.

"No."

"You mean I didn't hear you growl, and you don't look ready to stampede through the bar? Nah." His grin was quick. "Nothing's botherin' ya."

"It's her life." I turned my attention back to him. Archer hadn't touched his meal yet. Tonight was about getting to know him again, not about Aggie falling for Dr. Jake. "Tell me about the kids."

"I don't know if you'd be listening." Archer chanced another look over his shoulder. "When he comes to our place, he's a shameless flirt with Delaney. If you want to cockblock the bastard, say the word."

Word. A thousand times *word*. "I'm here to see you."

"You're here. You can come over every damn night for supper if you want, but I can't promise we won't put you on meal rotation. Emmaline thinks she should go vegan because she saw it in a cartoon, and Vaden throws half his meal on the floor before he takes a bite."

I nodded, hearing what he was saying but storing it to process later. The server deposited a glass of wheat-colored beer by Aggie. She shouldn't be drinking around a strange man.

Realizing I was tanking tonight, I shook myself out of it. Archer was missing a night with his family to stare at me while I glowered at Dr. Jake. "Sorry. Where were we?"

An amused glint reflected in his eyes. "Remember when

that family visited the ranch after the new owners took over and their kid told Mama she was nothing but the help, and he'd better not hear her make a sound?"

I couldn't forget. Dad had lost the cattle ranch he'd purchased with family money after leaving North Dakota. When he lost it, he'd been hired on as the ranch manager. We'd moved to "the help's" place, out of sight of the main house, and Mama had cleaned our former home to earn extra money. The little bastard Archer mentioned had slept in what used to be our bedroom and talked to Mama like she was trash. "And you said you'd keep him busy while I put dead scorpions in his boots?"

We both snickered. Archer and I had gotten away with it, and if Mama had figured it out, she hadn't mentioned a thing.

"I'll run interference again," Archer said.

I appreciated his offer, but it wouldn't be fair. I'd done enough to her.

Aggie was also getting even.

I should leave it alone. She might find what she wanted in the charming vet.

Stomach acid crawled up my throat.

I'd messed with her heart enough. "No, man. I'm fine."

Archer folded his hands on the table in front of him. "Ansen." My brother might have been dressed in a clean pair of blue jeans and a navy shirt with a loose black flannel over it, but he looked every inch the corporate guy he'd once been.

"Yeah?"

"Were you serious about marrying her?"

Some days, it was hard to untangle the motivation from reality. Other days, it was crystal fucking clear. "I would've made sure she was happy with me."

He studied me for several moments. "It took me a long

time to admit that my wife meant everything to me. *Everything*. I had to lose her a second time before I got my head out of my ass. I wasted a year and a half, Ansen."

Kind of like I'd wasted years not talking to him. Pissed away more years with Dad, who wanted to get to know his adult son. There were ten empty years between me and Aggie that were my fault.

Archer glanced at the couple chatting again. "If there's anything inside you that wants to rekindle what you two had, now's your chance. It'll be a lot harder to do when his dick's inside her."

I was sliding out of the booth before I could decide if I was making the right decision. After a lifetime of impulsive decisions that kept me from seeing how empty my years were, I went with it, grabbing my plate and water.

Archer threw money on the table, took his food and drink, and pushed past me. I followed him.

When we got close, Jake lifted his gaze. His trademark grin spread across his face when he saw Archer and surprise registered when he saw me. "Archer, buddy. You met the new arrival?"

Aggie glanced up, and her eyes widened. A beat of alarm, and dare I say relief, passed through her surprised expression.

"I used to change the new arrival's diapers." Archer chuckled as he took a chair next to Dr. Jake. "Ansen's my brother."

"No shit?" the vet said. "I guess I never caught your last name, Ansen." Aggie had intentionally not given it to him. I continued owing her. "Two Barrons. I'm in the presence of royalty."

"Something like that." Archer laughed, and I started to question the intelligence of my move. Way to run under the radar. I didn't know who Dr. Jake would tell, but with a town this small and the Barrons as prominent as I heard they were, it wouldn't take much for the news to spread.

Sitting next to Aggie, getting a hint of that coconut-sunshine smell, I wouldn't have made a different decision. I didn't have to look at her to know she was tense, but I acted like this was a normal night for us, and I tried not to think about how shooting the shit with people we knew in the bar had once been normal for us.

Archer launched into a tale about a goat pregnancy and Dr. Jake's help. I pushed my plate over, and Aggie absent-mindedly snagged a fry. She furrowed her brow and looked from the fry to me.

"Go ahead," I said casually, but nothing inside me was easy. She had a soft spot for fried food, and I used to let her have my french fries. *Wrap those pink lips around my fry.* "Did you eat yet?"

"I had a sandwich before I came here." She ate the fry, and I had to look away before I gawked at her mouth like a pervert. She tapped her mug. "I got a taste for the shandy they have on tap here. It's made at Reservoir Barrel outside of Coal Haven. This is your cousin's beer." I must've looked confused. Her mouth tipped up. "You haven't met the rest of your family yet?"

I shook my head. Archer had Dr. Jake's attention. "I don't know if I'm ready for it."

Her eyes softened like she sensed my sincerity. "Glad you and Archer got together."

I reached across her for the ketchup. Once I squeezed some on her end of the plate, I cut a chunk off my burger. She was a sucker for a good burger too. She snagged another fry and dipped it in ketchup. I took a bite from the burger and caught the way Dr. Jake's gaze jumped from Aggie to my plate, then to me. He slumped in his chair, a defeated look on his face. He laughed at Archer's story, but it was half-hearted.

Victory was mine, motherfucker.

A few moments later, Dr. Jake slapped his hands on his thighs. "Hey, I was going to ask you, Ansen—what kind of animals are you thinking of accepting?"

Irritated that he'd deferred to me but liking how his behavior reinforced my decision to cockblock him, I glanced at Aggie. "It's her call."

She finished chewing, her annoyance carefully stored away, but I could see it. "The pens need some work, but they can hold goats and pigs. Donkeys."

"I don't know a thing about pigs," I said. "Or goats or donkeys."

She patted my thigh. "You can learn."

Heat spread over my leg just as she snatched her hand back like I was made of hot steel. One part of me was getting there. "You gonna teach me?"

She rolled her eyes and took the section of burger I cut for her. She peeked under the bun to inspect the burger as if she was making a strategy for how to eat it without getting sauce on herself. "Google it."

"I can ask my niece."

Archer chuckled. "She's like her mother. She'll tell you what's up with goats."

Dr. Jake slid off his stool. "I have a call bright and early. Nice seeing you."

It was nice seeing him go away.

We finished our food. Archer made small talk about his ranch and his wife's goat and egg business. Then he pushed his plate away and stood. "Nice catching up, Ansen. Let me know when you have a free day. The kids would love to give you a tour of our place."

"Next weekend." Now that more of my old brother was

back, I didn't want to put off his offer. "Is that all right, boss?"

"After chores." Her tone was teasing. "You don't have to go," she said to Archer.

He backed up with a wave. No matter how aloof things had been between us for years, he had my back in a heartbeat. "I can get home in time to help tuck the kids in. Night, y'all."

Aggie's focus was on me. "Why'd he leave so quickly?" She glanced at the door again and worried her lower lip between her teeth. "Why'd you two crash my night when you're supposed to be catching up?"

The burger was lead in my gut. She would've been too smart for Dr. Jake, and I'd exposed my games because she was too good for me.

She pushed the plate closer to me. "You did it on purpose." Anger was hot in her tone. "You drove Jake away."

"He's just Jake to you now? Are you disappointed he's gone?" *Are you happy I'm here instead?* I was purposely antagonizing her, but my feelings were all over the place tonight. Connecting with Archer, seeing her get hit on, and sitting next to her sharing a meal like we used to—I wasn't as distant as I normally would be.

She sighed and wiped her hands on her napkin. "It's none of your business. It hasn't been your business for years."

She was off her stool and storming toward the door. I was hot on her low-heeled boots.

"Aggie."

She breezed out the door, her hair so tight in its bun only a few strands fluttered.

"Agatha, dammit." I jogged to get beside her. She was shorter than me, but the girl could make fast getaways.

She charged toward her pickup. The headlights flashed as she unlocked the door. We reached it at the same time, and I propped my hand against the window. "Why did you really hire me?"

"I told you why."

I caught her around the waist and planted a hard kiss against those frustratingly plump lips. She went rigid but didn't pull away.

It took the equivalent of eight horsepower to separate my lips from hers. I caught my breath and watched the green flecks spark in her eyes. She was familiar but new. She was intriguing, and I wanted to get to know the new Aggie as much as I wanted to dig through that smooth exterior and find the old Aggie.

I told Archer she and I were history, but after kissing her —I knew that wasn't true.

∩∩

Aggie

"Don't try that again." My heart hammered. I was ready to prance around him and raise my tail. One shocking but chaste kiss and he'd cracked my resolve to stay far away from him.

"Answer me, Aggie. Why'd you hire me?"

"I already told—"

He put a finger to my lips. I licked my tongue out, tasting the saltiness of the fries we'd been sharing.

"Christ, I forgot how good you are with that tongue."

Before I climbed him like a tree and proved I was still good with my tongue, I stepped back, attempting to put distance between us. He advanced and my back ended up against the cold door.

"Why, Aggie?" He towered over me, the parking lot lights casting shadows over his face, making the cut of his cheekbones and chin harder than they were in daylight. He wasn't wearing a hat to otherwise hide his expression. His gaze was intense, like he *yearned* to know.

I needed an answer to the same question too. "Revenge."

"Keep telling yourself that."

"Why are you still here? You could walk away at any time." Hope climbed a small notch in my chest. I'd been lying to myself. I wasn't over this man.

"I have nowhere else to go."

The hope shriveled. The bastard. "I've gotta go." I tensed to duck around him.

"I lied." His words made me stop. "I have one other place to go and that's back home. I miss Dad, but if I go back there, then everything I've done has only led me back to the same shithole I was running from instead of returning to make things right."

My stupid, soft heart cracked open for him, but in the end, he was living his life for himself. I didn't factor in.

A faint smile played over his full lips. "Then you sent me that email full of typos."

"It wasn't that bad."

"'Offer' only had one '*F*' and you spelled 'rescue' three different ways."

I winced. The screen had been pretty blurry by that point.

"I thought for sure I was going to get jumped and wake up to find a kidney missing, but you appeared. You'd seen what they were saying and plotted your *revenge* anyway. It means a lot."

My heart was going to be mush before I knew it. "Getting back at you means a lot?"

"You didn't question that the accusations were false. None of my other references had the same confidence in me. I was almost afraid to tell Archer and find out what he thought."

"I bet they believe you're not guilty of animal abuse." When one of Daddy's broodmares broke a leg, Ansen had been her biggest advocate. Daddy thought the animal was useless if she couldn't be mounted, but Ansen was willing to try every method possible to heal the break.

Daddy won in the end.

"There it is again. That unwavering resolve." He leaned in farther. "Why are you still single?"

"I told you."

His mouth was set. Again, he wanted more from me. At some point, I had to stop giving bits of myself to this man. He couldn't be trusted with me.

But I'd answer him. "I seem to be a magnet for guys who resent independent women. So I'm done with men." I struggled to sound nonchalant, but my pulse was kicking up thanks to his proximity.

"Done, huh?"

He was sending me off-kilter, spinning through the air like I'd just been bucked off. I had to right myself. "And you? Why aren't you married?"

A rod of tension slipped through his body. I didn't think he'd answer, but he brushed his thumb across his lower lip. "In case you don't know, emotionally unavailable men are catnip for women."

"I've heard that before."

"And those men are sometimes too clueless to know when they're leading someone on."

"Some women might consider it callous."

He dropped his head. Maybe I shouldn't have brought it up, but he was so close his presence scraped the rest of the haphazard bandages off my heart.

"I don't like how I hurt you, Aggie. I wish . . . I wish you'd had the same faith in me then you do now."

Was he suggesting I believe he would've married me without the money? He hadn't looked at me twice before getting paid. I wasn't falling for it.

But . . . his longing was hard to get past. I couldn't afford to look too deeply at what he said. "I'm not one of my rescues."

"I am." His lips whispered over mine. The pressure increased, and he crowded closer. I put my hand on his chest to push him away before he activated every last synapse until I was nothing but a live wire needing to be grounded.

I hit hard muscle and immediately curled my fingers into his shirt. So much for resistance.

A low growl left him, and he wrapped an arm around my waist, securing me to him. When his tongue licked out, I opened for him, desperate for a taste. His flavor was back in my mouth, and it was everything I never thought I'd have again.

Awareness nearly trickled back into my lust-filled haze, then he wedged a knee between my legs, and oh god, I remembered. He was just tall enough that when he did that, I'd grind perfectly against his thigh.

A whine sounded deep in my chest and I rocked against him. Shivers racked my body and the steady beat between my thighs grew. I listened to the demanding thrum and continued to shamelessly rub myself against him.

Two weeks of knowing he was so close had been hell on my nerves. Energy was coiled so tightly—I needed a release.

"That's it," he said and adjusted the angle to deepen the kiss until I thought he'd swallow me whole.

Another whimper. The bulge of his erection pressed against my belly, and memories bombarded me. The way he'd moved inside me. How he filled me. The heart-stopping explosions of the orgasms he could give.

"You're so fucking beautiful when you come." He ran his lips along my jaw. "Ride me."

I drank down air, the smell of frying steak and grease entering my nose. My eyes flew open. The lights of the parking lot shone onto my face, lighting us up like we were the main performance.

With a gasp, I shoved him away and straightened. My nipples were so tight the slide of the fabric almost elicited a moan. I was in bad shape. His tight stance and the rigidity of his shoulders were a small consolation. He was as uncomfortably turned on as I was.

"Don't touch me again." I needed to sound angry. Instead, I was breathless.

"You don't want that, and neither do I."

I glanced around. Had anyone seen me scaling him like a rock wall?

This man had a way of stopping logical thought. I couldn't trust myself around him, and I couldn't trust him. "The thing is, Ansen, I'm always going to wonder what your motives are."

With that, I got in and fired up the engine. He didn't step away when I backed out. I left him in my rearview mirror one more time.

Seven

ANSEN

Morning chores were done, and I put five more eggs into the carton on the counter. It'd been years since I'd had so many farm-fresh eggs, and I was becoming a spoiled man.

After last weekend, I was a starved, horny guy. That kiss in the parking lot had stolen sleep and solitude.

Was Aggie feeling the same? She'd avoided me all week. Yesterday, I had spotted her and Tex out with the horses when I was in my trailer eating lunch. The barns and pens were like neutral ground. She didn't come here and I didn't go to her house and we rarely met in the middle.

After that kiss . . . avoiding each other left me restless. Pissy. Cuddling kittens in the barn while brooding for way too long.

I washed up. I'd go back out after I ate breakfast, but before I ate, I had one thing to get out of the way.

I called Dad.

"Hey, Ansen. Everything okay?"

He was always the one calling me. Failure should be a familiar feeling by now, but maybe I'd gotten worse at ignoring it. "It's fine. I just wanted to tell you I'm working in North Dakota."

"With Archer?" He sounded both confused and delighted.

"No, not with Archer, but I've had supper with him. Met the family." That sounded less like the accident it was. Happy I could give Dad a positive emotional experience with me for once, I continued. "I'm going there tonight." Where I couldn't disrupt the visit in order to cockblock Aggie.

"That's nice to hear. What work are you doing?"

"Before I tell you, I've gotta explain some things." This was the reason I'd waited all week. I didn't want to add to Dad's worry, and even though Aggie and I were in the past—recent smoldering kiss notwithstanding—I also didn't want to flake out on telling him the truth. Talking with Archer again only showed what my resistance to telling them what was going on in my life cost me. I told him about Barnaby Knight and Aggie. The ten years after took a lot less time to describe, including the last six months.

"I didn't believe any of that nonsense."

Relief was a cool breeze in the middle of a Texas heatwave. I'd been spending time with the wrong people. Aggie, Archer, and my dad were in my corner. And for the last decade, I'd been avoiding all of them. "I was bought off by Barns."

He chuffed. "I would've married this Barnaby Knight for that much money, Ansen. Am I disappointed? Yes. But I get it. I wasted just as much money while my wife and kids witnessed. We all make mistakes."

I let my eyelids drift shut, soaking in his quick acceptance. Dad and Archer were both more forgiving with me than I'd been with them. That money . . . I'd had big dreams of starting my own business. Of growing so fucking successful, I earned my own millions, and then I could buy the old ranch. The place where my whole family was happy—before Dad lost the property and Mama died. A dream I wasn't meant to have, apparently.

"A rescue, huh?" he asked.

"I like it. No entitled owners telling me how to do my job. No bosses overriding my common sense. Aggie isn't a micromanager. She remembers everything even though she hasn't been around horses for years. You should see her out there. She's not the one working with them, but they love her. She got this place up and running on her own, and if she hadn't hired me, I know she'd be out there fixing fence until dark. Her chickens lay the best eggs—it's like they're pre-buttered—and when a cat with kittens showed up, she didn't bat an eye. Took them in too."

"Sounds like a special girl."

"She is." So fucking special. Regret could be a hard bitch. "I fucked that up."

"Second chances don't happen every day." His chuckle was wry. "Hell, I think it was my third or fourth chance when I got this job. Learn a little quicker than me, will ya?"

"Sure, Dad."

When the call ended, I drifted back to the picture window. The hurt and lonely kid in me had been hard on Dad. If I hadn't landed on my ass with nothing, would I have ever given Dad another chance? Archer? I hated to think I'd have let my ignorant pride push them away.

I caught a glimpse of Aggie's red, form-hugging coat. She was back in leggings today and a sweater dress like the one I'd admired her ass in last time. I was too far away to see her breath puff out, but she had her hands shoved in her pockets. She looked good. Sexy, but then she'd had an understated sexiness before that only a smart man bothered seeing. I liked this coat more than the old beat-up one she used to wear because of the way the new one showed off the flare in her hips. It made a guy thirst for the curves.

I was the guy.

Kittens barreled out of the barn to greet her, and the mama cat twined around her ankles. Fancy was filling out now that she'd been dewormed and was getting regular food, but she was an indoor cat tossed outside. Super friendly and dependent on us. Hopefully, she still had the instinct to teach six kittens to hunt. The barn had plenty of mice.

Several minutes of scratching and two kittens trying to scale her leggings later, she tossed treats into the barn so she could walk the path back to her house and leave for work.

Like a damn stalker, I watched until she was out of view.

I was used to running from place to place when complications arose, or I was angry enough at management. I wasn't used to second chances. Aggie gave me one with my career. I had written us off, but the longer I was around her, the more erasing of that notion I was doing.

Now I wanted a second chance with her, but her reaction after our kiss was a warning. She was still hurt, and it was my job to make it better. Yet her drunken decision to hire me was a sign. We weren't done yet.

Aggie

Walking to my pickup in the parking lot, I waved to a coworker as he drove off.

"Jackass," I muttered under my breath, tucking my

mouth into my collar to break the wind and keep my lips from being read. He was actually quite nice, usually one of my favorite coworkers, but not today. The guy had called a Friday afternoon meeting and then he'd kept asking the boss questions while the rest of us were squirming in our seats.

I lived for my weekends and resented having to stay five minutes longer.

Next week was Thanksgiving. I wasn't sure I would go to Buffalo Gully yet, but I'd taken Friday off in case I wasn't able to talk myself out of it by then.

Ansen hadn't asked for time off. Did he know he could? He was probably going to go to Archer's. The possibility was the only reason I entertained going out of town. Leaving Ansen alone on Thanksgiving tugged a little too hard on my conscience. It'd be hard to continue avoiding him if I was going to make sure he wasn't alone for Thanksgiving. After that kiss and the memories of what it was like with him, I didn't trust that I wouldn't fling myself at him.

Inside the pickup, I turned the engine over just as my phone buzzed. I hadn't caught up with Sutton in a while. Had she heard I might head there for the holiday?

I answered without looking. "Hello?"

"Is this Aggie with AKA Horse Rescue?" a gruff older man asked.

"That's me. What can I help you with?" Mentally, I scrolled through calculations. With Ansen working, I had a real rescue that was nothing but a money drain right now, but I could take on minor cases.

"My name's Samuel Gustafson." Just as I was digging through the depths of my brain to figure out where I'd heard that before, he added, "Gustafson Performance Horses. In Kansas."

Ansen's old boss. The one he'd had the falling out with.

I didn't give a shit where he was located. I only cared why he was calling me. Dread filled my insides. "Okay?"

"I've been made aware that Ansen Barron worked with you in the past."

"I know Ansen," I said flatly, not liking where this was going.

"You might not know what he can be like, especially around a young woman such as yourself."

I knew what he could be like—that was my problem. "I do know older guys like you tend to think we can't handle ourselves."

"What was that?"

I bit into my lower lip. Sometimes I couldn't outrun Daddy's influence no matter where I went. "Do you have an animal you'd like me to board?"

"That's not why I called. I wanted to give you due warning, professional to professional. He was roaming the state, and when he couldn't find work, he migrated north. If he's got connections, he's going to try to use them. That man shouldn't be around horses. Or women."

"Oh?" I chewed off the word but managed to make it sound like an innocent inquiry. *That man* around horses was a wonder. Dr. Jake and I would've struggled with the five rescues if Ansen hadn't been handling them. Ansen could read those animals like a psychic staring into a crystal ball.

"Being you're a newly formed rescue from what your brother said, I thought to warn you."

I dug my fingers into the phone. He thought to warn me? He was interfering with a person's livelihood. I thought about what Cody had said about someone calling him about Ansen. "You talked to Alcott?"

"Uh, no. Eliot."

Eliot barely talked to me, and he'd butted heads with

Ansen too. They were close in age, and Eliot resented Daddy bringing on more help after Austen left for the Army, but then he'd put Ansen in charge of Eliot. My brother had taken it as one of Daddy's many digs. When Daddy lacked faith in you, you knew it.

My brother had likely been extremely helpful in being a dick to Ansen.

"And you do this for every place where Ansen might work?" I asked.

"Yes, ma'am. It's the least I can do."

The whole situation stank. A bad reference was one thing. Tracking someone across the country to ruin their employment status was pathological. "Care to fill in some details, Mr. Gustafson?"

"He used my daughter. Planned to marry her to get the business. Then when she got savvy about how he was, I started having all kinds of issues. We lost two of the best horses I've been trusted to compete with."

"Lost how?" I read the articles after I hired him. The story came off as small-town gossip with nothing but weak speculation.

"Someone shot them in the middle of the night. Right on my property."

"Shit." I made sure to sound stunned so he'd keep talking. Ansen was the only one blamed, even though the hired help reported seeing Ansen run out of the living quarters at the same time everyone else did after they heard the shots, and no one had been charged. Something hadn't sat right with me after I finished reading. Killing horses wasn't a small offense, and a guy like Gustafson wouldn't just assume it was Ansen and deal with it by bad-mouthing him everywhere. He either knew who did it and didn't want to pursue them, or he'd done it himself and collected the insurance money.

"Yes, ma'am. We also found signs of abuse in other animals he handled."

I laughed. Each allegation should have given me pause. Instead, they sounded absurd. Gustafson's business didn't train racehorses. They trained cow horses for competitions. If the stock was how Ansen was making a living, why would he shoot them? Why would he want revenge if he was the one who broke up with the pageant queen? The deaths were awful, but they weren't at Ansen's hands.

"Ma'am, I'm serious."

I chewed the inside of my cheek. I'd had about enough. "What did Ansen do to you, exactly? This feels as much a personal issue as a professional one."

"Other than sweep my daughter off her feet so she'd ask me to give him a job?" Okay, that tracked, but I'd given Ansen a job while keeping my underwear in place. "She met him while he was at a cutting event, competing for another ranch. By the time she came home, it was, 'Papa, this guy knows what he's doing. Papa, this guy is great.' So, I listened."

The *she* in question had been a teen beauty queen and state pageant winner. Even though she wasn't a Miss Rodeo, she often rode at rodeos and competitions as their special guest, carrying the flag because of who her family was. Not that I'd stalked her social media, thinking she was beautiful in a way I never would be.

"So you gave him a job?" I asked.

"And then the problems started," he confirmed.

"Which were?"

"A higher rate of injury. Behavior issues. Then those two horses were killed."

"You checked his references and everything? No other employers had issues?"

"Doesn't mean anything."

Sometimes it did. Daddy still gave Ansen glowing recommendations. Half of them were to me. Eliot said he'd heard him once. Daddy would never mention a thing about Ansen breaking his daughter's heart, but he'd talk for hours about how the guy was a natural with training. *I see myself in that kid* he'd say about Ansen but none of his sons. I hated that Eliot had overheard. "Can I ask why you're not pressing charges?"

"Trust me—I would've."

"But?"

"The investigators said there was no evidence, but I lost a lot of goddamn business because of him."

No evidence. And no history of animal mistreatment. Just a known heartbreaker, which, to be honest, probably wouldn't have stopped Stephanie Jane. "If I may pry, what happened between Ansen and your daughter?"

"He strung her along. When I said I wasn't passing GPH to him, but he could purchase it when I retired, he bailed on her."

Tempting to believe, given my background. But would he dump her and continue working there? Again, didn't make sense. Ansen had proven more likely to leave a job than stay. "You have security cameras, right?"

"Yes, ma'am."

"Then why isn't Ansen in jail or out on bond? You said yourself there's no evidence he was involved."

"Honey, it sounds like you don't believe me."

"Humor me, Gussy."

A grunt sounded, and I wasn't sure he'd explain. "The horses died after the breakup."

"And the injuries?"

"After the breakup," he admitted with a growl.

I glanced in the rearview mirror. Yup. Looked as disbelieving as I felt. I used to be naive and sweet, but getting my heart shattered by Ansen had hardened me. Odd I'd use those shards to deal with this phone call. "So, with no evidence, no clear link of Ansen's guilt, you've been ruining his job opportunities since he broke up with your daughter—the same girl you accused him of using to marry into your little equine empire? Sounds like a helluva power trip."

"Listen, honey—"

"No, Gussy, it's your turn to listen. While normally I might appreciate the heads-up, I can't in good conscience buy one ounce of this uncured manure you're selling me. You might be sitting there thinking I've been dickmatized by the guy, and once that was true, but when it comes to horses, he's one of the best."

My heart rate was climbing, and yes, I was defending Ansen on little more than blind conviction, but fuck it. I could channel Daddy to deal with someone who reminded me of Daddy. Only for all of Daddy's faults, lying wasn't one of them, which made me all the more upset at Gustafson. "I don't believe for a split second he hurt an animal or did anything that led to its demise. I think he hurt your pride. I think your daughter's behind some of this. And I think you should watch yourself because a libel lawsuit can be quite expensive. But you know he can't afford that, don't you? Yet you don't know the same about me."

"He's gotten to you."

God help me, maybe. But I was sick of guys trying to walk all over me, and in this instance, it seemed like Ansen wasn't at fault. "No, he hasn't. He's gotten to my horses, and that's the way it's going to stay. If I hear about you calling one more place and shit-talking him, there's going to be some harassment charges coming your way."

"You don't know what you're doing—"

"I knew exactly what I was doing when I hired him." Under the influence of Fireball, I'd still known he was the best thing for the animals. I hung up, tossed the phone on the seat, and spun out. I'd heard one side of the story. Now it was time to hear the other.

Minutes later, I was pulling up in front of the old trailer house. Ansen had fixed the wonky railing on the front steps and repaired the trim by the windows I'd been afraid the wind would rip off. I had planted flowers over the summer in the flower beds around the base, and he'd cleaned those up too.

His pickup was parked out front, but that didn't mean he was home. I marched up to his door, the bitter November wind buffeting around me, and it swung open before I could knock. Savory smells rolled out, mitigating my adrenaline.

Did I come here so he could recount his Kansas experience . . . or as an excuse to quit avoiding him?

"Aggie," he said, surprised. Rightfully so. It'd been a week since the kiss.

"What happened in Kansas? The whole story?" My stomach growled, and the sound was thankfully smothered by my coat. What was he cooking?

He stepped back to let me in. The warmth of the place surrounded me and his scent crowded in. He'd only been here for a little over three weeks. How could every surface have filled with him?

I sniffed. Whatever he was cooking had my stomach's number. "What are you making?"

"Bacon to go with my everything omelet."

"With my eggs?"

His grin was lazy. "Was I supposed to bring those to the house? I thought they were part of my benefits package."

That smile of his went straight to the nexus between my thighs. I summoned the outrage from my talk with Gustafson. "*All* the eggs, Ansen?"

He snickered. "I was wondering how long it'd take for you to hunt them down."

I was still using the stock the hens had supplied me with before he arrived. The principle of the matter was my concern. They were good eggs. "Are you adding stealing to your repertoire?"

His expression shut down, and the cut of his jaw could crack those eggs.

I pinched the bridge of my nose. "Shit, I didn't mean . . ."

"It's fine." The Ansen from before never used to shut down like this. "Hungry?"

I kept my tone teasing. "For my eggs and bacon? Yes. What exactly is everything in the omelet?"

"I'll leave the bell peppers off yours."

He remembered. I hung my coat by his hat and followed him into the kitchen. All my furniture was in place, but touches of him were all over. His black cowboy hat hung on a hook by the door. Clean laundry was piled on one cushion of the couch. He hated folding. I could tell what chair he used when he ate at the table. I took the one on the opposite side.

"What brought up Kansas?" He took a sizzling pan off the burner and set it on a hot pad, then busied himself with a cutting board and ham and onions. I had nothing to do but stare out the sliding door to the sagging porch in the back or look at him. I should've called instead.

"Gustafson tracked me down. I just got off the phone with him."

He set the knife down and pressed his hands on top of the counter that cut between the dining area and the kitchen. Anger radiated over his strong features, and under the dark stubble along his jaw, a muscle jumped. I could swoon, dammit. "What'd he say?"

"I'm sure you know. I want to hear the story from you."

He let out a long breath. "I told you all of it."

"He said you broke up with her after he said he wouldn't pass on the company but that you could buy it."

"We never discussed a purchase. Maybe he told Stephanie that, but she never told me." He started chopping in tight, hard movements. Was it to have something to do with his hands or to keep from meeting my gaze? "He had to know I couldn't afford it."

His words from our breakup filtered through my head. I had all the resources I needed. When Daddy didn't provide, Mama had made sure I was taken care of. Now I was thirty-one, with a house, a fledgling rescue, and a good job I got because of the degree I used Mama's money to pay for. "I'm not here about that, and I can see it for the manipulation tactic it is."

He paused, his look questioning.

I cleared my throat, wishing I'd offered to help cook so I'd have something to do with my hands. "Daddy manipulated all of us, and he uses the ranch and the oil money to do it. Cody, Wilder, and Eliot are all at his mercy. I guarantee that's why Austen joined the military. Daddy used you to manipulate me into staying, and he used me and my brothers to coerce Mama into staying as long as she did. When both her parents were gone, they left her money, and that's what she did for me. After talking to Gustafson . . . "

Ansen and I had been pawns when we were younger. I could see it clearer than ever. Would Daddy have acted like Gustafson if Ansen had backed out before Cody busted him? I'd like to think not, but seeing the effects now . . . I could empathize with the position Ansen had been in. "I wouldn't be surprised if he saw your ambition and wanted to use it for himself. He probably told his daughter one thing and everyone else something else. His story sounds a lot better the way he's telling it now."

His brow furrowed. He dumped the ham and veggies he'd chopped into a bowl and grabbed a carton of eggs. "He went after me like it was his mission." He shook his head. "I thought I was doing the right thing when we broke up."

"And once you were married, you would've been at his mercy." It was Daddy's playbook.

"I didn't want his company. His stock. His legacy. I want to build my own. That's the way it's always been."

His words sank in, and I paired them with our argument from years ago and what he'd told me about growing up. He had nothing and Daddy had taken advantage of it. More empathy surfaced until my face warmed. "There's nothing wrong with that." I changed the path of the conversation. "The abuse? Did you notice it before?"

"One of the guys was rough with the animals." His gaze turned to steel. "Stephanie always seemed salty toward the horses."

On that, I could empathize. "They got all of Gussy's attention." He cocked a brow, and I explained. "He called me 'honey,' so I called him 'Gussy.'"

He tipped his head back and laughed. His Adam's apple bobbed, and I was riveted. The man—when he was uninhibited—was intoxicating. "You got some Barns running through you." His smile faded. "Gus is a hothead. It's his biggest downfall. He can compete, he can train, but he loses his temper, and the horses don't work as well for him. I think that's what really upset him when I finally quit."

"You, uh . . . might not have to worry about him anymore. Maybe."

He took his gaze off the pan to glance at me. "Why?"

I lifted a shoulder. "I mentioned harassment charges and legal fees and hinted that I had the time and money."

His gaze was steady on me. I twisted my fingers in my lap. Was he angry? The Ansen I used to know didn't worry about getting emasculated, but he'd been through a lot.

He turned his attention to the eggs and jerked into action. I didn't say anything as he finished the omelet. My appetite wavered. Had I crossed the line? First, I lured him here. Then I interfered on his behalf. Was I wrong to assume I could use my last name to help? I'd been so irritated with Gustafson and the holes in his story and his single-minded determination to destroy Ansen for making the right decision that I had to make the threat.

Once Ansen slid the food onto a plate, he picked up the other plate and carried them both to the table.

I didn't expect him to lower to a squat in front of me, his eyes brimming with concern. "You can't threaten him, Aggie. What if he tries to ruin your life like he did mine?"

"He knew he could take his wounded ego out on you. I'm nothing to him. Besides, I've dealt with Daddy. I can handle Gussy." Might as well use what little Daddy gave to me.

"Your dad used to call me every couple of years."

Shocked, I stared into his solid brown eyes. They were my anchor. "He never mentioned that."

"He just wanted to talk about how it was going and what my plans were. He didn't call after I told him I was seeing Stephanie."

"Oh."

"He never called you, did he?"

Numbly, I shook my head. Daddy never called me. He didn't chase after me. The news he heard about me came from my brothers. I'd been the one to reach out, and each time, I'd regretted it. I should be used to feeling unwanted and invisible when it came to him. Hurt was a full-body wrap that I didn't get to shed often enough, but new layers continued to be revealed.

"He didn't deserve you," Ansen said, his voice offering the comfort I'd gone without for so long. "You know that, right?"

"No."

"Ah, Aggie. Anyone's lucky to have you in their life." His fingers tightened on my legs, and God help me, I was dying for him to stroke upward. "Only the really stupid ones lose you."

Do not fall for this . . .

His warm hands left my lap to loosen my hair. Pressure eased on my scalp and the whisper of my plain, brown strands caressed my face. I no longer cared how sincere he was.

He tipped my chin up. "I'd hoped she wasn't far away."

"Who?" I whispered, terrified he was talking about another woman.

"The fearless girl who didn't care what others thought."

If he wasn't looking at me like I was a long-lost discovery, I'd wonder who he was talking about. "She found hair products and moved to a city with decent clothing stores."

"I thought she was amazing as she was—wild hair and worn clothes and everything."

"Ansen." How did I respond? He sounded sincere, but the hard feelings from the last ten years argued otherwise. The Aggie who got her heart broken standing in the door of her brother's office would disagree with him.

I didn't need a reply. He cupped my face and claimed my mouth.

∩∩

Ansen

. . .

Eternity and no time at all had passed since our last kiss. I wasn't sure it could happen again, but she was back in my arms. I didn't know how long she'd stay, but I knew I wanted it to be forever.

The thought humbled me. I didn't deserve her, but after seeing Dr. Jake skirt around her in a human's version of the mating dance, I wouldn't be content if anyone else was with her.

So that left one other option. Be a good enough guy for her. Be the guy I should've been when we were engaged. The man she thought I'd been.

I set one knee on the floor and tugged her toward me as I deepened the kiss. She came, compliant. Soft. Mine.

Resting her on my knee, I stuffed one hand through her soft hair and slid my other past the hem of her long blouse to massage her ass. She had padding in places she hadn't had before, and I wanted to reacquaint myself with every square inch of her and introduce myself to the rest I hadn't met yet.

"Ansen," she said between breaths like she couldn't quit kissing me. "We shouldn't do this."

"I know." I knew she thought we shouldn't, and hell, maybe she was spot-on.

But with her pressed against me, nothing felt more right. Nothing had been this right for a long time.

She whimpered and sank back into me. Licking my tongue against hers, I brushed my hand under her shirt. I needed more of her warm, satiny skin, and I didn't stop until I cupped her breast. She was fuller there too. This woman was branded into my head, and I was rapidly rewriting my memories, making them fresh. Relevant.

She dug her fingers into my hair and fisted, angling my mouth to plunder the depths better, and fuck was that ever a turn-on. The woman went after what she wanted, and what she wanted was me.

I rolled her tight nipple between my thumb and forefinger. She moaned into my mouth. Her sounds were as sexy as everything else about her. I left her mouth to trail kisses down her neck.

"Let me hear you, Aggie."

"Ansen," she whimpered, rocking on my thigh.

I abandoned her nipple and stroked down her belly and thank fucking God for leggings. I could wedge my hand between the material and her abdomen. She leveraged her legs to give me room, and I sank into heaven.

Finally, at least one part of me was where I needed to be. "You're wet for me, aren't you?" I rubbed across her clit and through soaked skin. She was hot enough to burn me.

She ground onto my hand.

"I need to feel you come for me, Ags." I pushed a finger into her, and she immediately clamped onto it. A groan left me. I threaded another one inside. My pulse pounded in my erection, and I probably had a perfect imprint of my zipper on my dick, but that could wait. "How bad do you want it?"

"I need it," she said in a ragged whisper.

Yes. "Take it." I nuzzled the base of her neck and nipped her lightly with my teeth.

She jerked like I was made of electricity, and right now, I thought I was. Flowing between us was an energy that had never been disconnected. This woman and I were tied together, and the question was what we did with it. I knew what I had planned.

Heat soaked my hand as she rode me.

"You're so beautiful when you come." I grabbed a fistful of her hair and tipped her head back. Her moans grew louder as I nibbled along her collarbone. "Come for me. Let me feel you explode."

"Ansen!" Her movements were erratic, and her body had a hold on my fingers that would've choked my dick, and I fucking loved it. Then she went rigid and rolled her hips. Her mouth was open and her eyes were closed.

Heat flooded my hand. So fucking perfect.

When she went limp, she opened her gorgeous hazel eyes. Vulnerability shone in them, and that wouldn't do. She needed to know she was safe with me. I failed her before. I wouldn't again. I'd figure it out.

I withdrew my hand, hating to leave her warm body, and brought my finger to my mouth. She tracked me with those shining eyes as I sucked my fingertip into my mouth like a promise of what I'd do to her clit when I got these clothes off.

"Mm," I said, taking in her riveted expression. "I missed the taste of you, baby."

She blinked. One slow drop of her eyelids and then an entirely different Aggie peered back at me. She pushed off, stumbling against the table and chair.

I could steady her around the thighs, but she spun out of my grip. "I have to go." She made a wide arc around me and darted for the living room toward the front door.

"Aggie."

"I can't do this again, Ansen."

"Why not?" I knew I broke us, but I needed to know where to start the repairs.

She yanked her coat off the hook but didn't bother to put it on. "I don't trust you."

Fuck, I hadn't earned it with her yet. The frustration was all mine, because of me, but I refused to give up. "I'm working on it, Aggie—but damn it. There was more between us than that damn money."

She hugged her coat to her chest. Her expression was scared and determined. "I worked for what I have. I know I got Mama's money, but she gave it to me so I could have my freedom. I'm not giving it up for a guy."

"I'd never ask you to." I ran a hand through my hair. My pesky erection was starting to flag, but physical pain was getting replaced with emotional torment. I couldn't cross to her, comfort her, or she'd gallop out the door.

She put her hand on the doorknob. "The thing is, you wouldn't have to ask. Last time, I was ready to ride along with you and let you make all the decisions. How long before that would happen again?"

"What the hell, Ags? I'm not like that."

She gave me a look like she knew better. "Gustafson should've known you'd never marry his daughter because you would've been tied to a place that wasn't yours. He should've looked at how often you've moved and changed jobs and realized that nothing would ever be enough."

I ground my teeth together. "It's not like that." Or maybe it was exactly like that—and maybe that was how all my relationships had been. I had goals, and the places and people I'd been around didn't line up with them.

"Did you know the ranch was Mama's? Her grandparents left it to her, and she married Daddy. Soon it was Barnaby's ranch. Barnaby's cattle. Barnaby's Arabians. She lost more control each year they were together and with each baby she had." She let out a scornful laugh when she noticed my confusion. "He plays off like he worked for it, and I guess he did. It was nothing but emptiness and cattle before him. Then with you—I dreamed of having four or five kids and being your partner. I ignored Mama's warnings even though they were still ringing in my ears long after she died. And when I found out why you were marrying me, I realized I wouldn't have been your partner. It would've been Ansen's training business. Ansen's house. Ansen's everything. And I would've been just like Mama."

"I'm not like your dad," I gritted out between clenched teeth. We would've been equals. Yet . . . I couldn't deny what she was saying. All our plans had been mine.

"But maybe I'm like Mama." She opened the door and a gust of cold air snuck around the screen door. "You asked why I was still single, and I gave you half an answer. The full truth is every guy I dated after you eventually grew to hate that I was in control of my assets. That I had significant power in the relationship. Do you think maybe you want something of your own because you're just another guy who can't stand not to have control over their partner?"

With that, she was gone, shutting the door behind her and leaving me with no real answer to her question.

Eight

AGGIE

I pulled up to my childhood home. After the weekend, I should have been relieved to get away—away from watching Ansen do chores and work with the horses while wondering what he thought of our parting conversation.

The finality of it left a haunted emptiness inside me. I'd said what I wanted to say after all these years. It wasn't that he'd hurt me. It wasn't that he'd shattered my self-confidence when he needed money to ask me out. It was that I saw what our marriage really would've been, and I was never falling for it again.

Instead of the vise around my stomach loosening, it grew tighter as I stared at the rambling log house I was raised in. I had thought growing up was the best years of my life. I was good at ignoring how miserable my brothers were. How much they hated Mama for leaving. The way Daddy's overbearing nature suffocated all of us. I'd been distanced from some of it thanks to being relegated to stock.

Now I was back, and I wanted to swing the pickup around and go home. The only thing stopping me was the thought of finding items left on my doorstep like they had been all week.

Saturday, after walking Tex, I found a plate covered with aluminum foil and the omelet Ansen had made me. Next to it sat a carton of fresh eggs.

For a bigger mindfuck, he'd left eggs every morning. Was he upset I called him a thief and was being an obedient employee, or was he being thoughtful? I was afraid of either answer.

I brought eggs with me for Cody and the kids.

To waste time, I looked at my phone. Message updates from Ansen. Nothing but business, yet he sent them more often than before. Photos of the kittens. They were at least eight weeks old and danced around the barn with their tails held high. I replied he needed to make an appointment with Dr. Jake to spay Fancy.

The cats were scattered among messages about the horses. Shelby was ready to take a saddle. Downy spooked at shadows and didn't like to be away from Melon. Morrow had been limping, but he'd dug out pebbles and grit from a rear hoof and didn't think there was an abscess, and he'd keep an eye on him.

We'd be able to find owners for Shelby once she was used to a saddle again. Downy would need more work. I could sell her as a pair with Melon, but I couldn't guarantee the new owners would keep them together or that there wouldn't be issues with either one if separated. The natural worries that came with a rescue were a nice reprieve from my personal conflict with a handsome horse trainer.

A knock racked against the window. I shrieked and dropped my phone. Tex woke up from the back seat with a sharp bark.

Sutton was grinning on the other side, and my heart settled back into my chest. Most of it, anyway. As long as Ansen was at my place and Daddy was in the house, there'd always be some tension in me. Laughing, I retrieved my phone. Tex licked the window, happy to see his occasional vet.

Outside the pickup, I gave Sutton our typical quick hug, neither of us super touchy-feely, and let Tex out to run. There was little traffic for miles. Crocus Valley was rural, but the county wasn't as empty of people as Buffalo Gully.

"You scared the shit out of me." I tucked my phone in my pocket and squinted at Tex sprinting up and down the driveway. The sun was out, but the strong wind could take the shine out of new paint.

"I saw you pull in and waited. Then I figured you might need reinforcements."

I did. "Where are the guys?"

"Cody's in his office. The kids are in the backyard with Wilder. Austen's coming home for Christmas instead, and Eliot's . . . " She waved her hand behind her. "Out there somewhere."

Eliot wasn't a sentimental guy. After working with Daddy his whole adult life, he was probably as closed off as a lagoon.

"The house looks the same." I shoved my hands in my pockets.

"It's exactly the same. Go on in. I'll take care of Tex. The kids have been so excited to see him again. I have to go pick up the food in an hour."

If I had stayed, it would've been my job to cook the Thanksgiving meal for everyone. It probably would've been my job to cook each night, and it wouldn't have mattered where Ansen and I built our house. The only fights Sutton had admitted to between her and Wilder had been about what Daddy had expected Sutton to do for the ranch as Wilder's wife.

Cody probably had absorbed the conflict to keep it from Meg. My brothers' wives had suffered for my absence, but I didn't shoulder the responsibility. That fell on Daddy.

I wandered to the door to the garage and stepped inside just as Cody pushed out the door from the laundry room.

He was dressed down in crisp blue jeans and a collared white shirt under a thick knit sweater. His dark-brown hair was brushed off his forehead, making his attention more direct and intense. His stern gaze landed on me and softened. "Aggie, you made it."

I crossed to him and gave him a hug. As my oldest brother, he'd been the father figure I could actually talk to. His hold around me was a brief band, but he kept it longer than normal.

"How is everything?" I asked. If I phrased it as "How are you?" he'd go on the defense and only say he was fine.

"Organized chaos. I was just coming out to check on the kids."

"Sutton said they're with Wilder."

"Exactly." A ghost of a smile passed over his mouth, then he was back to being my serious brother. "Barns is in his chair. He doesn't . . . he doesn't move from it often these days. It's close."

I nodded, my throat tightening. The swell of emotion had to be stronger because I was back home for the first time since that day, and it was harder to be there when I was trying not to think of Ansen living on my property.

I sucked in a hard breath. "Time to get this over with."

"Good luck. He's heard about Ansen."

"You're shitting me." Daddy knew, and he still hadn't called me? Had he talked to Ansen since his breakup with

Stephanie? No, Ansen would've said something. Daddy was probably waiting for today to pester me about Ansen again.

The grimness didn't leave his expression. "He's giddy. Eliot can't keep a secret."

"How'd Eliot find out?"

"That guy has a bigger network of gossips than a big-city high school."

"Thanks for the warning." I trudged into the house, straightening the material of my long-sleeved dress with the loose asymmetrical skirt. I had on my knee-high boots. My goal this morning in picking out my outfit was to find something opposite to what I would've worn when I lived at home.

Inside, I padded on the balls of my feet, just like the last time I took this walk.

In the living room, it was like Daddy had set out to be the exact opposite of how I'd last seen him. Instead of a big barrel of a man, he'd lost weight, shrinking to half his size. The steady hiss and click of an oxygen pump resonated through the quiet house.

Laughter from outside filtered in but couldn't block out Daddy's wheeze. His oxygen mask was sitting on his knee. He slumped in his chair. No glass of whiskey neat was sitting on the end table next to him. All the black was gone from his hair. A bushy white mass sat on his head. He never could be bothered with a comb, and now it seemed he couldn't spare a moment for clippers.

His mustache was gone. I blinked away a sudden well of tears. Shock resonated from head to toe.

When I regained control, I stepped all the way into the living room. "Hi, Daddy."

He swung his head around, a slow-motion move that was not him. "Birdie," he gasped. "You're finally home."

More tears threatened to crowd into my eyes. "It's Aggie."

He squinted. "Yes, yes. Aggie. I knew you'd return. Where's Ansen?"

My heart sank. Was this trip a bad idea? Would I have been better with the last impression of Daddy in my head when he did pass? Would it have been easier for me to pretend he was more invested in me than Ansen? "He's working. We're not together."

"He's with you?"

"*Working* for me, Daddy."

His smile was dreamy. "He's a good kid. That Gustafson fellow is full of shit." A cough sputtered out of him, growing stronger and shaking his whole body.

I took a step, but he lifted his mask and inhaled, his frail chest lifting and lowering a few times before his breathing settled into a wheezing gasp. My chest was tightening up, watching him struggle. This wasn't the big, burly man I'd grown up wishing saw me and not a pale copy of a woman who'd left him.

After he took the mask away, I asked, "Shouldn't you be wearing that?" Eliot said Daddy refused to wear a nasal cannula. The mask was one of his few concessions.

"Damn thing," was his only answer. He inhaled another rattling breath. "You and Ansen—"

"How are sales, Daddy?" He thought I was Mama when I walked in. Repeating that Ansen and I weren't a thing wouldn't go anywhere. I shouldn't have come. I was only hurting myself and confusing him.

He shook his head. "You're stronger than your mother." He gulped more air. "She was scared of everything."

"Mama? The same woman who swam with the dolphins and skydived when she was fifty?" Mama should've been afraid of more so she wouldn't have died in a car wreck after reported speeds of ninety miles an hour in her new sports car.

"Scared of this." He sighed a long raspy exhale and sagged in his chair, his gaze going out the window. "Scared of being a mom. Owning all this land." A cough. "Being responsible for all the cattle."

"Didn't you take it all over?"

He shrugged his narrow shoulders. "No one else around to do it."

No. He couldn't be right. His mind was foggy—from meds, from sickness. But his words tattooed themselves under my skin all the same. Mama was afraid to settle.

She'd told me outright not to be complacent in life, to live it to the fullest. For her, the only way to live free was to get away. From the shackles of the land that were the animals relying on her, the husband who loved her, and the kids who adored her.

"She was a runner." He took another gulp from his mask.

"Mama?" Which of us was confused? His conversation jumped while also hitting a soft target. "She did a few 5K races."

He feebly shook his head. "No. She ran from her responsibilities." His focus intensely cleared. "You were always like her."

I almost recoiled. I had a distinct reason for leaving the ranch, and while I took Mama's advice, I didn't emulate her life. "I have more responsibilities than ever, Daddy."

"Birdie . . . " he whispered. He settled his head on the back of the chair and let his eyelids drift shut. "Congratulations."

Concerned he was growing confused as we talked but terrified he knew exactly what he was saying, I asked, "For what?"

"Ansen. He's a good kid."

I pinched the bridge of my nose. He wasn't going to quit. "Yeah, Daddy. He's a good kid."

"He'll take good care of you." A shuddering cough. "You just have to let him."

I'd let Ansen *take care* of me in the trailer and I'd run. Just because I'd been trying to justify my actions despite my very solid reasoning didn't mean I was wrong to leave. If Daddy wanted to compare me to Mama based on my reaction to getting off with my ex while fully clothed, then I wouldn't argue. Fleeing had been the right choice.

"He'll make you happy."

For fuck's sake. Why not let it go? "I don't doubt it, Daddy." The only thing I had wanted Ansen to do was to love me, and I wasn't sure he could. And if he was capable, I didn't think I was the one he'd fall for. I'd had my chance, and I didn't want to try again. I shouldn't *want* to try again.

∩∩

Ansen

It was the Friday after Thanksgiving, and I'd spent the holiday with Archer and his family. He'd invited just me, but another cousin, Liam, had stopped by with his family too. If I could meet my relatives one at a time, maybe it wouldn't be as uncomfortable. Liam seemed like a laid-back person, and it was odd being in a room with guys who resembled me.

Now Archer was picking up Dad from the airport in Bismarck, and they'd stop out on the way here. For the first time since I left home, I didn't dread seeing Dad. I didn't have to steel myself against the tough inquiries only a concerned parent could have.

Dad was staying with Archer for two nights and flying out Sunday. Aggie was going to be gone all weekend, and she'd given me the okay to give him and Dad a tour.

First, I had an emergency appointment with Dr. Jake. One of the mares was biting at her belly and dropped little turds that weren't her usual.

"That's it." Dr. Jake patted Downy's neck. She wasn't as nervous around him as the last time he'd been here, and considering she was in pain, I couldn't be prouder of her.

Dr. Jake packed up his supplies, and we walked toward the barn to get out of the wind. I shoved my hands in my coat, putting "Get a heavier jacket" on my to-do list for the weekend.

"She'll be fine. The laxatives are pushing through, and her heart rate's going down. Keep an eye on her, and if she continues improving and her bowels are working, you can give her some hay. Glad you caught her early."

I bristled against the hint of a condescending tone. I wasn't a neighbor kid hired to do chores over the holiday. "She told me loud and clear something was wrong."

He bobbed his head. "Good thing you're around. Maybe I should've passed along the rescue's information the other day. I got a call about an abused horse. Deputy was asking if I knew who to call to take it, but Aggie's new, you know."

"How do you mean?" Aggie was new to town and that was it.

Dr. Jake gave me the *you know women* look. "This rescue. I mean, taking five on right away. I would've kept calling around, but Tanya insisted."

Tanya was also a woman and probably less of a dick. "Aggie knows what she's doing."

"Maybe," he said noncommittally. "I passed on a call about a pig the other day, but I can give them your number."

"Aggie's the boss."

"Yeah, but you know what you're doing."

"So does the three-time 4-H grand champion in the pig event who owns the rescue. And the five-time winner at the county fair in showing horses." Irritation turned me into a cranky fucker. She shouldn't have to pin her ribbons to her jacket to be taken seriously. "The only reason she didn't place first her entire childhood is because her brothers were competing against her."

Dr. Jake chortled. "It's eastern Montana. She didn't have anyone else to compete against."

My pulse thrummed in my temples. I wasn't joking. "You were ready with the compliments when you wanted to fuck her. What's up with this attitude?"

He recoiled, surprise crossing his face. "I never—"

"You sure as hell did. Take it from another guy who wants to fuck her, I can tell. Look, you may not be used to a young single woman not showing interest in you, but Aggie's serious. She won't take on animals she can't give one hundred percent to. Just like she wouldn't have hired the guy who broke her heart if I wasn't the man for the job." My heart was racing like Downy's had been a couple hours ago.

"I knew you two had something going on," Dr. Jake grumbled.

"A long time ago. Is that why you're constantly underestimating her?"

He sighed and brushed dirt off his coat. "No. I see people like her all the time. Big hearts, big pocketbooks, no damn sense about what caring for hurt and neglected animals really takes. I was worried when I heard about this place—and yeah, she's a nice-looking chick. But I'm not going to be complacent and load her up with rescues when I don't know she can handle them."

"She can handle them."

He tipped his head. "They all think that."

Some of my anger ebbed. I had to give him credit. He was using his best judgment, and while he might've come down harder on her when he realized getting into her pants wasn't an option, he was ultimately worried about the welfare of the rescues. "Just talk to her. She's got all this space, and I've got time. Melon and Downy are going to be ready to sell soon. The cats take five minutes of care a day, and the chickens don't require that much more time."

"I do feel better seeing what you've done with them." He held his hands up. "Don't take that as an insult to her. I know you've got a thing for her."

I had a big fucking thing for her. "There was a time we were going to go into business together. But she's the boss. Call her with the information. I'm just the help." And for once, I didn't suck on a big ol' lemon wedge saying that.

He snorted and started for his pickup. "From what I saw the other night, you're more than the help. Call me if Downy has any more issues."

Yes, I was more to her than the help. I was her past. Her present and future were what I wanted, and I had a bigger hill to climb than I first thought. I went into the barn to play with the kittens and give Fancy some love. She was curled into my jacket when Archer shouted for me.

"In here," I called.

They both wandered in together, same stance, same build. I'd be a triplicate. But this view was new. After Archer graduated and took off, and I did the same, the three of us hadn't been in the same place as adults. "Nice spread," Archer said. He was wearing the heavier winter coat I needed to buy. If it wasn't for Fancy and the kittens, I'd be frozen to the hay bale. Sunlight didn't reach this far into the barn.

I gently set the cat down, and she twined around Dad's legs. He chuckled and picked her up. "This one yours?"

"I'm just the guy who feeds her," I said. "She and the kittens were dumped about a month ago. Aggie would let you take her home with you."

Dad's brow crinkled with his grin. While he tucked Fancy into his elbow and petted her, I took notes. He looked hale, hearty in a way he hadn't while we were growing up. Signs he was getting older were there, but he looked good. Seeing him unknotted something I didn't know was tangled inside me.

"Nice to see you, Dad."

He aimed his smile my way and set Fancy down to give me a hearty hug. Dad was lanky but strong. The same citrus aftershave he'd used my whole life filled my nose. Hugging him was like someone shoved a cloak made of concrete off my shoulders.

"Been a while, Ansen. Having you two in the same spot was too much for this old man to resist. I had to make a flight work. It'll be nice to have the kids show me everything instead of seeing it through a screen."

Between his job and his finances, he couldn't travel often or very far. Guilt ate at my stomach. I should've seen him more.

"Look at us," Archer said, stooping to grab one of the kittens. A little tortie. "All in one place after how long?"

"Gosh," Dad said, adjusting a stocking hat he'd probably worn twice in his life. "Near fifteen years?"

"At least. Anyone want a cat?" I asked before we got too melancholy about lost time. Now that we were together, I wanted to enjoy my dad and brother. "The one you're holding, Archer, is Pepsi because she's the darkest tortie. Coke is the tabby with the whitest stripes."

Archer laughed. "Coke with the little white lines?"

"Aggie's idea. The tortie with more orange is Fanta. Root Beer has the most brown and then there's Pepper because she's still a little spicy."

"Not Dr Pepper?" Archer grinned.

"She's not that smart. And Tab because she looks like a traditional tabby cat."

"That's my kind of six-pack." Dad stepped out to check the horses, then twisted to scan the rest of the property. He tucked his chin into a navy-blue-and-silver North Face coat I suspected he borrowed from Archer. When he faced the trailer, he stopped. "That where you're staying?"

"Yeah." Showing Dad where I stayed the few times he'd visited me never failed to leave a stain on my pride. Someday, I'd show him something I was proud of. Someday, I wanted to show him my *home*. "I've been in worse." Rarely better. "Nicer than camping."

"Most definitely," Dad said. "I'm not made for the ground anymore."

He let out a gusty breath and circled. Snow had dusted the ground last week, but after a day above freezing, it was gone. The rolling hills were brown, and the random buttes dotting the countryside were the same color. Cattle graced the landscape in the pastures adjacent to Aggie's property. A large "for sale" sign had gone up across the highway. Hopefully, another rancher bought the land instead of having it parceled out for a subdivision.

"I didn't think I'd enjoy being back." He wandered past the pens and along the fence line. The horses nickered, their heads swiveling to watch him.

Archer came to a stop beside me. "He even asked me to

let Uncle Cameron know he was in town in case he wanted to meet up."

"Shit, seriously?" I vaguely remembered Dad's rants about his brother, but Archer would recall them better.

"Time makes a lot fade."

Dad had gone forty years without talking to his brother. Ten years hadn't wiped out Aggie's fear of me. I couldn't wait another thirty. Each day since she'd come on my hand, I'd only grown more determined to win her over. And each day, I was also stuck with her parting words in my head. I didn't want to control her, but I had nothing to offer her. Nothing.

Well . . . I had something to give back to her, but I wasn't sure when the time was perfect for it.

Right now, all I had was my growing obsession with all things her, and before I acted on my feelings, I needed to separate what went on years ago between us from how I felt now.

Hurting her again wasn't an option.

Nine

AGGIE

I stepped back from hugging Daddy's frail shoulders.

"Love ya, Birdie," he said gruffly. "Don't worry. Ansen will treat you right."

Hurt helped me refrain from rolling my eyes. "Sure, Daddy." He hadn't quit gushing about Ansen all day, excited my ex was back in the family no matter what I said. I gave him a kiss on his wispy hair. "Love you too, Daddy."

Thanksgiving night, after a tense but brief meal, I'd silently cried myself to sleep. Ten years of ignoring Daddy and I was no longer certain it'd been the right thing to do, but it was too late. The time was gone.

I walked through the house and stopped by my room. I remembered looking in the mirror on my wedding day, admiring my boots with Meg and Sutton in the room. How things had changed. Daddy never did make it into an office. The space was the same. Bed. Dresser lined with 4-H ribbons. I brushed my gaze over the empty shelf on the bookcase.

Eliot came in through the laundry room door.

"Whatever happened to Mama's old books that Tex tore up?" I asked. I'd wondered all weekend, but on Thursday, I'd been reeling from seeing and talking to Daddy after so long. Friday, I'd spent with my niece and nephew at Cody's while he worked. Saturday, Sutton and I caught up, and I managed to get in a visit with Wilder when he stopped for dinner during his shift. And today, I'd roamed through our land and marveled at how I felt like a square peg and the ranch was a round hole. I no longer fit here, and maybe I never had.

I liked where I was at now. It was mine. Thanks to Mama.

"I have no clue where those went." He leaned against the wall by the laundry room. His hair had more copper than mine, but he had Daddy's height and build. "That day was pure chaos. Barns never let anyone do more to your room than dust and run a Swiffer through."

My heart constricted. "I should've come back." I prepared myself for his barrage of accusations. I should've returned more often. I shouldn't have hired Ansen. How couldn't I know better?

"Consider it a gift to yourself." He shuttered his expression, but his voice was rough. "Watching him deteriorate has been . . . " He smothered a sarcastic laugh. "He made a shit patient, and once he couldn't get it up for the nurse, he gave up. I thought I'd enjoy watching him suffer a little, but . . . " He shook his head.

I should've thought of how hard this was on him. I stayed away because of Daddy, but I should've been around to help Eliot more—if he would've let me. "You've been here dealing with all of it."

His expression stayed even. "No one else was here to do it. Story of my damn life."

He meant more than Daddy's lung cancer. Cody had gone to business school. Wilder—the police academy. Austen joined the military. I'd run. Had we all assumed Eliot was grateful he didn't have to fight us to be the heir? Now we were all on our own tracks. "Daddy said Mama resented this place. That she never wanted to run it."

"Some days, I can't blame her. And I blame her for a lot." He pushed off the wall. "I loaded your luggage. I also tossed in a box of meat."

My taste buds were already watering. This spoiled ranch girl had a hard time with store-bought beef, and I hadn't stayed in one place to make connections with locals who sold their own meat. "Thank you."

He walked past me and turned, putting his back to where Daddy would be in his chair. "Look, when Ansen's old boss tracked me down, I didn't mean to reveal that he was working with you. I was shocked, but I would've never sicced an old prick like that on you."

I'd like to think he was looking out for me instead of thinking I wasn't capable of facing a guy like Gustafson. "He was a blustering dick, but I handled him."

"Don't get dragged into Ansen's shit again. I know he knows what he's doing with horses. I'm better at my job because of the time he was here—and I fucking hated that the dickhead knew more than me about training when we were the same age."

"You were a little cockier then."

"I'm not fucking ancient, Aggie." He rolled his shoulders. "I just feel like it most days."

"You doing okay?"

"Fine." As if a Knight would give any other answer. "You can't deny it's convenient, you know."

"What is?"

"He's somehow gotten close to you again, just as Barns is about to pass."

Money. Again with the thought he couldn't be with me for any reason other than money.

"I sought him out. He didn't know Daddy was sick when he took the job."

Ansen also hadn't known I would be his boss. But . . . he'd been chatting with Daddy here and there. No. It didn't matter. I wasn't falling into Ansen's strong arms with those talented fingers again.

"Did he stay after he found out?" Eliot wasn't dropping the topic.

I didn't have a reply that wasn't yes.

He gave a knowing nod. "Watch yourself with him. I don't want to go another ten years with you avoiding us because he hurt you. Anyway"—he backed up a step, like he was at his limit with the depth of emotion in our conversation—"a couple of the steaks aren't frozen, but the rest should stay solid for a three-hour trip."

His boots thudded on the floor as he went deeper into the house. I'd be at the peak of naivete if I didn't heed his warning, but everything in me wanted to wall off his words and shove them in a dark corner. I loaded Tex and took off.

Two and a half hours later, I pulled into my garage, sick of wondering how Ansen's holiday weekend had gone, tired of wishing I could just call and talk to him, and over how much my brain circled back to him. Tex popped up and panted against the window. I let him outside. I'd gotten the horses used to his presence, he was trained around the chickens, and I hoped he was tired enough from a day of frolicking on the ranch that I wouldn't have to chase him down after I hauled my suitcase and meat inside.

Once everything was carried in, Tex wasn't doing his

business yet. Confident he wouldn't go far, I got into pajama shorts and a fluffy, oversized, purple sweater. With all the people in Daddy's house, I'd stayed in jeans and a sweater all weekend. Tonight, I looked forward to lounging on the couch under a pile of blankets and reading.

I skipped unpacking my suitcase and focused on the meat. The two unfrozen rib eyes got set by the stove. I was putting the last of the roasts in the freezer in my mudroom when I heard heavy steps on the porch along with the skittering of claws.

I went to the front door. Ansen was squatting and nuzzling a delighted Tex. Opening the door, I shivered against the gust of cold air. Ansen glanced over and his gaze stuck on my bare legs.

"Hey," I said. I should've left the door shut, but I couldn't bring myself to regret opening it. It'd been a week since he'd gotten me off, and my body's craving for him would forgive this infraction. Seeing him should've put Eliot's warning at the forefront of my mind, but it tossed a nice blanket over the recollection. It'd been an emotionally draining weekend, and like it or not, Ansen was a friendly face.

He rose, continuing to scratch around Tex's ears. "I was bringing the eggs, but I wasn't sure Tex would stay out of them."

"He's been good about them, but yes, a package on the porch might not be safe." I drank him in. He was wearing a ball cap today, and his dusky-gray coat was new. "Are you keeping eggs for yourself?"

He shook his head and held out the carton. "They're not mine to take."

"Dammit, Ansen. There are plenty of eggs. Keep what you'll eat." A breeze snuck around the corner of the house, and I shivered. "Here—come in. It's too cold to talk outside."

"When you're in shorts, yes."

I playfully scowled at him. "Eliot sent me home with steaks. I have to use or freeze two. Are you hungry?"

Bad idea to offer to feed him, but he'd worked through the holiday and all weekend, and he hadn't asked for more compensation.

He paused like he wasn't sure if I'd kick him right back out. Tex had already raced into the house and was noisily drinking water in the kitchen.

I pinched the arm of his coat and dragged him in, then closed and locked the door. "I owe you a meal. The omelet was good, even reheated."

"I wasn't sure if you'd eat it."

I ate every morsel, and I'd replayed that orgasm with each bite. Sex and omelets shouldn't go together, but they were forever paired for me now.

He shrugged out of his coat, juggling the egg carton, and hung it next to mine. I blinked at the picture it made. I didn't have many visitors other than the few times my brothers had dropped by. I doubted seeing a guest's jacket hang next to mine would spark fantasies of the future, of sharing a home with this man.

I'd had all week to think about running away from him last weekend, and each day I was certain I'd done the right thing. After returning to Buffalo Gully and hearing Daddy go on about him and Eliot's warnings and being in my old room, I should've been ready to return home and fire Ansen.

The trip had flayed my insides raw, and Ansen's presence was comforting. He didn't look at me like I was a payday. He hadn't then, and he wasn't now. And we were no longer engaged.

Was I deluding myself? Was I looking for an excuse not to run next time?

Was I hoping for a next time?

He hadn't moved, looking around the living room with the peaked ceiling and rustic interior. I went for a cozy Western feel, decades more updated than Daddy's place. The kitchen was on the other side, a big open area where I envisioned the large family I once dreamed of gathering. I'd tried to talk myself out of the style and had failed.

"How was the visit with your dad?" I took the eggs from him and crossed to the kitchen.

I thought he'd sit at the island while I started pulling out seasoning for the steaks, but he leaned against the counter behind me, crossing one boot over the other. "Good. We drove across most of the county on Saturday." He chuckled. "We'd randomly park, so he could tell Emmaline and Vaden stories about what he and his siblings got up to at various places."

Smiling, I seasoned the steaks. How amazing would those memories be? All I'd gotten was what should've been and what could've been. "Sounds nice. How many siblings does he have?"

"Two brothers and a sister. All three live in Coal Haven."

"Did he talk to any of them? Cameron?" I nudged Ansen out of the way so I could get the cast iron pan for the meat.

"Actually . . . yeah. All of them. First, Uncle Cameron. I stayed back to do chores. That way, if shit went south, I wouldn't make it worse. Archer's more diplomatic than me. Also, I'm not ready yet."

I gave him an understanding smile. "He can be intim-idating."

"Archer said he thought Uncle Cameron almost cried."

I spun on him. "What?" My boss was a stern man. The only emotion I'd seen from him other than his usual stoic expression was irritation, and we all strived to avoid that. Otherwise, he kept to himself.

"I think there were a lot of general regrets about time apart from all of us this weekend."

I nodded at the roughness in his voice. "I might have to join that club."

"That bad? Or should I say, your visit went that good?"

"He told me again what a great kid you are."

He didn't crack a smile at Daddy calling him a kid. "Sorry. I don't know what I did to be the apple of his eye."

"You stood up to him. Looked at him without fear. Had a passion for horses and earning top dollar. You don't bull-shit, Ansen. That goes a long way with Daddy—and he didn't have to raise you. That seems to go further."

"Raising me would've been easier than raising you, from what I heard—if the story about the horse races with your friends is true."

I snickered. "Guilty."

His grin was lopsided. "Setting up a betting ring in fifth grade, Aggie?" My laughter grew. "I was going to ask you about that when I heard Austen ask Wilder if he had to arrest you yet."

"Come on now. I mellowed out by the time I was out of high school." By then, I'd wanted to be useful. I wanted attention for what I could do, like my brothers. "Besides, I'm sure you gave me some competition in the rebellious kid category, slick."

"Not at all." His eyes danced when he smirked. "I was an angel."

"How convenient your dad is back in Texas, scorpion-shoes boy."

"Isn't it a shame?" He went to my pantry. "What do you want with the steak?"

His broad back filling the opening gave me pause. The man had an ass and wore jeans designed to show it off. He bent to check out the options, and I gave myself a mental shake.

Quit staring. "Whatever you want."

He quirked a look over his shoulder, his eyes full of promise. "You sure about that?"

My mouth went dry. *Yes.*

No. "There are no baked beans if that's what you're looking for."

He closed the door. "You like potatoes with your steak. Got any?" He peered over the counters and went to the fridge.

"Snoop."

His chuckle was deep and went right down to my bare toes. I should throw pants on, but I liked the light atmosphere. Afraid anything I did would change it, I kept cooking.

While I busied myself with the steak, he found a couple of potatoes and tossed a bag of frozen peas into the microwave. Side by side, we worked at the stove.

"How's Barns?" he asked softly. "For real?"

The damn tears were back. I hated crying. I wasn't a pretty crier. My face turned red, my mouth looked like I had a run-in with a lip-filler scam, and I sounded like a moose on fire. But one salty tear escaped and rolled down my cheek.

"Hey, shit." He brushed a finger over my face to capture the wayward tear.

His gentle touch was like getting permission to let go. I couldn't stop the stream.

"Hey, hey." He pulled me into his arms until my face was tucked into his hard chest. "I'm sorry, Aggie baby."

Stupid nickname that I missed more than my next breath. "I should've gone back. I should've gone home."

He stroked my hair. "Trust that you had your reasons to stay away." His soothing touch helped stem the flow of tears. "You can't go back and make decisions for yourself with the information you have now. We all think we can, but we can't."

I inhaled a shuddering breath. "How'd you get so wise?"

"I've had a lot of time to think lately." He released one arm from around me, flipped the steaks, and moved the potatoes around.

Taking care of me and the meal. He was too good to be true. Always had been. Eliot's warning rang loud in my ears, but I pushed it away. I'd rather have the comfort.

I sniffled and pulled away. My tears made wet spots on his shirt. I brushed at them. "Sorry."

"Not the first time I've had your body fluids on me."

"Gross." I laughed and wiped my eyes, focusing on my steak.

"Trust me—it's anything but gross."

The wicked grin returned, and laugh lines in his dark scruff were an invitation I had to refuse. I had to get my mind away from riding his knee. After my tears, thinking about the way he could make me feel versus the sadness I'd brought home with me was too much of an allure. "Is there a reason why Dr. Jake is blowing up my phone since he treated Downy?"

Ansen took his pan off the stove and set it on a hot pad. "How exactly is he blowing up your phone?"

Hating how much I liked the hint of envy in his voice, I dug out my phone. "He could use some help to rehome an abused pinto, a Mangalitsa pig that was found on the side of the road, and a donkey needs a home after it recovers from getting hit by a tractor and has a bad case of laminitis. Either he saved them all up, or . . . "

Ansen propped one hand on the counter. He'd rolled his sleeves up to cook and those forearms . . . A lock of hair fell over his forehead, and my fingers itched to run through the strands. "He wasn't sure about you. Thought you might not be the real thing and he was hesitant to direct rescues your way. He asked me, but I said you're the boss and you're the real thing."

"That asshole." I couldn't blame Dr. Jake for being cautious, but to talk to Ansen instead?

"Yup. Just remember that next time he smiles at you real nice and his eyes twinkle."

I felt nothing when Dr. Jake looked at me. I burned alive when Ansen looked at me. "He's a flirt."

"He wants to fuck you."

My cheeks warmed. I pulled my pan off the stove. The savory scent of seasoned steak filled the kitchen, and my stomach rumbled. "I'm not interested in getting fucked by the vet."

He folded his arms. His biceps bulged—through flannel. Wasn't fair how easily he was so hot. "Who are you interested in getting fucked by?"

Fire swept across my face. I'd walked into that one, but there was a serious question buried under his teasing tone, and I wasn't about to tackle the answer. "I'm about to fuck this meat up. Get a couple plates."

His laughter was a lot like when he made the omelet. Head tossed back, throat working. His big shoulders shook. That damn scruff made it hard to keep my hands on the food prep and not running over his chin.

We sat at the island. I crossed one leg over the other and sat straight like Meg taught me. He leaned over his food, poking his fork into steak and potato and running the load through steak sauce. His ass was half off the stool, and his weight rested in his boots on the floor. He ate like it was his last meal, and it was a relief. I slumped and dug in.

My exes were like Daddy in a way, using their resources to control aspects of their lives. Food had been one of them—Lawson with his persistent critiques of what I ate and when, and Penley acting like every meal was a five-course event served by Gordon Ramsay himself.

When we finished, Ansen took both plates to the sink and stuffed all the dishes we'd dirtied into the dishwasher. "Goddamn, that hit the spot, Aggie baby. Want to catch a movie?"

My breath caught, and I was back in his cabin. We'd cook together, and if he didn't have to go back to work, we'd watch a movie, all curled up on his little discount couch. I'd sleep over, and he'd make me come at least three times before morning.

I had thought that would be the rest of my life, and losing that dream had been devastating.

He froze when he noticed my expression. His jaw worked before he finally said, "I guess a movie's out."

"I can't do this. I can't always wonder what your intentions are. I can't . . . "

His shoulders fell. "I understand. Thanks for the meal." He gave my shoulder a reassuring squeeze, a *friendly* gesture, which made me feel like shit, and went to the door. He paused. "Hey, before you settle in, I need to run and grab something for you."

I nodded, not trusting myself to speak. He slipped out, and I looked around my empty house. Tex snoozed on his dog bed in the corner of the living room. The meal was nice. Cooking with Ansen had been more than pleasant. I didn't care about making meals otherwise. Preparing food was something I had to do, like my bedtime routine. I would look forward to cooking with Ansen every night.

I stayed at the island, staring at the faux marble. He told me we couldn't remake past decisions with present-day facts. Had I made present-day decisions based on facts I had years ago?

When he returned, he knocked.

Wishing I didn't feel like my heart was breaking all over again, I pushed off my stool and answered the door. He had a shopping bag in his hands, an old one full of a million wrinkles, and handed it to me.

"These are yours. I should've shipped them back to you. I didn't know where you went, and by the time I talked to Barns . . . I don't know. Thought it'd be weird." He lifted his hand like he was going to adjust his hat, but he wasn't wearing one. His coat crackled in the cold.

I opened the bag, and he turned to go.

"Wait."

My books. The ones Tex had torn up during my argument with Ansen. They weren't in their original used condition, but they'd been taped back together. I took out *Murder on the Orient Express*. The cover had been painstakingly pieced together and taped. I set the bag on the end table and ignored the cold flowing through the open door. Paging through the book, it felt different than when I was a kid. Though heavier from the tape and less pliant, the cover had been puzzled together from the shredded pieces, and he'd taped the interior together too. The first two chapters were nearly laminated with all the tape he'd had to use.

He did this . . . and held on to them for *years* . . . for me? He had so few possessions, but he'd kept these, and they weren't even his. Just like I'd taken Tex and cared for him, Ansen took my books, fixed them as best he could, and kept them. Just in case.

"I felt like crap Tex destroyed those. I knew how much they meant to you." He cleared his throat, his voice gruff. "Took me forever."

This man. I let out a soft exhale. Stunned. Touched. Flayed open. There was no hiding what I really felt for him after seeing these books.

He was complicated but so simple. He hurt me. We hurt each other with what we said, but he still tried to fix something that got wrecked because of him, and he'd carried these around all those years.

"Ansen." I carefully set the book on top of the others. Then I grabbed a fistful of his coat and yanked him inside. "I can't believe you held on to them all this time."

"They were important to you."

"So was your dog."

The corners of his eyes crinkled with his small smile. "And you took care of him. But you don't need to give him back. Good night, Aggie."

I hadn't let go of his coat. I snaked my hand around the back of his neck and brought his mouth down to mine. "Stay."

Ten

AGGIE

He didn't push the kiss fast and deep like before. This time, he gently broke away. "What am I staying for, Aggie?"

I ran my tongue over my tingling lips. His gaze touched on my movement and heated. Was I brave enough to tell him I wanted him to take me to bed and destroy me? "I want . . ."

He crowded closer. "I want you to be clear. We've done this dance before. Only I *know* what it's like between us. I know it's going to be good. I've been dying to get back inside you, Aggie. I want to hear you moan my name while I'm buried deep, but I need you to be sure about what you want. If you want a quick fuck, I'm not strong enough to say no. If you want to hang on to what's left of what we had and see where this goes—I want that too."

"You do?" My entire focus was on his answer. This moment wasn't real. It couldn't be.

"More than anything. I've never felt like this with anyone but you."

It was like I'd been falling for so long and he was there—a net to catch me. For years, I thought I'd been a fool, and maybe I had been, but not for the reason I originally thought. Could a guy as sexy as Ansen, someone who could have whoever he wanted, really have a thing for me? No dollar signs attached? I had thought so once, and the heartbreak had been staggering. "I'm scared."

His exhale gusted across my cheek, and he touched his forehead to mine. "You were so damn beautiful that day, and even with everything going on when you appeared at the office door, I thought about how I couldn't fucking wait to rip that dress off you."

I cupped his face with my hand and rubbed my thumb over his stubble. I had no idea how much I needed to hear him talk about that day with anything but anger and regret. "Do you mean it?"

His dark irises drew me in. "I never thought I'd get another chance with you, Ags."

"Then you'd better not fuck it up."

He growled and caught my mouth. This time, he slid his hand around the back of my neck, tilted my head back, and made promises with his tongue I wanted him to live up to later. Without letting up, he shrugged out of his coat and dumped it on the floor. I held on to him as he toed off his boots.

I was dragging his shirt out of his waistband when he trailed kisses over my jaw and down my neck. I gulped in air. Disbelief was setting in, but I refused to let my mind wander far from the heat he ignited under my skin.

His big hands bracketed my hips. I put mine on top of them and he stilled, looking up at me. Dammit, I never used to be self-conscious with him. I bit my lip. "I'm ... different ... "

He squeezed my hips. "Ags, do you know how often I stroked myself off to the memory of you on your hands and knees in the barn?"

"How often?"

He hooked his thumbs in my waistband. "Every fucking night."

Dropping to his knees, he took my pajama bottoms with him. I lived out in the country, but the drapes were open and the lights were on. I was fully exposed to him, but there was no criticism in his expression. Nothing but naked desire.

He wanted me. No one could fake that. I didn't have time to second-guess him or myself. He spread his hands on my pelvis and stroked his thumbs over my bare pussy. A brow was cocked when he glanced up.

"I got into some girly stuff after I moved."

"How much of you do I have to devour before I find the wild girl I used to know?"

"I ... don't know."

"Oh, I'll find out, honey. Don't you worry." He hooked one of my legs over his shoulder and held my gaze while he flicked his tongue out to tap my clit.

I jerked, hitting my back on the wall. "Oh my god."

"Keep shoutin', honey. You're gonna get louder."

He cupped my ass and held me to his face. I could do nothing but hold on. His tongue was fire, and he didn't hold back. He licked through my seam, dipping into me and then back out.

"Ansen—I'm almost there." I'd never orgasmed so quick.

"You're fucking soaked." The way his voice rumbled against my body could be packaged into its own sex toy.

He deliberately circled my clit, and a long moan left me. I arched, shoving myself into him, and slammed into my peak. I should've lost my balance, it was like an out-of-body experience, but he was holding me. I gripped the wall and his hair, crying his name much louder, like he promised I would.

Tex ran into the room with a bark. Laughter bubbled out of me as I tried to catch my breath. Ansen prowled up my body and covered me as if the dog would be scandalized about the position I was in. His protectiveness only reinforced my decision to invite him in.

He aimed a crooked grin toward Tex. "She's just fine, bud." Ansen lifted me and carried me through the room. I wrapped my legs around his waist, his jeans digging into my inner thighs and his hard bulge pressing against my core. "You're more than fine."

He stopped at the hallway. "Which one is your room?"

"Farthest back."

Each step he took, I rocked against his erection.

"You keep bouncing against my dick like that, we're not going to make it to the bed."

"I don't care."

"Fuck." He swept into my room, kicking the door shut behind him, blocking out the sound of Tex's claws on the floor. "Now we're alone." His gaze swept the room. "Still don't make your bed?"

"Still don't see a point."

He grinned and laid me down. "Get this top off." He shoved the hem up, and while I struggled to get it over my head, he was sucking a nipple into his mouth. He couldn't seem to keep his hands off me. A heady experience.

"You're still dressed."

"Mm-hmm." Unbothered, he continued nibbling and licking from one side to the other. My nerves were alive, tingling, dancing against his touch. Pulling away, he smacked his lips. "You want to do something 'bout that?"

I sat at the edge of the bed, and he stood while I unbuttoned his shirt. Undressing him was better than unwrapping a Christmas present I'd been waiting years for. I pushed his shirt off, stroking my hands over shoulders more muscular than I remembered. He was the same but different, just like me, and that was what brought us back together. Once the material reached his fingertips, he tossed it on the floor.

I feathered my fingers over the tan lines ringing his arms and the base of his neck and the tiny mole right over his heart, partially hidden by the scattering of dark chest hair. I followed the trail of hair to his jeans and worked his waistband open, my pulse kicking up with the flick of the button and the undoing of the zipper.

Catching his dark gaze, I tugged his waistband down, leaving his underwear in place—for now. That look. His fathomless yet hungry stare had kept me from listening to the critiques of my exes. Maybe I'd filled out, and it wasn't with muscle, but I'd once had a man look at me like this while I was naked—and that was before the highlights and the lotions and the shopping consult. And that man's gaze continued to burn into me until I thought the sheets would combust.

Taking my time, I eased his boxer briefs over his erection. I hadn't imagined how nice his cock was. My brain hadn't made it out to be better than it had really been. Long, thick, and veined in a way that spelled pure magic.

He made a choking noise. "Keep lookin' like you want to eat it, and I'm goin' to make a mess of this."

I lifted my hand to run my fingers over his length, loving the way his cock jumped at my touch. I did this to him.

He caught my wrist. "Uh-huh. If your lookin' almost

does me in . . . " He pushed me to my back and stretched out over me.

This. I missed so much, but definitely this.

I brushed my fingertips over his face and along his square chin and spread my legs. He prodded my entrance.

He blinked and froze. "Shit. *Shit.* I don't have any condoms." He held his hips back like I had a restraining order for his erection. "After what happened, I've been firmly in the abstinence lane."

Not having sex when we were this close would be a damn shame, but I also believed him. We'd been honest up to this point about the years between our last time together. "No, it's fine. I mean, you said you got tested and I . . . Same." I caught my lower lip between my teeth. "It's been a long while, and I'm still on birth control."

He ran his knuckles over my cheek. "I never thought I'd get this again, Aggie." He kicked a leg out to spread mine wider. "Feeling you pulse around my dick."

When the broad tip of his erection pushed in, I let out a whining whimper, a wordless demand.

"Fuck, that's it. That sound. And when I do this." He shoved all the way in, filling me and pausing to give me a moment to adjust. My breath hitched, almost a gasp. "That fucking noise. I think about it every time I have my dick in my fist."

He rolled his hips, and I had to let another moan escape. It only added to the intensity. Determination lined his jaw, and I knew I was coming again before he let himself finish.

His mouth and hands were everywhere. I could only hang on to him for the ride. I arched to meet every thrust, another storm building inside me, ready to rage, but when he slipped his hand between us, I was done.

"Oh god, Ansen."

He punched his hips in. "Louder, baby."

"Ansen!"

His growl was it. I loved the noises he made too. This wasn't fake. The chemistry hadn't been an act then and it wasn't now. Later, I'd decide what to do with the knowledge.

∩∩

Ansen

Aggie rode me, her lush hips working up and down my length. After the first time tonight, we lay in her perpetually unmade bed, and she told me about her visit to Buffalo Gully. It hadn't been long before I was ready to go again, and since I hadn't quit playing with her body since I'd pulled out, she'd been primed.

I'd wanted to drive into her soft body again, but she'd pushed me over and climbed on top. Far be it from me to argue.

She braced her hands on my chest and her hair fell over her eyes. She pushed it back and smoothed the strands down like she was self-conscious.

"Let them go," I grunted, gripping her hips.

She rolled her eyes and kept riding me.

"I'm serious, Aggie. I'm going to fuck that polish right off you."

"Try it."

I flipped her, and the way she landed, her head was almost hanging off the bed. She let out a startled cry and then broke into laughter.

I was still inside her, loving her giggles, and kept pumping away. "I'm serious. You're hiding in there."

She gripped my shoulders like she was afraid to fall, but I

wouldn't let her. I just wanted to unlock her. The girl who used to stand in the saddle because she could. The girl who wasn't afraid to trudge through the mud to tag a calf. The girl who was willing to defy expectations, marry young, and build a business with her new husband.

That girl sometimes felt buried farther inside her than I was. I angled my hips to drive up.

"I'm not—" She moaned. "Hiding."

"Do chores with me in the morning." I shortened my thrusts, just barely tapping the spot inside of her that drove her wild. "Wear nothing but your riding coat."

She laughed again, rolling her hips, trying to get me to hit that special spot.

"Naked chores. They're a thing." I gritted my teeth against the way her body gripped me. I meant to tease her, but I might've caused my own downfall.

"It's freezing out."

"I'll keep you warm."

"I work in the morning."

"So do I." I gave her one full pump, and she groaned.

"Fine—I'll let the chickens out and get the eggs."

"Nothing but a coat?"

"And boots." Fuck, would she really do it? I could blow just picturing it. She dug her heels into my ass. "And a hat and gloves."

"As long as this pussy is mine." I put a thumb on her clit.

When she arched, I finished us both. Her body milked mine, stronger than ever. My release shook through me, and I growled her name.

Holding her to me, I righted us and curled my arms around her. Christ. This comfort and intimacy had been missing in my life since she'd walked out.

She danced her fingers over my wrist. "Why are naked chores so important?"

"You're uptight." She tensed, and I squeezed my arms around her. "You never used to be."

"I matured. Is that a bad thing?"

I kissed the shell of her ear. "No, but I feel like you think the immature Aggie was a bad thing."

Her breathing was steady, if a little quick, from the recent orgasm. "I do," she finally said. "Immature Aggie was brash when she felt ignored, then she switched to compliance. She was content to have what others let her have. Mature Aggie finished college in three years with a rambunctious puppy everyone told me I should give away. Mature Aggie didn't let guys decide her future. Mature Aggie has a mature job that helps fund something I really want to do in my life."

None of her points could be argued with. "Did you think I was trying to control you?"

She looked over her shoulder. "Like I told you, I would've let you. I don't want to train horses for a living. I never did. I want them in my life, but not to breed like Knight's Arabians."

She'd been so excited. I thought she wanted it as much as I did. Shocked, I pulled back and coaxed her to turn toward me. "You didn't want to start the horse-training business?"

"I could watch you work with horses forever." Her gaze went liquid, and I rubbed a thumb over the crest of her cheek. The blush I put there was still visible. Goddamn right it was. I put it there. "I'm red, aren't I? Meg compared me to last year's beets when I'd get flushed."

I hated to think ill of the dead, but fucking Meg. She'd looked through me the few times she'd grudgingly gone to the ranch with Cody, and I hadn't liked the way she'd treated Aggie like a pet project. "When you're red like this, it means I did something right."

Her light chuckle was intended to play it off, but her gaze softened. "Anyway, that's what I was wrapped up in. You—not what I wanted to do with my life."

I understood what she was saying, but I couldn't pair it with where she was now. "Working in an office is what you wanted?"

"It gives me the freedom to run AKA." She poked me in the chest, then spread her hand on a pec. "Which reminds me, I have to run the numbers for the cases Dr. Jake talked to me about."

"Every time you say his name, I want to put my dick inside you to make sure you only think about him as a veterinarian."

She mock frowned. "Wouldn't that make me think of sex when I said his name?" I narrowed my eyes and she laughed—carefree like she used to. "He's good-looking, but I saw his womanizing tendencies as soon as he drove that Dodge dually into the yard."

"That's my girl." I mulled over what she'd said about running the numbers. "How tight is the rescue?"

Her playfulness faded. "I can handle a few more animals. Thankfully, the horses were mostly healthy and vet bills were a minimum, but I have a full winter of feeding them. The nonprofit paperwork is complete. I'll brainstorm some fundraising activities."

"The sales from the horses will help." I'd make sure they went to the best homes. Especially Shelby. She was burrowing her way into my heart. It'd be hard to see the mare go.

"Yeah," she said almost regretfully. She'd probably miss the mornings she'd walk down to the horse pasture to let Tex stretch his legs. Aggie was popular with her herd, and they always moseyed to the fence when she appeared. If it wasn't winter, she could probably get on Morrow, but I wanted more predictable footing when we went riding. "When they're ready to sell." She draped a sheet over us and stared at the ceiling. "I can funnel some income from my job into the rescue. Mama's life insurance covered the property and the down payment on the house." Her smile was sheepish. "I wasn't prepared for five horses at once."

"Or me."

"I only took them because I could hire you."

Shit, she was serious. "You wouldn't have opened the rescue?"

"I could've taken one or two. Not five."

The decision came easily. "Pay me half my wage."

Her brow crinkled and the green in her eyes shone from the kitchen lights we left on filtering in under the door. "You're already getting paid less than what you should."

"It's not a forty-hour-a-week job."

"Only because it's too cold to do half the projects. I'm not paying you less. It's been hard enough keeping my guilt at bay."

I stroked my hand over her belly. Now that she was next to me again, I couldn't quit touching her. I didn't care about the pay if I was with her. I'd figure the rest out later. I wanted her to quit worrying about her rescue. "Call it temporary. I'd rather earn a little less and make room for more animals."

The startling truth of what I said rang in my ears. Years of clawing my way up the training ladder, taking one pay jump at a time, having my dream dangled in front of me twice as long as I danced to their tune—and I realized I needed the same as Aggie. Freedom.

"You're really good with them."

I crunched the pillow under my head and traced circles

on her abdomen with my fingers. "I like animals better than people. They don't expect me to do anything other than try to listen to them."

"They don't manipulate."

I smirked. "Some of the really smart ones do. But not like humans."

"Not like my dad."

I continued tracing circles on her skin, grateful we could talk over the hurt. Glad I could finally say my piece. "You were off-limits. It's why I didn't seem interested until . . . I was."

"And after that?"

"You became my favorite person to be with." I flattened my hand, soaking in her warmth. "Your brothers aren't going to like this, but I'm not letting them run me off again."

She twined her hand into mine. "They acted like they had a hard time letting me go, but I think they never knew what to do with me in the first place. When Mama's life insurance went to only me . . . it hurt them, and I always wondered if there were hard feelings. If they were relieved that I left and never came back."

"They care about you."

"They feel responsible for me. But they had their own problems with Daddy, so they were content to ignore me if I wasn't getting in trouble." She studied where our hands were laced. "How did they run you off?"

That day ran through my head. I'd avoided thinking about it for so long, the memory was distant, yet the words rang clear.

You're a fucking loser.

Piece of goddamn shit.

You came from nothing, and you wanted to use my sister to get something that would've never been yours.

I still didn't disagree with them.

"They gave me ten minutes to pack my shit and get off the land. Barns argued with them, insisting he was still the boss, but I left." There'd been nothing for me there.

I hadn't found anything for me anywhere.

In Kansas, I thought I'd be able to make a home. Fall in love with Stephanie. Talk her into moving to Texas. Do it right. Yet nothing would be right as long as I was living off someone else, and by the time I pieced together the clues as she mentioned her friends' engagement rings, what she'd like, bridal magazines by the shitter, and talk of who I'd want standing up for me, I figured out I was defunct. I wasn't capable of falling in love, and if I missed that many signs, I had no business stringing her along. The panic I fought off, worrying she'd think I stayed in the relationship with ulterior motives, had been the biggest signal I had to break up with her.

"Where'd you go?" I asked, knowing the general outline of her life after me. Barns had glossed over major details, and I hadn't wanted to sound too interested in case he started with more manipulative plans.

"Bozeman first. Then I did an internship in Denver before moving to Cheyenne." She smothered a yawn. "Tex kept me sane as much as he drove me crazy."

"I'm glad you had him."

She laughed, then bit her lip. "He hated my exes. Peed in one's shoes, and he ate the other one's underwear."

"Good boy."

Still chuckling, she rolled to the edge of the bed and paused, looking over her shoulder and holding the sheet to her chest. The curve of her back and her bouncy curls gave her an ethereal quality—a painting on the edge of the bed. "Are you staying the night?"

It'd be so easy. To stay over one night. And then

another. Moving in little bits here and there until there was nothing left in the trailer but the furniture that was left in it when I arrived. But we couldn't just pick up where we left off. There were too many years between now and then, and this time, I really wanted to do it right. I wanted to have something to offer, and that wouldn't happen while I was getting paid in kibbles and bits.

I had no clue how to remedy my situation, but I couldn't start by fucking things up with Aggie. "I'll stay in my trailer. I have to get Fancy kenneled so I can take her for her spay appointment in the morning."

Disappointment filled her expression. "That's right. Thanks for arranging it. I'll pick her up after work."

I couldn't leave her thinking I didn't want to be with her, only that I wanted to take it slow, to make sure I did it right this time. "I also want to ask you on a proper date. Friday night? Wings and dancing? Or darts?"

"I haven't played darts since I lived in Buffalo Gully."

"Let's see what Crocus Valley has for a wings-and-darts situation."

"Friday. It's a date." Her grin was in her voice when she slipped out of bed and took my shirt off the floor. She draped it over her shoulders and wrapped the sides around her like a robe. "I'll give this back in a minute."

"I didn't forget naked chores either," I called after her.

<h1 style="text-align:center">Eleven</h1>

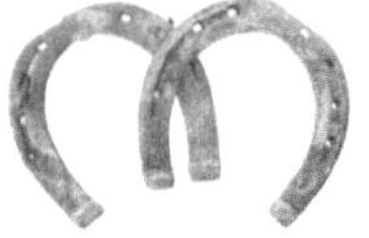

AGGIE

I swung by the vet clinic after work to pick up Fancy. A young vet tech with a long ponytail set Fancy's brand-new carrier on the counter. A bleary-eyed tortie blinked back at me, her golden eyes slits in the black fur of her face.

"How are you doing, kitty?" I cooed.

"She did just fine. Still a little groggy, and she's not a fan of the cone of shame."

Ansen had picked up a fabric cone-type contraption that should be easier for Fancy to wear. I could swap them out when I got her home. Seeing her like this, doped up with a shaved belly, gave me pause. Ansen had set up an old, large dog kennel I'd had in the shop for Fancy's recovery, but I hated to keep her in this while the outside temperature was dropping.

After the tech rattled off instructions, I paid and loaded Fancy on the floor of the back seat. In the pickup, I called Sutton.

Her voice floated through Bluetooth. "You miss me already?"

"Always. I have a drowsy cat who is sans one uterus, and I thought of you."

"People always do when it comes to cat uteri."

"Put that on your business card." I grinned and pulled out of the parking lot. Time for the reason I really called. "There's been a new development."

"You slept with him."

"Sutton, dammit. Yes."

A scandalized gasp filled the cab. "You did?"

I had to tell her it wasn't an impulsive, thoughtless move. "He kept Mama's books all these years, and he fixed them as best he could."

"Gah, that's sweet. He should give lessons."

"So you can sign Wilder up?" I joked.

"I don't think Ansen has a thick enough marker to spell it out for my husband."

I laughed, but she couldn't see my grimace. I never interfered in my brothers' relationships, and it wasn't like they'd have listened to me anyway, but should I say something to Wilder? *Don't fuck up and lose her. Did you marry Sutton or your job?*

"Is it weird to be, like, back in a thing with him?" she asked. "This isn't like meeting a guy and going on a few dates."

"It's different but the same."

We were different but the same. Maybe I was more different than him.

"You're sure he's not buttering up his boss?"

"He did a lot more than buttering." The quickie inside the barn this morning was cold and hot at the same time. I'd frozen my ass off while letting the chickens out, but he'd warmed me up to a point I could've stripped everything off again. "We're going on an official date this weekend."

"Like a fancy restaurant date?"

"Wings and darts."

"Oh my god, he remembers. How long has it been since you've played darts?"

I bit my bottom lip. The answer was easy enough to remember. But for a girl who'd been determined not to let her life get controlled by a guy, I'd also quit doing some activities I enjoyed because of them. "Since before Lawson."

"I don't take uptight Penley for a darts guy."

He hadn't been. Before him, I'd been flying through college as fast as I could and hadn't had time. I missed my old dart league in Buffalo Gully.

I'd thrived on playing in my hometown. Guys who'd thought little of me in high school got their asses cleaned during league. I had a good arm and a sharp eye, and Ansen had delighted in my wins. No sign of jealousy.

I had never played with Lawson, but I doubt he'd have thrown one more dart if I'd beat him. "Maybe Ansen wants to try to kick my ass."

"Tell me how it goes," Sutton said.

"Cody is going to lose his shit." I wasn't hiding my relationship, and I refused to think about me and Ansen as temporary. My brothers would learn about us sooner rather than later.

"So will Wilder. And Eliot. Austen might even call when he hears."

Ansen's trailer came into view. A few flakes blustered into the air, hitting the windshield and melting. "I don't know where this is going, but we don't have a deadline." That I knew of.

"Then you already have an advantage you didn't have last time. But . . . " My heart pounded, waiting for Sutton to finish. "When your dad passes and the inheritance is dispersed, the guys are going to be suspicious as hell of Ansen."

I didn't want to think about Daddy dying, or I'd start crying. And my brothers were already distrusting of Ansen. "I know. I don't want to deal with them."

"As far as I'm concerned, this conversation didn't happen."

"I don't want you to hide things from your husband just because he's my brother."

"Your brother would have to be home first. But he prioritizes the safety and security of the people and property in this damn county."

"I'm sorry."

"Yeah." Her voice was soft, resigned. "It's not like I didn't know what I was getting into." Fancy let out a mournful meow as if she didn't trust road trips—not after getting dumped and then having surgery at the end of a couple. "I'd better let you go."

"Talk to you soon." I pulled up in front of the trailer. The old garage twenty feet from the trailer was full of old, rusted equipment the previous owners had left and discarded metal parts that might have once been used for decoration. I'd have to let Ansen know he could make room for his pickup inside. The structure wasn't heated, but it'd save him from clearing snow off and scraping windows each morning.

I got out, my face getting dotted with snowflakes. I brought the cat carrier with me to Ansen's door and knocked.

He opened it, not wearing a shirt. I'd been all over that chest last night, and I was ready to do it again—with my tongue.

He grinned, not shivering at all from the blast of cold

air. "Hey. She do okay?" He took the carrier from me and let me in.

"She's good. Can you take her?"

"Sure, I'll get her set up in the spare room. There's nothing in there she can jump up and down on and pull her stitches."

"No—can you take her? I feel so damn guilty making her recover in the barn right before it's going to snow." I fluttered my hands, oddly nervous about pushing an animal on him. "Want a cat?"

He carefully set Fancy on the floor. Golden eyes watched us from the slats. His brown eyes were confused. "You're giving her to me?"

"Her kittens are used to the outdoors and hunting, but she's an indoor cat. Seems harsh to put her back out if I don't have to."

He folded his arms and his biceps bulged. I had to get home and walk Tex, or I'd undress right now. "You think this makes up for stealing my dog?"

"Tex is the only one who preferred me over you." I smiled, but there was a catch in my chest. Sure, my family had been upset with Ansen once they learned of the bribe. Before the truth got out though, he'd been like another brother to them.

Ansen's gaze softened. "Now you're exaggeratin'."

"So if I go out into the pasture, Shelby won't go running to you?"

He smirked. The other four would too. They adored him.

My phone buzzed. I checked it quick to direct my gaze at something other than his pecs. "It's Dr. Jake."

"He'd better be callin' about animals."

"He had his hands all over my pussy earlier." I couldn't suppress my grin as I flicked my gaze to Fancy.

"You're playing with fire, girl."

I read the message. It was about the pig he'd texted me about earlier. I hadn't studied the books yet, but I made some quick calculations. Before I messaged Dr. Jake back, I asked Ansen, "Want to help me pick up a pig after work tomorrow?"

He nodded. "Give me the details, and I'll get a pen ready." He squatted in front of the carrier. "What do you think, Fancy? Want to be my cat?"

She blinked at him, and he trailed a finger over the purple plastic frame. I couldn't get a good view of his expression, but his brows knit together. Was he frowning?

"You don't have to. I don't want to pressure you. She might do okay in the house until she's recovered, and Tex hasn't been chasing her when we've been outside. He's not used to another animal in his space, but—"

Ansen hooked a hand around my calf. His thumb stroked just below my knee, the warmth sinking through the cotton-polyester blend of my pants. "I'll take her. I was just thinking . . . other than Tex, I haven't had a pet since . . . before my mama died."

"Surely you have."

He shook his head, his gaze solemn and a touch sad. "Not even a horse. Thankfully, no one pointed it out—a horse trainer without a horse. But I moved around so much it didn't make sense to have a pet, and when I pumped money into a horse, I wanted it to be mine, on my property, on my land."

My guilt sparked. He wouldn't be able to care for more than an independent cat with what I paid him. And he'd offered to accept half of that.

I lowered into a crouch. "I'd like you to stick around for a while, but even if—if we don't—if you have to move, a cat will travel with you just fine. She'll always have a home here no matter what." I couldn't look at whatever this was reigniting between us as forever. Ansen had made no promises. His silence on the matter spoke volumes. I'd have to be careful with my emotions.

"You got a big heart, Agatha Christie Knight."

I pressed a light kiss to his lips. "Remember that when I kick your ass at darts."

∩∩

Ansen

I peeked at the message on my phone, then I looked at the woman dominating an impromptu dart game of 501 with the table next to us. Aggie was holding back her grin. She'd just finished the game.

"I can't believe you nailed that so fast," Vienne said. She had flinty blonde hair piled on top of her head and was dressed like Aggie. Slouchy sweater over tight jeans and stylish winter boots that would get trashed with one trip to the barn. Aggie's had rubber soles that wrapped high around her toes. She could jump through puddles on her way to a board meeting or a nice meal, and they worked for the quasi dive bar on the edge of downtown Crocus Valley.

Snow was falling heavier outside. The forecast said several inches, and everyone in the bar had shared stories all night of getting snowed in when only two or three inches were anticipated. Eight inches of snow was bragged about almost as much as a guy would boast about his dick size.

It was fucking cold. I wasn't a total newb when it came to winters, but I'd only been through two Montana winters, the most brutal of my experience. I was only there a year and a half, but that specific season was long. I had bales and feed within easy access for the horses and the new arrival—Skinny, the Mangalitsa pig. She was eight years old, six and a half years past the intended slaughter date, and when she outlived her owner, the rest of the family didn't want anything to do with her. So they just let her go, and a driver spotted her munching her way along the interstate. She lived up to her name, but Aggie and I were balls deep in internet research about the Mangalitsa breed and how to rehabilitate neglected pigs.

Vienne collected the darts, the multitude of thin metal bracelets around her wrist chiming together. "We should probably call it. I don't want Catherine to worry." Vienne said her daughter, Catherine, was twelve and preferred being anywhere but around her mother.

"As if she would," her boyfriend, Theo, grumbled and chugged his beer while Vienne returned the darts and put her coat on. He was close to my height but looked like he'd been trudging to a nine-to-five since he was six years old. His messy hair didn't look intentional and half his dress shirt was hanging out. I wouldn't have pictured the two together. Was that how people saw me and Aggie? The corporate girl and the farm hand?

"Thanks for the game," Aggie said, sliding off her chair. "It was so nice to meet you."

"You have my number, and I have yours. Call me anytime. I like playing." Vienne waited for sluggish Theo to maneuver his own winter gear. I'd had root beer that apparently my cousin brewed, but Theo had drunk enough beer for both of us and we'd only been here for a couple hours.

I stood with Aggie and held her coat for her to put on. She'd passed over her red riding coat for a heavy winter jacket with a quilted insert.

I shrugged into my new outerwear, which needed a wash after a few days of chores. My appearance next to her was a juxtaposition of how it used to be between us. I never paid attention, but she'd made comments about the gossip. I'd reassure her they were all dicks while feeling like shit, knowing I had money in my bank account that ensured I took her out.

Now she looked like she was dating down. A beat of insecurity drifted through my head. I'd never thought of it like that before. Aggie had always been out of my league, but she'd mentioned back then everyone thought she was dating up, and I'd brushed it off. No wonder someone like Meg had gotten into her head.

I wished I had a chance to go back and show them all what a catch she was.

"Ready?" she asked, tucking her arm into mine.

"You might have to guide me. I'm not experienced on winter roads."

"If we hit the ditch, you were going too fast."

I smiled and led her through the tables to the exit.

She huddled into me as we walked to my pickup. Our winter gear didn't block the feel of her body next to mine.

The snow was only a couple inches deep yet. "This, I'm used to. It's the other shit coming I don't care to experience."

"You remember that one storm?"

When I glanced down at her, I could've stopped and lost myself in her luminous eyes. They were bottomless and open. She'd never hid her feelings, not from me. I hadn't realized how much she'd closed herself off over the years until now. "You mean when you claimed to get snowed into the cabin, and we spent three days in bed?"

She giggled. "I guess I know now why Daddy wasn't pissed you missed helping move snow."

"Eliot was spittin' mad." We hadn't been able to trudge through the drifts to get to the main house thanks to the wind that had kicked up for a solid forty-eight hours. Too risky. But while we'd been lazily fucking the snow days away, her brothers had been moving tons of snow and rescuing animals. The house and shop and barns created enough of a windbreak they could actually work.

"Eliot's always upset about something. I wish he'd find a way to be happy."

"Working for Barns can do that to a guy." All of my bosses over the years had been similar to Barns. Gruff, growly, and controlling. I was easygoing enough to handle those personalities. I just realized too late those types of employers wouldn't give you a hand unless it was on their terms.

I opened the passenger door and helped her in, sliding a hand over her bottom and grinning shamelessly when she lifted a brow. I hopped in the other side, shaking snow off my head and shoulders.

Aggie finished buckling. "It's not just that. I don't know. He's not the same carefree brother who used to climb bales with me. I guess none of them are. I wonder if Mama was afraid to see them all turn into Daddy."

She hadn't drunk enough to get morose, but Aggie didn't do sullen when she was tipsy.

More likely that she didn't have anyone to talk to about her mama. The woman had died before I'd come along, and Aggie's brothers got dark and moody whenever she'd been brought up by Barns or the people in town.

"Did your mama change?" I asked as I pulled out of the parking lot, going slow and peering through the wipers. "When she was on her own, was she different than when she lived at home?"

"She never saw the ranch as home." Aggie rubbed fog off the passenger window. "Meg was a lot like her. Mama wasn't as snotty, but she had the same distaste for living so far away from a bigger population. She felt stuck, and I think Meg . . . I think she would've either talked Cody into moving, or she'd have left too."

"It's not a life for just anyone."

"I think that's what we didn't understand. We wanted that life. The freedom. The horses. The cattle. The challenge." She drew a little smiley face in the condensation on the passenger window that refused to stay wiped away. "What was freedom for us was walls for Mama. The guys didn't understand that. I didn't either until . . ."

Until she'd been willing to settle for a career I wanted.

She drew curly hair sticking up from the smiley face with her fingernails in the condensation that was turning to frost. "Theo's a real drip, isn't he?"

I barked out a laugh, accidentally jerking the wheel, and the pickup felt light as air for a moment. Nothing happened, and the next second, it all was normal again. Scattered fucking ice. I clutched the wheel. "Shit."

"Aren't you in four-wheel drive, slick?"

"One, yes." I pointed at the windshield, where the snow was getting heavier. "The temperature's dropping. And two, Theo is not who I would've pictured someone like Vienne with."

Her attention burned into me. "Vienne's a lot like the women you used to date."

There was no censure in her tone. Only observation. Vienne was attractive in a way that I'd notice but could move on from in a heartbeat. She didn't capture my attention, and over the years, it'd been harder for women to stay on my mind for longer than our initial conversation. "All except for one, and that's the one who tied me in knots."

Aggie clucked her tongue against her teeth. "You are slick."

"I'm being honest right now, Ags—and you *were* spying on me for the last ten years."

"Maybe a little."

I concentrated on the road, holding in my smug grin, but she wasn't the only one with a confession. "I did the same."

"Thanks to Daddy?"

"Barns liked to talk about himself, and I didn't want to ask him about you and get his gears turning. So I did the checking myself." I gave her a pointed look. "Penley? Really?"

She winced. "Don't remind me. Theo made me think of him, but I don't know whether Theo is ambitious enough to stalk Vienne if—hopefully, when—they break up. I know we've only known them for two hours, but I hope she ditches him."

"Small towns don't have the biggest dating pool. What happened with Lawson?" Yeah, I'd fucking spied on her. And with the few guys who'd made it into her social media accounts, I'd wondered if she was happy. If the couple I saw in her old photos was genuine. Because she'd seemed posed like the pictures were meant to taunt an ex who regretted his fuckup more each year.

"Lawson called me cold."

"Unless he's talking about your hands when you crawl into bed, he's full of shit."

"He didn't like that I made more than him. He didn't like that I was fine on my own. He didn't like that I could change my own oil when he couldn't even change a windshield wiper on his car."

"Why'd you stay with him?" As if I didn't know how easy it was to get complacent.

"It was nice to not be alone. I had Sutton to talk to, but I didn't meet a lot of people like Vienne—women I hit it off with right away. My coworkers were all older than me, and I worked with Lawson, so we had something to talk about. It scares me to think I would probably still be with him if he hadn't broken things off."

It scared me too. The only thing I liked about the guy I'd never met was that the breakup was the catalyst to get her to Crocus Valley. The dominos of circumstances fell, and here we were.

"He met Daddy, you know."

I carefully turned off the highway and onto the gravel road that thankfully had more traction but, unfortunately, less visibility. I slowed, but I didn't mind. I had to hear this story. "And you thought that'd go well?"

"Absolutely not, but he was insistent. I thought fine, see for yourself, smart guy. We went to visit Cody and the kids. To introduce them. Lawson thought he was a big shot. He thought he could go to the ranch and win Daddy over. Daddy was just starting to get home health care, so I think Lawson thought he'd be facing this old man who could barely spoon-feed himself." The emotion in her voice told me Barns was at the fragile stage now. "But he got all of Daddy's attitude. Lawson was so stunned, he couldn't talk about it right away."

I'd faced some type *A* cock-of-the-walk employers before, but none had blustered louder than Barnaby Knight. I hadn't needed long to see the man was all bark. His bite came in the form of control, which I could handle. Most of my life, I'd had no control. "How hard did you try not to laugh?"

She snickered and tried to cover it like she should be ashamed of her father. "Daddy was seriously offensive. I was so upset with him." A laugh bubbled out. "Daddy told him that I'd never be happy with a fancy-assed little twit who'd piss himself during a straight-shave."

I chuckled. "Barns told me, on the first day I was hired, that if I couldn't handle the winter, just hand my balls over and he'd light a candle under them in my honor while I packed my bags and left."

"You never told me that. What'd you say?"

"I asked him if it would be a scented candle and to please make it purple. I like to spoil my balls."

Her laughter rang through the cab as I pulled to a stop in front of her garage and breathed a sigh of relief that we'd stayed on the road the whole trip.

"No wonder Daddy liked you," she sighed, staring out the window at the falling snow. "It's getting heavy."

"Yes. Good thing we left when we did." The road would be hard to see soon.

"I suppose you need to get home before you can't see the road." The hint of uncertainty in her voice made me want to kiss it away. Which I planned to do.

"Just so happens I gave Fancy extra food in case I got a chance to sleep over." I'd regretted passing last time, and only a week had gone by, but I could only be an honorable man so long when it came to Aggie.

Her lips curved up. "I'm trying to decide if that's presumptuous or savvy planning."

"Wanna see how prepared I can be?"

Her laughter was everything I'd been waiting to hear for years.

Twelve

AGGIE

I thought I'd wake up earlier than Ansen and have time to sneak into the bathroom to tame my hair and put on some makeup before I let Tex out. Ansen had seen me at my most unrefined—full of dust, dried sweat, and cow shit, but that didn't mean I wanted to deep dive back to that point this quickly. Instead, I woke up to Ansen's deep rumble talking to Tex as he put him outside. Then the bathroom door upstairs closed. I'd told him I had extras in that bathroom for guests I hadn't had stay over yet.

When I bought the toothbrushes, toothpaste, and combs, I'd had no idea it'd be Ansen using them. Giddiness curled through my belly, but my brain threw in a healthy dose of caution. An insidious warning drifted through my awareness.

Was this temporary?

How much did it matter? I wouldn't change what I was doing. Resisting him right now was a moot point. I couldn't do it, so I'd take it a day at a time. My heart would stay wrapped in a box and tucked on the shelf.

Rolling up to a sitting position, I stretched for a moment before going into the bathroom connected to my room. Building this house had been a test of optimism. After a few failed long-term relationships, I'd still designed this place for a family I wasn't sure I'd ever have.

Cody didn't fail to remind me that a four-bedroom home for a single lady might be overdoing it. *Do you want to clean on your days off? How do you plan to care for that place when or if you get sick or injured? What if you're still single when you're eighty?*

Wilder wasn't any better. Austen stayed out of it like he often did, and Eliot had made some caustic comment about Mama's money.

Thoughts of their criticisms faded as I brushed my teeth. Squinting in the mirror, I made a game plan. First was taming my hair. The frizz had returned after a night rolling around in the sheets. A messy halo of brown tangles framed my head.

After my teeth were brushed, I dug for a hairbrush. A quick bun would do. The style was the best way to keep it out of my face and prevent me from looking like I'd been lost in the wild for a few months.

I grabbed my tinted moisturizer to cover my freckles.

"What does that do?"

I jumped and nearly dropped the vial. "Jesus, Ansen. Give a girl a heart attack."

"If I give you a heart attack, it'll be pleasure-induced." Ansen leaned against the doorframe. He was wearing his boxers and nothing else. The doorway was a marquee for the broad expanse of his chest. He hadn't bothered to tackle his hair, but where mine would embarrass a feral animal, his looked magazine ready. Some guys paid good money for the tousled look, and all Ansen needed was a night of fucking.

Heat swamped my body. Wind blew snow against the windows. It *sounded* cold, but I was ready to finish stripping out of my nightshirt and underwear. "It smooths out my complexion."

His frown was sexy and adorable at the same time. "You don't need that."

"You know how much more seriously I got taken at work when I covered my freckles?"

"That's bullshit."

"No, it was really apparent—"

"I mean, it's bullshit you were treated differently in the first place."

I agreed, but I lifted a shoulder. "I caught on quickly that I was treated better if I looked better."

He took the bottle from my hand and stepped behind me. His body outlined mine. The man had always made me feel dainty.

Putting his hands on my hips, he caught my gaze in the mirror as he leaned down to whisper into my ear, "I want to treat you really naughty right now."

"You did that all night."

He circled around me and put a hand on my stomach. "I'm going to do it again. Don't cover those freckles. Fuck everyone."

"Ansen—"

He slipped his hand under the material of my underwear, then he dragged them down. As I stepped out of them, he lifted my nightshirt over my head.

Naked in front of the mirror, on full display for his perusal, I'd never felt more exposed. I couldn't touch him back. If I lifted my arms to bring his head down for a kiss, my boobs would be at full attention. I'd look like I was auditioning for a centerfold. Would posing be better? A kick of the hip, an arch of the back? How would that look?

This man made me feel vulnerable in a way no one ever could. He stripped me down literally and figuratively, burrowing in like he had to understand and read me as well as he did every other creature he worked with. But at the same time, he built me up. He made me feel like Agatha Christie Knight again.

I planted my hands on the counter, deciding not to care about what the hell I looked like. My gaze was riveted on the way the tanned skin of his arm stood out against my abdomen as he stroked his fingers through my wetness and hit my ultrasensitive clit. My body filled with crackling lightning.

Once he earned a groan from me, he used his free hand to pull down his boxer briefs.

How could he have so much sex and he was already rock hard and pushing into me?

He locked eyes with me again in the glass and took the holder out of my hair. "There," he murmured, lazily thrusting while he stroked casual circles over my swollen clit. "Properly soaked and getting fucked."

"What do you have against hair and makeup being done?" I could barely gasp the words out.

"Nothing as long as I get all of you. Everyone else can have what you want to give them, but I want all of you, Aggie."

"Why?" The stark question dulled the sensations rolling through me.

His expression shuttered for a moment as if he didn't know the answer, and it was like the window opened and blew frigid air on me. The moment didn't last. He kept up the steady thrusts and increased the pressure of his fingers.

"Because you've gotten all of me—the good and the bad, and you're still here."

I didn't know what to make of his answer, but his words and the vulnerability I heard were enough for me to sink into the movement of his hand and the way he filled me.

We made an erotic picture in the mirror. I'd had a few images saved in my brain from our previous time together, and they'd gotten me through some lonely stretches, but we were making new ones. Just us. No family pressure. No money. No plans for the future.

Just us together. And that was enough. For now.

My climax built, and this time I did bend back to wrap my hands around his neck, tipping my face up and to the side to rest against his cheek. He angled to lick across my lips and cupped a breast, his fingers lightly massaging.

"You're so fucking beautiful." He kicked his hips forward. "Watch yourself come."

Normally, that'd be the last thing I wanted to do. My wispy hair sprayed in every direction, but his fingers kneaded my breast and glided across my tight nipple and the muscles of his arms flexed. I didn't recognize myself or the way I moved and shifted as he thrust. My climax hit hard.

"Ansen!"

"That's it, Ags. Let me see you come."

I was captivated by the sight we made. His big body behind me. The way he didn't let up as I shuddered in his hold. How he went rigid behind me, his lips pulling back and his embrace banding me to him as he spilled his hot release inside me.

He didn't let me go when he was done. I held us up with my hands planted on the counter. Outside, Tex barked by the front door.

The corner of Ansen's mouth lifted. "Finished just in

time." He kissed my neck. "Now that I'm done plowing you, I'm going to plow some snow."

"That was bad." I giggled.

He grinned and pulled out of me, then slapped my ass as he sauntered out of the bathroom.

"You don't have to move snow," I called as I rescued the band he'd tossed on the counter to keep my hair out of my face. "That part's not your job."

He appeared back in the doorway, his flagging erection tucked into his underwear. His brows were drawn together. "This part isn't about work, Aggie. You know that, right?"

"I know." I tied my hair back and faced him. We'd just had sex, but his gaze trailed down my nude body. Like that, I was hot again. "I want you to know that it's not expected."

He studied me, then a sly smile crossed his face. "What I know is that we both want to play with the skid steer in the snow."

"Dibs."

He laughed as he walked away. "Save some for me."

When I looked back in the mirror to double-check my quickie ponytail and the cloud of fluff it made, I caught my gigantic grin. How long had it been since I'd smiled like that?

I bit my lower lip and finished getting ready. If I kept going down that line of thinking, I'd start wondering where we went from here or whether I was *absurdly* optimistic when I had built a big house. The one time I'd had those thoughts before, it ended. So I'd enjoy today and quit worrying about the future. For now.

∩∩

Ansen

. . .

The sun had come out with a vengeance, and the temperature was approaching freezing. I didn't have sunglasses, but the glare of the sun on the snow was going to sear my retinas. Cowboy hats were no good for the glare coming off the ground, and I wasn't wearing my hat anyway. I had stuffed a black stocking hat on my head.

On the plus side, the snow kept the dust down, and the hard work was welcome. I'd been fixing as much as I could around the property, but winter wasn't a good time for construction projects, installing new fences, or landscaping of any sort. It felt good to work up a sweat, and I welcomed the cold air.

I was shoveling by the garage door when a thud hit between my shoulder blades. I turned to find Aggie, in her dusky-blue stocking hat with the fluffy ball on the top that reminded me of her hair, giggling.

"You're playing with fire, Aggie baby." I stooped to grab a handful of snow, but before I could form a snowball, she fired off another.

I twisted, but it struck me in the shoulder. Finishing mine, I lobbed it at her half-heartedly.

She rolled her eyes. "Is that the best you can do, slick?"

It was the slick. It got me every time. I rested the shovel handle against the garage door and gathered more snow. Before I could get a second decent snowball made, one busted against my hat, raining cold snow into my collar. "That's it."

I abandoned my snowball attempt and sprinted for her. She squealed and rounded the skid steer. Tex barked from somewhere behind me as I chased down his human.

Her black snow pants made whisking sounds as she ran. I slipped and skidded in the snow she'd moved with her equipment, but I caught up to her as she was climbing the ridge formed from pushed snow.

Tackling her, I twisted to take the brunt of landing in the frigid bank. She was laughing and trying to wiggle away from me and succeeding with her slippery winter clothes. I hooked her with one arm around her legs and dragged her toward me. Then I took a glove off, grabbed a handful of snow and weaseled my hand under her coat and over the waist of her snow pants.

She shrieked, and it was my turn to laugh. Tex's barking got closer.

I grinned at the concerned dog. "It's okay. Your human's being naughty."

"You play dirty," she said with a smile.

"You mean like lobbing snowballs at me before I even get one made?" I helped her sit up so we were side by side, then put my gloves back on. Tex mellowed, his tail slowly wagging as he eyed me.

"It's not my fault you're slow."

"I didn't grow up in Montana with four brothers."

She patted my legs, residual snow falling from her gloves. "Speaking of, you need snow pants."

"I have long johns on underneath these."

"Not enough."

"I didn't even have snow pants when I worked for Barns."

"You were a trainer there. Here you're a jack-of-all-trades." She wiggled off the snow pile and brushed herself off. Icy wetness seeped into my jeans, but I stayed put, watching my very own snow bunny. If she had a pair of ski goggles, she'd look ready to hit the slopes—wherever they were in this state.

My vibrating phone got me to stand. "I'll buy a pair when I'm in town next."

Her smile turned satisfied and cinched around my heart like a warm hug.

The call was from Archer. "Hey," I answered, wandering around the freshly shoveled driveway to keep warm. "Y'all get through the storm okay?"

"Just dug us out. Emmaline wants to make snowmen with her uncle. I told her—"

"Yes." My niece was quickly winding me around her tiny, demanding finger. I had time to make up, and while being around my brother and his family made me think of everything I thought I'd have by now, I was happier for him each time I got to witness a slice of his life. If I couldn't have it, one of us should. "When should I be there?"

"Oh, she's goin' to be thrilled." I deserved the surprise in his voice. I would've thought I'd say no not long ago too. "I think it'll warm up a little more, so the sooner, the better while the snowman-making is still good, but I know you've got a lot to do."

"Not really." When I had a boss who let me babysit the weather and plan for it, these kinds of things weren't terrible. Aggie and I did chores before we moved snow. The horses and Skinny were doing good, and the kittens got extra cuddles. "Hey, uh . . . " I turned my back on where Aggie was kicking off heavy snow that had collected on the edges of the skid steer. "Can I bring Aggie? If she wants to come."

"Absolutely." He paused. "Just know . . . Emmaline is going to ask questions."

I chuckled. My niece had a lot of questions. I'd learned that quickly. "No problem. Just don't tell her until we show. I'm not sure if Aggie will think it's too soon."

"Got it."

I hung up and cleared my throat. I should've talked to her before I mentioned a thing to Archer. What if she didn't want to join me? I was tired of evading the truth around my family, but I also didn't want to show up and announce she was still leery of me and meeting family was a little much.

Both Aggie and the dog looked at me. Too late now. "You want to build a snowman with me and Emmaline?"

Her shock was more pronounced than Archer's. "At Archer's?" I nodded. She blinked. "Sure. You don't mind?"

Did I mind? I was damn near giddy. Years ago, I would've loved to introduce her to my family, but it hadn't been an option, not with Barns's money in my account. Today though? I was broke as hell, and she wanted to go with me. "I'm going to warn you—I know I just met my niece, but she could ask us to build one snowman or an entire army."

"Let's go find out."

∩∩

Aggie

After stopping to get Ansen some proper snow pants at the farm and tractor supply store, we went to Archer and Delaney's place. I'd been properly introduced to Delaney and then Emmaline had towed us around the property, introducing us to the goats, chickens, horses, and even a few of the cows. She reminded me of my niece Ivy—outgoing and uninhibited. She'd be a force one day.

I missed my niece and nephew and made a mental note to check in with Cody between the holidays. Our relationship had shifted. He'd still have his strong opinions about what I should do with my life and business, and he'd always be the oldest brother, but it was time he had someone butting into his life.

We were on our third snowman and the little girl was

going full steam ahead while my body reminded me that it'd been years since I'd spent the day in the snow.

"What's your favorite book?" Emmaline asked as we packed snow around the seams of the largest snowman.

"I'm supposed to say *Murder on the Orient Express* since I was named after the author, but I loved *Where the Crawdads Sing*."

"Never heard of them. Do you know Peppa Pig?"

"No?" I struggled to recall the books I'd read to Cody's kids over the years. With Meg, I was surprised she hadn't started them on *War and Peace* right away.

"Uncle Ansen?"

He grinned. "No Peppa Pig for me."

"*Fancy Nancy*?" she asked earnestly.

"If it's a little girl's book, I can guarantee I haven't heard of it. I probably haven't heard of any kids' books."

She put her hands on her hips in a move that must have come straight from her mother. "I'll have to read you mine."

"You can read?" I asked. My niece, Ivy, was only a little older, and she could read some books, but Emmaline spoke with the authority of someone who could recite *Pride and Prejudice*.

She nodded, beaming.

Laney poked her head out of the front door of their little farmhouse. "Ready for some hot chocolate?"

"Hot chocolate!" Emmaline sprinted away, leaving me and Ansen facing a sideways-tilting snowman.

"It's not the worst I've ever made," I said.

He chuckled and straightened. His cheeks were red and his gaze was lighter than I'd ever seen, including when we were younger. "I suspect Laney's saving us from making three more."

"Emmaline is quite the taskmaster. She's almost as bossy

as Daddy. He used to make us redo a snowman if we half-assed it."

"Probably because he wanted you to quit playing and go back to work."

My brothers, maybe. "Once, he came out to help me build one. He and Mama had a fight, and I think he wanted to prove he wasn't the bad guy she thought he was." I waved off the memory. It brought more humor with it than it used to, but the bitterness was still there. "Never mind. I don't want to rain on our snowman parade."

"He might've just wanted to have fun with his kids." We started for the house. "Everything your brothers do around the ranch, he used to do himself."

"Daddy wasn't a deputy like Wilder—or in the army," I joked, but I knew what he meant. Wilder and Austen still helped around the ranch—during horse sales and for calving season and working cattle, but Daddy used to run the oil business and Cody was now. Daddy had been the ranch manager until his lungs forced him inside, and even then, he'd clung to his role with white knuckles. Had Daddy known what it was like to have fun, or had work always been a priority? Had taking care of us been the reason behind his drive?

Mama hadn't helped with anything. She'd go horseback riding and make meals and then curl up in her chair and read. We hadn't done much as an entire family before Mama left. I didn't think work needed to be a family affair, but play should be.

As we took our winter gear off in the entryway off the garage, I saw Archer buckling Vaden into a booster seat, Laney lining the table with various mugs of hot chocolate, and Emmaline carefully doling out mini marshmallows by each spot. It struck me that I didn't have these types of family memories. I'd grown up in a big family, and size made it feel like we were closer than we were.

This was a close family. Parents who were still a couple. Kids who thrived and wanted to be included and were. A familiar ache ignited in my chest. Grief for what my brothers and I had missed out on, and maybe some residual longing for what could've been.

I shook it off and grinned at Ansen's niece. Her hair was in a ponytail that was now crooked and hanging low, but she positioned herself in a chair like she was royalty. "Please, y'all have a seat."

I slid into the spot she beckoned me to. "Thank you for inviting me."

She pointed to the chair next to her. She was in the middle of me and Ansen. Laney and Archer flanked Vaden on the other side of the table. The house was smaller and had been added on to, but it was cozy and warm. The living room spilled over with dolls and books and large, plastic musical instruments.

Emmaline wiggled in her seat and dumped her mini marshmallows in her cup. "You're welcome, Aunt Aggie," she said primly.

Startled, I looked around the table. I was used to being called Aunt Aggie, but that was Cody's kids. Laney just lifted a shoulder like she didn't care if I didn't care. Archer bit back a smile, and Ansen slid his gaze toward me as if asking me if I minded. I didn't, but it also struck me that I would've been her and Vaden's aunt, and maybe if Ansen and I had gotten married all those years ago, we would've been around since they'd been born. Eventually, I would've realized there was a rift in his immediate family that was more than distance and work obligations. I would've noticed his relationship with his brother and father was little more than what he had with his extended family. Would I have encouraged Ansen to close the distance?

But that was in the past. Looking back on a time line that never happened messed with my head. Best to focus on the present.

I gave Ansen a small smile to tell him I didn't mind. The same realization floated through his eyes, and he dropped his gaze to his hot chocolate.

"I have a question, Emmaline," I said. When I got her attention—and everyone else's, I leaned toward her. "How many marshmallows is just right?"

She grinned and started touting the benefits of the more the merrier when it came to all sizes of marshmallows. Ansen's gaze softened, and when he looked at me, I had to distract myself by taking a drink. I saw my desires from long ago reflected in the bay-colored depths of his irises. The longing. The loss.

I'd never allowed myself to ask what would've happened if I hadn't left that day. But I'd done the leaving first. I'd listened to my mother, the woman who hadn't stuck around to learn what was best for me. Leaving was better than watching him go. Had I known I wasn't strong enough then? Had I known it would've devastated me to keep living and working on the ranch where everything reminded me of him?

Was the real question whether I was strong enough now if he decided I wasn't the one for him and that Crocus Valley wasn't where he wanted to be?

AGGIE

I was leaving work when Cody called. Instead of talking to him on the drive home, I sat in the pickup and let it heat up. The temperature hovered at ten degrees, and the wind was bitter. More snow had fallen since the last storm. It'd be a white Christmas.

"Hello?" I braced myself, never sure what news I'd be getting from him with Daddy's health continually deteriorating.

"Is that Christmas offer still on the table?"

"Yes," I said without thinking and sucked in a relieved breath. Even if I had realized I'd have to tell him about my relationship with Ansen, I would've said yes. The only decision I had to make was whether I'd hide it or not. "When are you coming, and how long are you staying?"

"Meg's parents wanted the kids for all of Christmas break—and I'm not gonna lie, it'd be easier. Austen's only taking leave for a few days, but Sutton said she'd help watch them over break when their day care's closed. I'd hate for them to miss their uncle when he's in town, so I thought maybe we'd make sure to go and see you too."

Meg's parents probably had issues with the day care in the first place, and this was Cody's justification. Cody took them to a small, in-home day care with a woman who was born and raised in Buffalo Gully and wanted to support her family while she stayed home with her kids. It was cozy, intimate, and convenient. He'd known the family forever. But Meg's parents thought the kids should be getting early education like they were going from preschool to an Ivy League college. It didn't help that Meg hadn't liked living in Buffalo Gully.

"I have a three-day weekend over Christmas and the week after. Stay as long as you want."

"We'll get a hotel."

"I have plenty of room, Cody. I even have all that furniture you complained I was wasting money on."

"Grayson's been asking to see your new place."

"Skinny's pretty friendly. I even have a donkey called Shrek now." Shrek had arrived shortly after Skinny. After the worst of his car-accident trauma had healed. Ansen had studied up on all things donkey, and he'd recited his research and facts when we'd gone to pick the animal up from Dr. Jake's office.

"Ansen?"

My eagerness vanished, and I turned guarded. I wasn't ready to tell Cody *today*. "He's doing good."

"How good?"

I chewed the inside of my cheek. The same thoughts ran through my head as the last time I talked to him. If I kept evading his inquiries, I'd look like I had something to hide. I'd come off as immature. If I wanted things to be different with my brothers, then I had to act differently. "We're seeing each other."

"For fuck's sake, Aggie." The heat in his words hit swiftly, but it was accompanied by a resigned *I knew it,* all in the same sentence.

"It's not like that."

"Like he has a pattern? Like he's done this before? Like maybe he found a way to live the good life because now he can sleep with the boss and not just the kid of the boss?"

Anger and defensiveness mingled inside me. I shifted in my seat and let the drone of the pickup's heat dull my ire. "Stay out of it, Cody. You don't know him, and you don't even know me that well. It's not like I'm sitting out here made of money. AKA has some ragtag animals, not horses that can be sold to make a name for the business."

"I don't trust him," Cody growled. "But I guess you'll see what he's really like when Barns is gone and that inheritance is yours."

"Doesn't mean he'll get access to the money. But hey, thanks for thinking that I'm such a catch that he can't resist me." I infused my voice with as much sarcasm as it could hold.

Cody blew out a tired breath. "It's not like that. Any guy would be lucky to be with you. One thing I've learned is that you don't make it easy on them."

He almost sounded grateful about that. I hadn't made it easy on Penley and Lawson. With Ansen, I didn't have to. "You have a lot going on. I know you don't trust him, but can you trust me? I've done okay up until now."

"I know." His fatigue filtered over the line. Was it the in-laws? His job? Grief he probably hadn't let himself experience? "You've done really well, and you're less than three hours away. I don't want him to hurt you and you up and leave and then we don't see you more than once a year again."

I . . . didn't realize how much that had bothered him until I heard the heaviness, the fear in his voice. Eliot had said something similar. I had up and left and assumed my brothers had each had their own lives and would barely notice. "I would've had to leave eventually. I know you don't agree with how Mama abandoned us, but she and I were in the same boat. There was nothing there for us. I kept wanting to do more, and you all kept me doing less."

"You're the baby. We had to take care of you."

With Ansen, I wasn't an obligation. I wasn't someone he had to care for. We moved snow together. He cleared his training ideas through me. While I didn't disagree with anything, he would've listened if I had. We worked well together. I didn't feel like his boss. We were more like colleagues.

"But I see what you mean," he said. "If it's going to be too uncomfortable to have us there—"

"Not at all—I want to see all of you. I don't know what Ansen's going to do for Christmas. He has family too."

"Since when?"

"He hasn't met much of his extended family, but his brother lives in the next town over, and his dad was up for Thanksgiving."

"Guess we all have to grow up someday. Dammit, it's Curt calling."

Curt Smith was Meg's dad. A lawyer who couldn't retire because he would miss being in everyone's business and calling the shots. "Tell the others they're all welcome too." My entire family hadn't been to my place yet at the same time.

"Eliot's going to bitch about Ansen and claim Barns needs him there. Austen's flying in and out so quick I don't know what the point is, but he's going to stay and help Eliot. Wilder took the weekend for another deputy. Maybe check with Sutton?"

"Will do." After we hung up, I stared out the windshield. A woman from HR walked by and waved. Heat was finally kicking out of the vents, and I could go at any time.

I dialed Sutton instead. After what Cody said about Wilder, I didn't want to wait on her call. When she answered, I said, "Cody and the kids are coming for Christmas. Want to come and guess about everything Cody's going to critique?"

She laughed. "He hasn't let up about the square footage."

"The whole second story."

"He told you Wilder offered to work for Kaplan?"

I immediately knew why Wilder did it. Kaplan had three kids and his in-laws lived outside of Sioux Falls. Sutton had made Wilder take Labor Day weekend off so they could hike in Yellowstone, and he'd felt guilty all vacation because Kaplan's in-laws had driven up for a few days. "Sorry."

"Yeah." Each time I apologized like I could make up for my brother's workaholism, she sounded more defeated. "You know what—I'll drive down. I work on Christmas Eve, but I can come down for Christmas Day. I'm on call the day after. Want me to bring anything?"

"Your pudding salad." It was anything but a salad, and I could eat a gallon.

"See you then and—Aggie?"

"Yeah?"

"Thanks."

"Any time." I'd been alone enough Christmases, but I'd always been single. I didn't know what it was like to spend a holiday by myself when my significant other seemed to go out of his way to avoid being home.

I pulled out of the parking lot and hit the highway toward home. I was having guests for the holiday.

ᏌᏌ

Ansen

I'd purchased presents for Emmaline and Vaden weeks ago. I'd gone to Bismarck and had even paid for someone to wrap them. Last Christmas, I'd been part of a big family dinner that was more for showing off how much money the ranch I worked for was making than to concentrate on any large family gathering. Stephanie had made me dress in a black western-cut suit that had reminded me of my wedding tux. So the day had started out shitty.

I couldn't have pictured the changes I'd been through since then.

Watching my niece, still in a fancy red nightgown, helping her brother tear into a spring rocking horse he could ride, just like Archer and I had when we were kids, wasn't it. But it was one of the improvements.

Just like Aggie. She was at her house hosting Cody and his kids and Sutton. She'd invited me, and I'd love to watch her with her niece and nephew and see her enjoy their visit, but I didn't want to add any awkwardness to a milestone day for her.

"It says good for kids up to six," I said as Emmaline crawled onto the horse to show Vaden how it was done. He stamped his little legs and screamed at her.

"I might have to drop it to five and under." Laney grinned and beckoned Emmaline toward her. "Come on, Em. Let Vaden enjoy his present. You have yours."

She had barely let go of the three-foot cowgirl doll almost as tall as her.

"Besides," Archer added, "you have a real pony you can ride. Vaden doesn't."

Emmaline didn't look convinced, but she dropped to her butt and fiddled with her doll's hat.

"Did you go to the mall and ask for the biggest presents to get a kid?" Archer asked, his mouth in a wry twist.

"You said nothing noisy. I didn't hear a thing about big as hell."

My niece threw a censuring look my way. "Mo-om."

"Those are words adults can say," Laney replied. She curled her feet beside her and snuggled into Archer's side. They were going to another cousin's later today, and I'd been invited, but I hadn't decided. The longer I waited, the weirder it got. How many relatives had I come across in my months here and didn't know? But staying by myself in the trailer didn't seem like a valid option. It wasn't progress.

After I'd first arrived, I'd been ashamed to show my face. Since Dad's visit and being with Aggie, I wanted to see my brother more. According to Archer, the Barrons were all decent people, and after the Gustafsons, I needed more of that in my life.

"I'll go," I announced. "Tonight. I'll go."

Archer didn't break out in a grin like he knew what a shift in my life this would be. "You sure? Once others hear you're there, they'll come running."

"No, I'm sure. Aggie likes Reservoir Barrel, and so far, we've stayed away when we've gone out. It's not fair to her and . . . I need to get over myself."

"I don't think that's possible." Archer's quick smile would've made me flip him the finger if kids weren't present. "Wanna help me in the kitchen? Delaney wouldn't play fair when it came to deciding whose job it was."

"It was a coin flip," Laney interjected. "Strip potatoes isn't a thing."

Emmaline's head popped up. "What's strip—"

"Something adults do," Laney said.

Archer snapped his fingers. "Hah—so it is a thing."

Laney rolled her eyes but giggled.

I trailed Archer into the kitchen. He dug out a pot and two peelers, then pointed to a ten-pound bag of Yukon gold spuds. I took the bag and followed him to the dining room table on the opposite side of the kitchen as the living room.

When we sat, he tipped his head to speak quietly. "Have you talked to Dad recently?"

I shook my head. "We sent some messages back and forth." Mostly about how everything was going and if all was well. I initiated the messages like I was making up for lost time.

"We had a video call last night, and he was really tired."

"They've been getting ice and shit down there."

He shook his head, his eyes pinched at the corners. His worry went further than skin deep. "This is different, and he insists everything's fine."

"He wouldn't say otherwise."

"I just . . . " Peelings flew as he attacked his potato. "We're all finally talking again."

Losing Dad would be the worst sort of irony. He'd been there, waiting for me for years. He couldn't be fading now. Maybe it was the time of year. Maybe he was taking extra hours so others could have time off. "He's healthy, right? I mean, he's lived a mostly healthy life."

"Yeah . . . mostly," Archer said in a way that told me he was remembering the stress of Mama being sick, morphing into losing our home, then making a living on barely anything in the same place he'd lost, and then years with two sons who hardly talked to him.

"He owns his house and land, right?"

Archer lifted a shoulder. "He's making payments."

"So the bank owns it." Meaning Dad still had to work. There was no retirement for him. Part of why I'd wanted to achieve my dream so badly. "I've mentioned him moving out here where he could be closer to family, but he's so damn proud of that place. You should see him with the kids. He lives for showing them around and seeing Emmaline ride his horse. After losing everything, he won't leave that land and move somewhere all his family members, but him, have land and houses and farms and ranches. He'd feel like he failed twice."

"Can't blame him." If I had a place to call my own in a state that didn't flex over you by dumping loads of snow on your head, then take a few layers of skin off with the bitter wind, I'd stay too.

"Short of winning the lottery so he can buy his own place around Coal Haven, I don't know what to do."

"Wish I could help." I'd have to win the lottery too. There had to be some way to help Dad. I didn't want to leave Aggie, but if Dad needed me . . . He'd never say he did, and he'd gushed so much about Archer and me being in the same place, it'd bother him if I left on his account.

"I'm glad we can talk about it." When I nodded, he stopped whipping his peeler against the potato like it'd wronged him and insulted his entire family. "Don't underestimate that, Ansen. If I met Delaney tomorrow, you'd be the first one I told."

"You were the first to know Aggie meant something to me." He was the only one.

"Have you told her?"

I concentrated on peeling the most pristine potato in the county, if not the planet. "I'm still trying to figure it out. I think about back then . . . " I shook my head, tossed the spud in the pot, and grabbed another. "I didn't know what I had back then, but at the same time, I did. I also knew how badly I fucked up and didn't think about her or what went on between us—it wasn't happening again. After a couple of shitty relationships, I started realizing that what Aggie and I had wasn't . . . common." So I'd made sure to think about her less. Except when I was cyberstalking her on the really bad days.

"Tell her."

I ripped through the tater skin. "I have nothing to give her, Archer. Nothing. She's putting the roof over my head. She's paying me to work for her." And she refused to pay me half my wages to direct the rest toward the rescue. "Hell, she's even feeding me by splitting the eggs with me. I have nothing to give her."

"Don't discount yourself."

Disgusted, I dropped the peeler and potato. "There's nothing to discount. I'm in the one place in the world where I'm surrounded by my successful brother and my business-and-land-owning cousins. Even my uncle is her boss. How long before she looks around and realizes there wasn't much to me back then without the money?" I picked up the items. I wasn't going to let Archer do all the work, and he was diligently peeling like he was afraid if he made any sudden moves, I'd stop talking and leave. Maybe I was afraid of that too. Maybe I was afraid of a lot more. Like not being worthy of my boss. "You know what I wanted to do with that money Barnaby was paying me?"

"Weren't you going to start your own training business?"

I nodded. "That—but it was where I was going to do it. I planned to talk Aggie into moving to Texas if our old place ever went on the market." It hadn't seemed pertinent to bring it up to Aggie until after we were married, when I would've actually had a substantial amount of money. Oddly enough, Barns had let me wax poetic about my ideas. I thought that was half the reason he made the deal. I hoped the other half was because he cared about Aggie.

"Where we grew up?" Surprise lined his brow.

"I'd buy the guy out, give Dad a job, and it'd be good again."

He sat back. "I didn't think you thought about our old place."

"You don't?"

A ghost of a smile played over his lips. "When I got my head in the right place, maybe, but by then, I wanted a home with Delaney. Our own place."

Our old home was always on my mind. It was the pinnacle of every goal I'd ever set. It shimmered at the unattainable end of every failure. "I think about the good times."

His smile was faint. "There were some of those." He blinked the humor away. "Since I've been here with Delaney and the other Barrons, I can see why we had such a hard time."

"Mama dying didn't clue you in?" I was half teasing.

"Yes, jackass. Losing her was . . . " He shook off the melancholy. "But it was just us. No extended family. We were an island, and the world was a storm around us, hammering at our walls. We had no help, and it was sort of self-inflicted."

"Mama's family refused to get over her marrying Dad and moving across the state." Mama was supposed to stay in El Paso and take care of them and help her sisters and their families. She'd fallen for Dad and moved far enough away to keep from being beholden to them. They spoke to us even less after the funeral, blaming Dad for her being gone.

"Just like Dad did with his family. We could've had someone who gave a shit around us." He waved his half-naked potato around. "Listen, I'm not throwing blame. I'm just saying that you can't wall yourself off on an island and expect to thrive."

"Aggie's not an island. She still talks to her family, and they don't trust me. When her dad passes and the inheritance gets spread around, they're going to trust me less. I have no way to prove to them I'm with her because I want to be."

"Fuck what they think. You make sure you're solid with Aggie, that you're honest with her, and it won't matter."

I'd like to think it was as easy as that, but I had a hell of a blemish on my record.

Emmaline danced into the room, her gauzy nightgown bouncing around her like a ball gown. Her new cowboy boots completed the look. "Can I help?"

My brother, the traitor, handed his peeler over, letting me and Emmaline do the work. I flashed him a look, and he smirked.

"Uncle Ansen, are you going to have kids with Aunt Aggie?"

I pushed the picture out of my head of Aggie and a kid or two dancing around the living room during the holidays. The clarity was startling, and the yearning was daunting. "I don't know. We only just started dating."

"You should get married." She carved random spots from the spud. "Girls like rings."

Aggie had loved hers. She hadn't worn more than earrings once in a while, citing sensitive skin, but she'd loved the solitaire diamond ring I had picked out. The platinum setting matched my plain platinum band.

It'd been my first purchase with my first payment from her dad.

"If you know we're not married, why are you calling her aunt?" I liked the sound of it.

"She's nice. You like her." That was all she needed. "How many kids are you going to have?"

"Em," Archer interjected. "It's intrusive to ask personal questions."

She shrugged her tiny shoulders. "He doesn't have to answer them."

"That's her grandma right there," Archer muttered. "Blunt and don't care."

Laney walked into the kitchen with Vaden on her hip. "I'm going to tell Ma you said that."

"She'll take it as a compliment."

Laney chuckled. "Yeah, she will."

"Are you going to meet all my cousins, Uncle Ansen?" Emmeline asked.

"Yeah." I gave her a quick smile. "They're my cousins too."

She launched into an explanation of all the kids and what they liked to play, some of their favorite foods, who'd gotten her dolls muddy before. Her stories made the potato chore go quickly.

I couldn't escape the desire to have Aggie at my side while I met my extended family. She had her own family, and we'd kept a separation between me and them. Perhaps that was the real reason I finally accepted an invite. I needed people to be on my island with me, and I wasn't sure if Aggie would stay or if she'd listen to everyone telling her to get off.

Fourteen

AGGIE

Christmas had turned out to be a good day. Cody arrived yesterday with the kids, and they'd delighted in running all over the yard with Tex and getting introduced to the horses, but Skinny and Shrek were the stars of the show.

Cody didn't have pets. Meg had forbidden it. They were at the ranch a lot since Cody also maintained the books for Knight's Arabians and Cattle Company, but Eliot kept the cattle side of the ranch going and, of course, the horse-breeding business. So unless it was a cattle dog and mousers, Cody didn't raise any other animals.

Sutton and I had coaxed the kids inside for the meal. The dishes were done and put away, and I'd promised ham and farm-fresh eggs for breakfast in the morning before they took off.

Cody was inside the house, getting them to sleep, and Sutton was with me outside. She had helped with chores.

My gaze kept straying to the trailer house. No lights were on.

Had he gone to his cousin's? How'd it go?

Did he miss me?

Had he thought about me all day like I'd thought about him, worrying and wondering and wishing him a good day?

I shook the thoughts away. He hadn't tried calling, and I'd take it as a sign things were going well. But I wanted to know. My thoughts were never far from him. Ugh. I had it bad.

I'd always had it bad.

Sutton leaned against the fence post and watched the horses graze on the hay we'd just fed them. Her beige stocking hat was pulled down to her eyebrows and the tip of her nose was red, but she didn't seem in a hurry to head for home just yet. "Can I tell you something and swear you to secrecy?"

"Absolutely." She'd been quiet the whole day, showing up before noon. She planned to leave after we were done in the barn, even though it was dark, but there was no wind to blow snow over the roads and the weather wasn't supposed to change until the middle of the week.

She went quiet again, her brow furrowing and her breath puffing out. "I'm going to file for divorce."

My shock detonated in my head. Divorce? I'd heard her unhappiness in our snippets of conversation, but she'd been with Wilder for over ten years. They went together in my mind. A pair, even when they weren't together. From the anguish swimming in her gray eyes, the decision wasn't easy. Neither was the loneliness. "I'm sorry."

"Me too." She didn't look at me. "So damn sorry." She inhaled a long breath. "But I have to leave before I hate him so much I can't stand myself. I'm going to move."

"Where?" We'd grown closer over the years and now we

were only hours away. I'd seen her more in the last year living in Crocus Valley than in the ten years before that.

"I don't know. I have to figure that out before I file." She kept a hand propped on the fence post. "I didn't want to put you in the middle, but I wanted to ask if it'd be weird if I moved closer to you."

"You'd move to Crocus Valley?" Excitement that I'd have my closest friend nearby warred with my sadness that she felt she had to move in the first place.

Her gaze scanned the dark land. The barn light cast over the pens and corrals and the quiet landscape stretched out beyond, dimly lit by the moon high overhead and the faint glow from the city. "It's quiet here. Rural areas always need more vets. Maybe I can build the life I've wanted in Crocus Valley. Start my own practice like I once planned."

Did she mean she wanted to meet someone new and start a family? My heart was breaking for her. Anger built toward my brother even though I knew he had a shitty example of family life growing up. I wanted to make her feel better, but I didn't know what to say. "I'll be your first customer."

"You sure that Dr. Jake you were telling me about won't run me out of the county?"

"No. He'll probably hit on you."

Sutton's laugh was empty. "I don't know if I'd recognize his attempts." She chewed on her lower lip and tears glistened in her eyes. "I wish it would've worked out. You guys are family to me. I got three brothers and a sister when I married Wilder."

"It's not going to be easy for you, but you'll always have me as a sister."

"I know," she whispered, then offered me a watery smile. "And with that, I need to get going. I'm on call tomorrow."

I gave her a hug. "Drive safe."

"Thanks for inviting me. This was a needed distraction."

I walked her to her pickup and stood on the porch to give myself enough time to process the passing sadness of her announcement. I wanted her happy. I wanted my brothers to be happy. But it seemed like dark clouds hovered over all our relationships, ready to dump on us.

No wonder Eliot and Austen stayed single.

Cody eased outside with no coat, only his nice pullover sweater. He was actually in jeans and cowboy boots. The guy worked an office job, and he usually dressed the part. I was almost relieved to see he took a break from being on all the time.

"It's quiet out here," he said.

"It's quiet at your place too."

"Not as much mooing or whinnying."

"The owner of the cattle across the road lets them spread out more." Daddy maximized space and efficiency, not always in favor of the cattle.

His gaze landed on the dark stretch under the sky. During the day, the gently rolling hills were brown and white. "How many acres are for sale over there?"

"It's two quarters. Three hundred and twenty acres of paradise." I leaned against the porch. "I would've bought it if it was open when I was looking."

"Then you wouldn't have the rescue."

"True." Or a reason to hire Ansen. "But it'd be nice to rent pasture, get hay shares, and not have to do any of the work."

"I would've been more supportive of that idea."

"Which is probably why I would've bought this place anyway. I might've decided to cut and bale the hay instead of splitting the shares so someone else could do it."

"You miss the work?" He crossed his arms. If he was cold, he didn't show it.

"Yes," I said wistfully. "But Mama always said she wished they'd never found oil on the land, so the ranch would've failed and we could've moved."

"Mama would've said that if the ranch was lucrative."

"Isn't it?"

He lifted a shoulder, ever the professional and not divulging business that wasn't mine. "I'm glad you prioritized college and got a job elsewhere."

He might as well have said he was proud of me. I glowed inside like he did. I recalled what he said about Mama. Barns and his gruffness weren't the only imprints on me and my brothers. "She had that effect on all of us, didn't she?"

"What do you mean?"

"You do the books for the Knights' businesses, but you could pull up stakes and go anywhere. Wilder and Austen went into other careers. Eliot got stuck managing it all, but it sounds like he'd have rather gone to do something else."

"Maybe it's because we learned not to trust our family when it comes to money."

I tipped my head down. Mama's life insurance.

"I'm not talking about that," he said like he could read my mind. "Well, not only that. None of us can predict what Barns wants done with his assets once he passes."

"You don't know?"

"Nope. He and his lawyer are thick as thieves with that shit. You know, Meg offered to do some legal work for the ranch, and Barns canned the idea so fast *I* got the silent treatment for a week."

My mouth crooked. Sounded like Meg.

"I'm not saying any of us are waiting for him to pass away with our hands held out. I'm just saying we don't trust he has our best intentions in mind."

"'Thy Knight's will be done.'"

"I hate that fucking saying." His breath billowed around his face with the heat of his words.

"Me too. Ansen threw those words at me right before I left." I gazed at the expanse of land for sale. At the time, I thought Ansen had thrown those accusations at me because he was in the wrong and grasping. "Said I wouldn't understand why he did it because I grew up with everything and had the town wrapped around my finger thanks to my family's money."

"He wasn't wrong." I glanced at Cody in surprise and he shrugged, keeping his arms crossed. "We had a different upbringing. Money helped in a lot of ways. But it also ruined a lot because Barns used it to control Mama and the rest of us. I want to make sure it doesn't affect my kids the way it did us."

"I know we had our troubles, but our last name opened a lot of doors in Buffalo Gully that would've been closed."

"To be fair, there aren't many doors in Buffalo Gully." He huffed out a breath. "Fuck, it's cold."

"There are these things called coats . . ."

"Ha ha, smart-ass."

I laughed as we went inside. I hadn't seen Cody this loosened up for a long time. Probably since before the kids were born. Maybe even before he met Meg. With her, it was like he had to be Alcott Knight all the time and not just Cody. Showing her and his in-laws that being the CEO of the family business didn't mean he worked in a barn and got dirty as if there was anything wrong with that.

"You've done good," he said as he sat on the couch and tossed his arms out to the sides, taking up half the space. This was like having teenage Cody back. My brother before he started wearing suits and running numbers. Before he had to start buying groceries and signing us up for school activities and 4-H events because Daddy would never bother himself with what he considered woman's work. "I know I come off as critical"—he rolled his eyes when I made a "No, really?" face— "and maybe I wouldn't have started the rescue. I definitely wouldn't have hired someone before the rescue was earning money, but you're making it work. You seem happy."

After my brother's constant nitpicking, his words made me feel like a little girl with my prize pig at the fair. It wasn't a coincidence I had a degree in finance. So did Cody. "I'm happier here than I have been anywhere else."

"Your boyfriend never showed."

"I'm going to need wine if you're starting on Ansen." I went into the kitchen and found the sweet red wine Sutton had brought. It was still half-full, but Cody wasn't a big drinker. He drank whatever fit the situation, and since the pumpkin pie had been cleaned up by Grayson, this would have to be in place of a second dessert.

"I'm not starting on him," Cody said, raising his voice only enough for me to hear but hopefully not too loud to wake the kids upstairs. "I'm making an observation."

Back in the living room, I handed him a glass. "You never verbalize an observation without reason. You're more subtle than Daddy, but I know you're digging for information."

"Do you blame me? Lawson seemed nice enough, a little arrogant if nothing, but I didn't take it as a good sign that he handled us so poorly."

"Wilder practically fingerprinted him. You interrogated him. He thought Eliot wanted to kill him and make it look like an accident when he invited him on a trail ride. And Austen did not need to be cleaning guns that weekend. All of that was minor compared to Daddy's insults."

"We went for target practice that day. Besides, if Lawson

had nothing to hide, he wouldn't have cared about feeling interrogated."

I sighed. "That's not how it works. People get offended when you treat them like a criminal."

"You can't blame us after Penley."

"You knew about that?"

"Mr. Stalker? Yes."

"How?"

Cody's face went blank, but he held my stare.

Sutton. She must've leaked my problem to Wilder. I narrowed my eyes. "What'd you do?"

"Nothing."

"What'd Wilder do?"

"You know Wilder never talks about work." The corner of his mouth twitched. "So . . . Ansen?"

I wasn't getting answers about Penley, and however they'd intervened, Mr. Stalker had ceased to bother me, making it hard to be more than mildly annoyed. "Coal Haven is full of Barrons, and he didn't want to make anything uncomfortable. But I assume I have you to thank for the warning messages from the others?"

Wilder: If I ever find anything on that guy, I'm going to have him arrested so fast.

Austen: Do I gotta come back there and kick some ass?

Eliot: I know you have bad taste in men, but making the same mistake twice isn't like you. You know he's after the money again. His was the worst.

Cody grumbled as he took his drink.

"What if he's not after the money? Will you guys be decent to him?"

Cody drained his drink. "The thing is, Aggie, how are we going to know?"

ANSEN

The dark highway stretched out in front of us. Tonight was New Year's Eve, and the place we were going would be busy, but I wanted to make tonight special.

"Can I open my eyes yet?" Aggie asked. Her arms were crossed, like I'd had to drag her out kicking and screaming for our date, but in reality, excitement poured off her. In the passenger seat, she sat with her legs pressed together and her heels lifted off the floor mats. Her eyes were squeezed shut, but she was biting back a grin.

I turned into the brightly lit parking lot. This area was probably beautiful in the daylight, but the way the old, repurposed train foundry and repair shop was highlighted by ground lighting and the artful Christmas lights around the doors, windows, and lining the roof made it a master-piece. I could just sit and admire it.

I found a spot facing the brewery. "Okay, open them."

When her eyelids fluttered open, the view sparkled in

her hazel eyes. "Reservoir Barrel!" She aimed her grin toward me, and a spot in my chest tightened—hard. I'd earned her happiness just by taking her out to a place I knew she liked. She bit her lip and concern edged out her jubilation. "Are you sure?"

"I should've brought you here earlier."

"Have you met the owner?"

"My cousin Isla? Yes. And her husband." I'd met all my relatives in the last week. The experience was overwhelming but welcoming in a way I hadn't expected. There was no simmering hostility like how my mama's side of the family looked at me, Archer, and Dad, like Archer and I should've abandoned everything as soon as we'd been old enough to walk and go back to a family that was nothing but strangers. The situation would've been different, but a similar animosity to how the Knights would look at me. "I told her how much you gushed about this place."

Pink dotted Aggie's cheeks. She wasn't used to wearing her heart on her sleeve anymore. "She's going to think I'm a weirdo for not mentioning I knew you."

"She doesn't think you're a weirdo, and I only said I worked as hired help for your family. Just Archer and Dad know the details. Come on. I heard from a reliable source the shandy on tap is the best." I hopped out and pulled the collar of my coat up to cut as much wind as possible. Aggie rushed out of her side of the pickup, and we trotted across the parking lot to get into the warmth.

A vestibule had been added to help cut the cold and hold the heat flowing in and out of the doors during the seasons. The dull roar of steady conversation grew louder as we entered. People filled the high-top tables and stools. Regular wooden tables in the back were covered in various board games, their players concentrating and chatting with their mugs of beer.

Beams arched over us, much of the metal securing the joints looking original. I was told they used as much of the building as they could, and it showed in the burnished wood grain. The windows couldn't be the same ones from a century ago, but the frames around each one weren't comprised of new slabs of wood.

I put my hand on the small of Aggie's back and steered her toward two empty stools at the edge of the bar. Isla said she'd save them for us so we could chat. My tall cousin with the long blonde braid was at the row of taps that were separated from giant, silver, chilled brew tanks by a decorative wooden half wall.

She turned to hand the glass to a customer, her gaze falling on me. Her face lit up, and she waved like I was a friend she hadn't seen in forever. "You made it! Cold enough out there for ya?"

"Bitter," I said good-naturedly. I made introductions, and Isla nearly bodysurfed on the bar top to shake Aggie's hand.

"Aggie, nice to see you again. How's the new job?" She wrinkled her nose. "I guess it's not so new."

"Great. Your dad is a good boss."

She tilted her head, and her long braid slid off her shoulder. "Now that's odd to hear. He's loosened up a lot. I never thought of him as being the guy everyone wanted to work for, but he's been at the refinery for almost forty years. I don't know what he'll do when he retires."

Surprise flitted across Aggie's face. "He's retiring?"

Isla winced. "I shouldn't have said anything. Nothing's concrete, but I actually heard him mention it. Years ago, I'd have guessed he'd never retire."

Cameron could've quit ten years ago and still be fine for retirement. He probably didn't have to work. Dad would work until he was in the ground and then he'd want to keep going after that.

Archer's question about Dad seeming tired resurfaced. I made a mental note to call Dad again. I'd talked to him at Christmas, but the urge to call him more than once a week was strong.

"Your secret's safe with me." Aggie smiled. "His secret."

"Where's McCoy tonight?" I asked.

The blue in Isla's eyes danced. "He opted out of the New Year's Eve chaos to stay home with Ian. The baby will be in bed by eight, and McCoy will probably be asleep on the couch by eight thirty." A customer at the end of the bar called her name. She patted her hand on the bar. "Shandy and root beer?"

"Whenever you get a chance," I said. "I can see you're swamped."

When she was gone, Aggie peeked at me, curiosity and gratitude in her eyes. "We didn't have to come tonight."

The noise made it hard to hear, but I had no problem twisting on my stool so I could prop a leg on each side of her and rest my hands across her hips. We had no place for our coats, but I didn't know how long we'd be here. "I wanted to. Just like I wanted to bring you."

"I know you said you met all your relatives, but I'm really glad." She finished so softly I almost didn't catch her words.

"Me too, but I have to say, the longer I'm here, the more I think Dad really left to get out of working outside in this weather."

"It's not Texas."

"Hell, I don't remember Montana being this brutal."

Isla swung by to slide us each our drink. The label of my root beer was a picture of my cousin Liam's twin boys sitting on a barrel with the name Twin Boots.

I nodded my thanks and took a drink. Sometimes, I had a beer or something stronger to fit into a social gathering, mostly to keep shit-talkers off my back. I resented having to repeatedly explain that I didn't have a taste for alcohol, and I was happy to let Aggie enjoy herself while I chauffeured us around the county.

"Those were mild years," Aggie said, turning into me until we formed our own little unit tuning out the rest of the place.

"We also spent a lot of the time in the cabin."

She tipped her head toward me. "In bed."

I lightly kissed her lips. "And in the shower."

"On the counter."

"My favorite was the table. You were my feast."

The flush was back in her cheeks, only this time, it wasn't from embarrassment about gushing over my cousin's beer. Those blushes were my favorite.

"Whaddya say?" I asked. "Can I have you for breakfast in the morning?"

"Before or after the frigid chores?"

"I need to warm up somehow. I won't even ask you to do naked chores again." There would be naked chores again one day when the temperature was well above zero. Thinking about round, pink ass cheeks peeking out from under the hem of her coat would make me hard in this crowded brewery. I took a drink to cool off.

"Next time, it's your turn to wear only a coat."

I coughed into the bottle. She laughed, tilting her head back. The lights played off the red highlights in her hair. She'd left tendrils of curls out of her bun to frame her face. The uncovered view of her freckles delighted me.

This morning for chores, she'd worn an old pair of cowboy boots and a pair of new Wranglers she'd grumbled about getting dirty right away.

I'd tried to beat her to chores, but she was determined to give me the weekends off.

Off to do what I didn't know, I wanted to spend all my time with her. The animals were a close second. My family, of course, but I couldn't hang around them every spare second of the day. Besides, the horses made my day fun.

Shelby pranced to the fence every time I showed up, and the others weren't far behind. Their personalities were distinct, and each day I got to see a little more. There were horses I missed working with over the years, ones I wished I could've afforded to have as my own, but Shelby was both. When it came time for Aggie to sell them, the pasture would be awfully empty.

She traced the line of my jaw. "What are you thinking about?"

"The horses."

Her eyes twinkled. "That hasn't changed."

"I was thinking that I'm used to getting temporarily attached to each horse I'm working with, but those five have a hold on me."

"And Gingerbread?"

Gingerbread the pinto hadn't warmed up to me yet, needed to be corralled separately next to the herd because he couldn't behave with Shelby or Bruno, and was a right challenge. He was ornery because of pain from poor care over the years and being forced to endure riders who weren't a good fit for the smaller-built horse. He was at the point of shunning all humans to keep from hurting all the time.

I loved the challenge, and he was full of promise. "I'll get him used to me, but the exercise has been strengthening his sway back."

"Good. The sooner he can get chiro treatment, the better."

Vienne leaned over on the other side of Aggie, a myriad of necklaces hanging from her neck. "Hi!"

"Vienne! How nice to see you." Excitement glowed in Aggie's eyes. She'd known people in Buffalo Gully, but when we'd gone out, she'd never had this reaction. Crocus Valley was good for her.

"Happy New Year!" Vienne said, pulling back. She had a purse in one hand and her coat in the other. She set the purse down and juggled getting her coat on. Theo lingered a few feet behind us. He gave me a casual wave but didn't otherwise help his girlfriend. "I wanted to stop and say hi before we go."

"I didn't see you," Aggie said, looking around like she was trying to figure out where they'd been sitting. "I'm sorry we missed you."

"It's getting too loud for Theo, so we're calling it early. How are you?"

"Good. How was your Christmas?"

"Come on, babe," Theo broke in, sounding bored.

Vienne glanced at her boyfriend, crushing the annoyance in her eyes. "Sorry." She squeezed Aggie's arm. "Let's meet up soon. Maybe another darts night?"

For as loud as it was, Theo's can't-be-bothered sigh made it right to my ears. "Darts again?" he whined.

Goddamn. If Aggie wanted to bring me along to hang with her and her friends, I'd be there with a grin in place and a cup full of darts ready for everyone.

Vienne's grin was apologetic. "Clearly, he's not a fan. Gotta go—happy New Year!" She rushed off.

Aggie watched them until they slipped outside. "It wasn't my imagination. He really is a downer."

"Definitely not your imagination." I liked sitting this close to her, cozy. This time, things were different, and it wasn't just her. "This isn't like Buffalo Gully, is it?"

"How do you mean?"

"When we'd go out in Buffalo Gully, people were . . . "

"Standoffish unless they were kissing one of my brothers' asses."

"Both men and women. Here, you've met Vienne, and Isla was excited to see you again."

She gave me a placating look. "Because I'm here with you."

"She said you were really nice, and she wished she'd had more time to talk to you."

"She said that?" She licked her bottom lip like she was embarrassed about what she was going to say. I kept still, waiting for her to speak. "I haven't, uh, had a lot of friends. Other than Sutton. Meg was like a big sister-ish figure. I wished we could've been closer, but she was distant."

"Aggie baby, Meg and your mama made it about them, not you."

She frowned. "No, they didn't."

I gave her a solemn look, tracing over the fine tendrils of her hair. "Didn't they?" Reaching up, I smoothed them between my fingers. The yellow flecks in the brown of her irises sparked.

She blinked, and her eyes became unfocused, like she was recalling a hundred conversations over her lifetime. "I guess I never thought of it that way. I wanted to make Mama proud, and she'd have loved Meg." She let out a sardonic laugh. "It's a miracle I didn't go to law school."

Because Meg had been a lawyer.

I feathered a curl through my fingers. "Good thing you didn't, or I'd be locked into a hell of a contract."

"I would've put so much small print in that thing it would've made your head spin."

"You already make my head spin."

She groaned. "Oh my god, that was sappy."

I chuckled and took a drink of my root beer, glad to see some things hadn't changed. Aggie preferred her mama's beat-up, taped-together books over new copies. Just like she'd liked the simple ring I'd gotten. She'd be glad to get another chicken as a gift for her birthday rather than receive jewelry she wouldn't wear.

Dr. Jake appeared at Aggie's side, standing closer than I would've preferred, but there wasn't much space, and it was obvious she and I were a thing. To make sure, I slid a hand around her waist. Couldn't help it.

He wasn't looking at her anyway. "Ansen, how do you feel about draft horses?"

"You'd have to ask my boss how she feels," I said good-naturedly but annoyed. I thought our talk would've been enough, but when it came to horses, he deferred to me. "She'll tell me how I feel."

He gave a self-detracting wince. "Sorry, Aggie. I'm used to dealing with your man when it comes to the details."

She leaned into my hold. "Send me the information, and I'll see how I can help."

"Will do." He pushed away without looking at her.

"If Sutton moves here, I'm firing him so fast," she muttered.

"Sutton and Wilder are thinking of moving?"

Alarm passed through her gaze. "Shit, I'm not supposed to tell anyone." She grimaced. "They're probably getting divorced. I'm not sure if Sutton's going to go through with it, but she mentioned moving here if she does."

Damn. I had fond memories of Aggie's brothers, even Eliot, up until the day of our wedding, and I'd been envious of how well they fit each other, like a tailored pair of boots. They were evenly matched, while I'd been like a pauper trying to infiltrate the castle.

If Sutton moved to Crocus Valley, Aggie would have her

best friend pretty much next door. Her family was only hours away. She had her own business and a place that was her dream. The same thought from earlier filtered through my head. Crocus Valley was perfect for her. I had no plans to leave Aggie's side soon, but she was growing deeper roots in the area with each passing month, and I still felt like a transient.

∩∩

Aggie and I tumbled through the door from her garage into a mudroom. I hauled her toward me.

I buried my face in her coconut-sunset-smelling hair. "I miss you wearing jeans so I could hook my fingers in your belt loops and you couldn't get away."

"I'm not going anywhere." She twined her arms around my neck. We'd barely made it inside. After kissing her when the new year hit and thinking about how much differently the year had ended compared to when it'd begun, I wanted our clothes gone and to be inside her.

I kissed up the column of her throat, and she tipped her head back. Wrestling with her coat zipper and mine, we finally dumped them on the floor.

Claws tapping on the floor alerted us to Tex's approach.

"Shit. He might need to go outside."

The dog's potty break put my lust on hold. I gave him some ear scratches and let him outside. I leaned against the front door and watched Aggie step out of her tall boots. She caught me watching.

"Can I help you?" The suggestion in her voice was enough to make me think we could fit a quickie in during Tex's potty break.

"One day, you're going to wear nothing but those boots to bed."

She tossed her head in a cocky way that did it for me. It'd always done it for me. "I thought you wanted to fuck the polish off me?"

Chuckling, I strolled toward her, slowly, deliberately, so she'd know once I reached her, all bets were off. "I'll still do that. But I'll take you any way I can get you."

Just as I reached her, the sound of Tex thudding up the steps preceded his bark at the door.

I let him in on a rush of cold-dog-smelling air. "Your dog doesn't like the cold."

"Just like his former owner."

"He can piss outside in Texas without his stream freezing before it hits the ground."

She leaned against the frame of the entrance into the mudroom. Our frenzy from earlier was put on pause, but I enjoyed the familiar air between us right now. "You miss Texas, don't you?"

I missed a lot about Texas. "There's always been some homesickness. Talking to Dad has reignited some feelings."

"I thought you didn't have the best memories of living there."

I held out my hand and led her to the bedroom, turning off the living room light as we went. Being cast in shadows made it easier to speak. "Dad's there now by himself. He has his own place, but the ranch he lost? That's where we were a family. When my mama was alive."

"You don't talk about her much."

As much as I wanted to ravish this woman, I also wanted to answer her question. I had never talked about Mama much when we were first together. "I was young when she died. And she was sick for a while before that. Breast cancer. But I remember a cozy home. The way she'd shoo me and Archer out the door to play. Dad was always touching her. If he wasn't doing something, his hand was on Mama's ass, I swear."

She giggled. "Sounds sweet. Can't say I got to witness that kind of affection growing up."

"I'll give it to you now." I picked her up and tossed her over my shoulder.

"Ansen!" She swatted my behind, laughing.

I tossed her on the bed and jumped on after her. She widened her legs to cradle me. I could undress her, but sitting so close to her all night, I had to taste her. I licked across her lips, and she opened for me. I explored her mouth, the sweetness of the shandy she'd been drinking on my tongue. My erection was pounding at my jeans. Seeking relief, I rubbed against her. She answered by moving her hips with mine.

I broke away to kiss down her neck. "You know," I said, nipping her sensitive skin, "it's best to start the new year naked."

"We're already late."

I licked along the base of her neck and gently blew on it. She shivered. Yep, I'd do the same thing all over her body. "It's never too late to take your clothes off."

Just as I reached for the hem of her shirt, a buzzing sound made me stop. "Is that your phone?"

Frowning, she rolled up, and I scooted back to make room for her.

"It's after midnight." Alarm passed through her features. She reached behind her and pulled it out of her pocket. "Oh god, it's Cody."

I moved to her side so she could sit all the way up. Tears were already filling her eyes when she answered. Cody's voice drifted through the phone, loud enough for me to hear. "It's Barns. He's gone."

Sixteen

AGGIE

Eliot and I stood in the kitchen. Cody and Wilder, in his various shades of brown deputy clothing, were getting ready to leave, but we were having a last-minute discussion about the funeral the next day. The reception would be at the church. No one felt like entertaining at the house in its faded glory with the faint smell of Daddy's cigars. The house could still use a good dusting, the kitchen a wipe down, and boots cluttered the floor by each door. A mopping would do wonders.

"I can clean before I go to bed," I said, still trying to be useful two days after I'd arrived. Yesterday, I'd deleted messages from Lawson asking how I was doing, sending me his condolences, and asking if I needed anything. As tempted as I'd been to reply, **"I don't need anything from you, wasn't that the problem?"** I'd made each communication disappear. Lawson was in the past, and now his obsession with getting into Daddy's good graces was too.

"There's a lady coming in the morning," Eliot said. "I don't pay her to clean a clean house."

I'd sat around for two days and watched my brothers rush everywhere. "Are all the arrangements—"

"Done," Cody said, back to his abrupt self. His in-laws were in town and already offering to take the kids to Helena for the week and up to indefinitely. He was on edge and cranky.

I made another attempt to contribute. "I can pitch in for chores in the morning."

Eliot brushed that offer away too. "The guys are working as normal. None of them worked under Barns's time. They don't feel the need to go to the funeral."

"Everything's arranged." None of it by me. The same antsy feeling from when I'd grown up wove through me, making me want to pick the orneriest mare to ride or sled down the hill straight toward the stock pond after a stretch of forty-degree days. I'd lost one sled doing so and flirted with hypothermia after another attempt—and I'd even seen the open water before I started. Then there was the time I was eight and my brothers wouldn't let me help work cattle, so I'd ridden out on a green, broken filly—and broke an arm.

"Barns had it all done," Cody said, residual bitterness in his voice. "Everything's been planned down to when his lawyer will read the will."

"Just like Barns," Wilder said. "Controlling everything with his cold, dead hands."

His words landed in the middle of us like a heavy emotional load made tangible.

My brothers were tense, probably wondering if Daddy had some surprise up his nonexistent sleeve. An axe waiting to drop. But I was different. I was waiting to see if I'd be forgotten one last time.

I gave myself a mental shake. Enough. Being at home for this long was a subtle mindfuck, making me feel like an impulsive fifteen-year-old all over again. Thanksgiving had been a holiday. A lighter mood had rested quietly over the place. The start of this week had been different. Daddy's death brought relief. With that came guilt. And being under the roof without him was haunting.

"I gotta get back out there." Wilder adjusted his utility belt. When I'd first seen him in uniform, I had thought it odd, so different for my country-boy brother who'd rarely been out of ratty jeans, a dirty hoodie, and his cowboy hat. Now, I wondered if that kid was anywhere in this guy who was hardly out of uniform. He hadn't taken a single hour off since Daddy passed and said he'd be at the funeral in his uniform. To honor Barns. Sutton muttered it would be because he was on the clock.

"I need to get home as well." Cody ruffled his fingers through his locks like he was making sure every strand was perfect to go with his slacks and stylish cream pullover, or his in-laws would drive off with Grayson and Ivy.

Eliot pushed off the counter after they left. "You okay all by yourself?"

"Why wouldn't I be?"

"Austen won't be here until tomorrow." He briefly clenched his jaw. "Have you ever slept here by yourself?"

"I have an entire house by myself."

He rolled his eyes to the ceiling as if he was sick of my shit when we'd hardly talked since I arrived. "It's not this place, and it's not in the middle of nowhere."

"Eliot, are you asking your thirty-one-year-old sister if she needs a babysitter?"

"Fuck's sake, Aggie. Barns died in the living room."

I snapped my mouth shut. Point taken. "I'll be fine, and you're in the cabin." The cabin was on the edge of the property, but Eliot had made a makeshift dirt road by traveling so much between there and the house. The path was no longer the two-wheel trail I'd used when Ansen stayed there.

"And the whole town knows Barns is no longer in the house. I don't want any lookie-loos thinking they can roam the place because they know I'm in the cabin and the guys are in the bunkhouse."

He sauntered out through the door in the garage, flipping the dead bolt on the other side. I stubbornly unlocked the door after he left.

I'd lock it later—after my pride was properly assuaged. I knew when to lock a damn door.

My emotions might be making me extra defensive.

Getting into loose sweatpants and an old long-sleeved shirt, I crawled into bed. While packing, I'd randomly grabbed the repaired copy of *Murder on the Orient Express*. I kept the light on and sank into the familiar pages, not seeing a word.

Memories streamed through my head like a film instead.

Mama's voice, so soft and lilting and always a touch sad, sounded off between my ears. *Your daddy comes from a different time. Don't settle for what Barnaby Knight says you can have.*

Make your own way in the world.

Ensure whatever you have is yours.

"I did all that, Mama," I murmured. Yet here I lay in my childhood bed, wondering why she'd had five kids before deciding we were a prison. She'd blamed Daddy. I'd heard her say baby-trapped once and hadn't understood what she meant. Now I knew that we were the chains holding her down, and Daddy was the warden.

I set the book down, unable to stomach the memories of Mama telling me about how she was going to travel the world someday. How she'd be on a fancy train, wearing classy clothes, just like the characters in the book.

She'd died alone and with nothing. Seducing men like a game of leapfrog around the world.

In the end, I'd listened to her advice, and my life was better for it. Earlier in the kitchen showed me how it'd have been if I'd stayed. I might've had my own place in town. I would've worked shifts at the bar and gotten called Birdie by the owner. My brothers would've teamed together to convince one of the hired men to take me out—without being paid. Didn't seem much better.

Had Ansen done me a favor?

I couldn't answer that. But I could admit that I missed him, and I'd been away only two days. He'd had to stay behind to care for the animals, and I was starting to wish he'd come with me. Between the chores, Tex, and the attitudes of my brothers that would be sharper this week, it was better he stayed. But I could wish.

I lay staring at my childhood ceiling. Daddy hadn't changed this room to an office, but Eliot probably would. He'd probably redo the whole house now that Daddy wasn't around to argue with him and be militantly tightfisted with all the money tied up in the business and investments.

Tapping my fingers on my chest, I wished sleep would come. I left the light on because Eliot's words had fucked with my mind. Alone in a house where my daddy had died. I couldn't look cowardly and call Sutton to ask to stay with her and Wilder.

My phone buzzed. Worried there was more bad news since it was after eleven, I checked it. Ansen's name was on the screen.

"Hello?" I answered quietly, even though I was the only one in the empty house, which might be contributing to my inability to sleep. Shit, I had to lock the door.

"Checking in on you."

Warmth settled into my bones. After Cody's call about Daddy, I had unexpectedly broken down. Ansen had held me all night. Being in his arms while I was crying was the first time I'd had someone to comfort me. After Mama left, everyone had been short-tempered, and I'd kept my distance. After she died, my brothers were dealing with their own grief, and Daddy had shut us all out. I'd been alone after I broke up with Ansen. Any heartbreak after him, I'd messaged Sutton. But to be held and comforted?

I wished he could be in bed with me now.

"Restless. The house is so quiet. I keep walking out and seeing that empty chair . . . " That no one was in the chair wasn't unusual. It was that Daddy would never sit there again.

A door creaked open. I bolted upright, my heart clawing into my throat. "Eliot?" I was going to get attacked, and my life would end, proving my brothers right after all.

A dark form appeared in my doorway, a phone to his ear. "Why isn't the door locked?"

"Ansen!" I flew out of the bed and into his arms. He was cold from walking in from outside. His leather-and-soap smell filled my nose, and I buried my face in his jacket. "What are you doing here?"

"I asked Archer to cover chores for a day or two. Emmaline is delighted to host Tex. Thought I could at least stay the night if my presence is an issue with your brothers, but I didn't think you should be alone the night before your daddy's funeral."

Having his deep voice speak into my ear in this big, empty house was unbelievable. I hugged him harder. "You don't have to."

"I wanted to."

His simple answer was more than I wanted and everything I needed. He wanted to be with me because he was worried about me. "Do you want to go to the funeral?"

His smile was small. "No, I don't need to go, and we both know it'd cause problems. The town will already be gossiping about you and your brothers. My arrival would turn the chatter into a storm."

I didn't want him to leave. His presence made me feel . . . secure. Like I wouldn't be wandering aimlessly around my childhood home, marveling over how it didn't feel like my home. "Can you stay until the will is read? Daddy arranged with his lawyer to do it the night after the funeral. In Cody's office."

"That's ominous."

"Right?"

"I'll stay as long as you want me." He brushed a hand over my wild curls. "Let me go out and grab my bag." He fisted my hair and planted a hard kiss on my mouth. "And lock the door."

I was in bed by the time he returned. He dropped his coat on my dresser and took a pair of shorts out of his duffel. While he stripped out of his hoodie, black T-shirt, boots, and jeans, I watched. He tossed the shorts on and crawled in next to me. I shut the lamp off.

Cuddling close, he wrapped his arms around me, my back to his chest. "How's it really been?"

We'd only been messaging back and forth, but it had mostly been about the rescue and the time line for the week. "My brothers are still my brothers."

"That bad, huh?"

"No, not terrible. I keep expecting there to be something here for me, but they've got it all taken care of. Like always. Honestly, I'm surprised Cody talks about the issues with his in-laws as much as he does." My oldest brother didn't have anyone to talk to, and the others probably wouldn't understand how much it bothered him his in-laws were trying to control his kids. He instinctively knew I'd understand. "How are things at home?"

"Fancy has claimed the whole trailer as hers. The barn cats left me a mouse when I got back to the barn from working with the horses. I'm not sure if I should be flattered or insulted."

"That's sweet. You can't hunt them yourself, and they need to take care of you."

"Dr. Jake came to check on Shrek. He said a family has ducks they need to get rid of."

"I don't know a damn thing about ducks."

His chuckle vibrated through my back. "You and me both. We seem to be saying that a lot."

He splayed his hand over my stomach. He wasn't making a move, like he sensed I only needed to be held. If his fingers found their way under my pajamas, I'd be there for it, but right now, I wanted this. Him with me in my queen bed from my childhood.

"Can we sell ducks?" I asked.

"Maybe. If they're layers."

"I don't know a damn thing about duck eggs."

"And again, we have something in common." The humor in his voice made me smile. "But that's never stopped us. I'm caring for a donkey. Dr. Jake says Shrek's hooves are almost healed. Then he can be sold. I think he'll be a good livestock guardian. He's been braying lately when Tex is outside."

"He is feeling better. Good." I didn't doubt Ansen could rehab Shrek. The job was more than a challenge to him. He cared about the animals. "I'll prepare a sales ad and find out if anyone wants a donkey."

"Since there are enough ranchers around, you should get some hits."

We fell quiet. "Shrek would be my first sale. I'd have a real rescue."

"You do have a real rescue."

"I mean one that brings in money instead of hemorrhaging it."

"I told you, you can pay me half—"

"Absolutely not." Since he refused to sit out weekends and holidays, I owed him overtime he'd never ask about.

"You can find another Mangalitsa and breed Skinny. She's got some good breeding years."

I glanced over my shoulder. The yard light filtered through the room's blinds, but the rays highlighted his serious face. "Then I'd be a rancher. I have a job."

"A lot of people in the area ranch part time and work full-time. Besides, you have me for now."

This time I rolled around, too raw from Daddy's passing to see his face when I asked my question. "For now?"

"I didn't mean . . . " He let out a sigh. "I'm not going anywhere—I can't afford to. I know this thing between us is old and new, but . . . is Crocus Valley where you want to be your whole life?"

"Yes." I'd found everything I wanted in Crocus Valley. Including him. "You don't like living there?"

"It's like any other place I've lived. I've gotten used to adapting."

But he'd never had a place that was his.

He flexed his arms, bringing me closer to him. "Anyway, you're stuck with me."

And when I wasn't?

The question echoed in my head as I drifted off to sleep.

∩∩

The heavy end to our conversation the night before was forgotten as he pumped into me while we were both in the shower. My legs were wrapped around his flexing ass, and I was holding on to a soap holder. The shampoo and conditioner had already been knocked off their shelves.

"Oh god," I gasped. He'd already gotten me off once. I didn't know how much water we were wasting, and I didn't care. My body tightened right before lightning exploded across my vision, and I started bucking against him.

He licked up my neck and sucked on my earlobe. "I can feel you coming—you're fucking fisting my cock." He groaned and went rigid, his strokes shortening.

Water streamed down my face. He was blocking most of the spray, but with his head tilted while he caught his breath, I was getting pummeled.

A giggle eased out. He narrowed his eyes.

"It's stupid. I'm getting hammered by the water, but I just got hammered . . . "

His grin was lopsided, good-natured, and he flipped the lever to shut the water off. It was so damn simple between us, but what he'd admitted last night rushed back. He liked being with me, but what about when he had other options?

Yet he still offered to take less pay, knowing it'd take him longer to save up money to get his own place.

What did it all mean?

I handed him a towel and wrapped another around myself. Grabbing a smaller one for my hair, I stepped out of the tub-shower combo and went to my old bedroom.

Ansen's hair was tousled when I turned, softening his hard edges and giving him a boyish charm that was irresistible. I'd stay with him until he broke my heart again, and maybe I'd accepted that. I had everything else I wanted, and I was gambling on him.

We dressed together. Not the first time. I put on a pink,

collared blouse that I'd wear with a long, flowing gray cardigan, some black slacks, and my ankle boots. Daddy would hate everyone dressing up. Cody would probably throw a suit coat on with his normal button-down and slacks. Eliot and Austen would likely be in black jeans and a dress shirt. Anyone else who showed would most likely be in jeans or business casual.

I went back to the bathroom to wind my hair into its normal tight bun to contain the curls, but I got caught on my flushed cheeks. I might cry—and I hated crying in public—but tears or not, I'd definitely get red. Daddy would dislike me all gussied up too. Probably made me look too much like Mama, which likely made him *feel* the anger, hurt, and bitterness from her leaving, and Daddy hated that as well. As an ode to him, I left my hair down. The wind would kick it into a frenzy. I'd look a little wild, like he'd known me to be.

Just as I was finished attempting to tame my hair, Ansen leaned against the bathroom door. His gaze stroked over my hair.

I met his stare in the mirror. "It's going to get taller as the day goes on."

"The bigger the hair, the closer to God."

We grinned just as the front door banged open. "Aggie, who the hell is here with you? And it'd better not be who I think it is!" Eliot shouted.

My heart rammed into my throat, and I choked on a gasp.

Ansen jerked like he'd been jolted with a cattle prod. His eyes flared, but he set his jaw and tipped his chin down. "I don't want a confrontation. Not today."

My heart rate dipped back to normal. I hooked my arm through his. "I refuse to let them make it a big deal."

Daddy would've loved it, though.

Eliot and Austen piled through the entry on the other side of the kitchen. Eliot wore exactly what I suspected, but Austen was in a polo and jeans with a camouflaged backpack slung over one shoulder. His dark hair was buzzed to the scalp with a little length on top, same as usual. He and Eliot could almost be twins. Except Eliot wore his hair longer and usually messier, but he'd styled it to the side today and hadn't worn a hat yet.

Both of them aimed identical glares at Ansen.

"Eliot. Austen," Ansen greeted. "I just came to support Aggie. I'm not looking to start trouble."

"You should've thought of that before Barns paid you a dime," Eliot said.

"That was a decade ago," Ansen said patiently. "Things are different."

"You're broke, and Aggie's about to come into a shitload of money," Austen said, his voice rougher than usual, like he'd had a late night or an early morning or both.

Ansen straightened, his chin held high. "If I cared about money anymore, I'd already be married. I'm here for your sister, and I only care about what she thinks."

"Since when do you care about more than yourself?" Eliot countered. "You probably left that other woman when you found out her old man never planned to turn a thing over to you."

"Knock it off," I said. Eliot and Austen were worried, but their reactions were signs they didn't trust me to make my own decisions, and this confrontation lacked respect for me. "You both assume Ansen and I haven't talked about what people might think or our individual histories when it comes to us. The way you're both acting is disrespectful to me more than him."

Cody and Wilder piled through the door, dressed exactly how I'd assumed.

Surprise filled Wilder's brown eyes, then something I couldn't identify took over his expression when he looked at me. He glanced toward the door he'd just come through, then back at me. "I found this guy roaming around, lost."

A third man entered, a few inches shorter than my brothers, and my stomach dropped. What the hell was this morning turning into? "Lawson?"

Seventeen

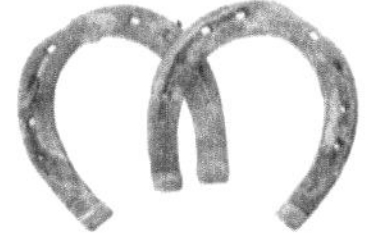

ANSEN

I should've been nice and relaxed after my shower with Aggie, but Eliot and Austen's arrival had wiped away the calm. Now I was facing all of her brothers and this guy. If a stranger entered the house and was told to pick the guy who'd never worked cattle or wore a cowboy hat, it'd be an easy guess. This was the fucker who discarded Aggie once he realized he could never be man enough for her?

Lawson's hair was neatly styled, rising up in the middle and shining from product. He wore a black suit coat over a pale-green shirt and black slacks with shiny black loafers. He looked like an office manager or whatever position he yanked out from under Aggie.

He was my opposite and didn't that burn. I drove Aggie to a pompous dickwad like this.

Austen covered his mouth like he was hiding a grin. Aggie had described him once as the mischievous one of the bunch. Wilder was biting the inside of his cheek, probably giddy at the possibility of using his law enforcement skills on his family. Cody was stern as always, and Eliot looked twice as pissed to be dealing with two of Aggie's exes. Only I was no longer an ex.

"Aggie, hey." Lawson's blue gaze scanned the gathering. His face was pink from the wind and from his expression, he was trying not to shrink under the scrutiny of her brothers.

It wasn't them he had to worry about. I didn't know him, but I didn't trust him. Aggie told me enough, and I'd been around enough guys like him. Guys who used people until they reached the next stepping-stone and discarded them.

"Why are you here?" Aggie asked. A simple question, but she managed to sound stunned and irritated.

I wanted to tell him to get the fuck out. I'd gladly help him on his way—if that was what Aggie wanted. She might want to talk to him, and I'd have to eat my hurt and let her. She needed to make her own decision, but I also trusted what was between us more than what she'd had with this dick weasel.

Her brothers' heads swiveled from me to Lawson. Their own personal tennis match. Lawson was probably the only one of us who'd touched a racket in this room.

"I heard about your dad, and you aren't answering my texts." He could stuff that hint of accusation up his ass and shit it out on his way out of town.

"For a reason," she said bluntly.

That's my girl.

His lips pursed like he was annoyed she wasn't falling over herself for him. "I know how hard this can be, even though you two weren't close and thought . . . " He shrugged. "I wanted to make sure you're okay."

Good damn thing I'd gotten here first. I was upset I hadn't come earlier, but she needed time with just her brothers. That this asshole thought to do the same thing rankled. What if he was legitimately concerned for her? What if he realized he fucked up the best thing that happened to him and was willing to work to win her back?

Too bad. She was mine now.

Aggie cocked her head like she couldn't believe Lawson had the audacity. "You're the one who said I was cold and emotionless."

Lawson was an idiot. Aggie was warm inside and out, and her emotions ran deep and true.

Cody sucked in a breath. Austen choked, holding in his sputtering laughter from the delight dancing in his eyes. Eliot's mood darkened, but I had always thought he thrived on being in a shitty mood. Wilder crossed his arms like he was the one waiting for the answer.

Lawson's gaze dropped to the sidearm on Wilder's belt, then drifted to the living room where Barns's most prized rifles and shotguns were mounted as the centerpiece over the fireplace. The ones he'd used to kill rabid skunks and scare badgers were probably still in the coat closet. Easy grabbing on the way out. There'd been no such thing as gun safety to that man.

Don't be a fucking idiot. That's all you need to know, he used to say—about everything.

"I, um, wasn't talking about a parent's death, and I'm sorry about that. Look, I can go, but I wanted to check on you. Really."

He wasn't welcomed, and he acted like he'd expected to be. I almost felt sorry for him.

Nah.

I'd low-key hated this guy since I saw the first picture she posted of them together. I'd despised every man I saw pictures of her with.

"You don't have to leave," Austen said, failing to hide

the delight in his tone. "There's a reception after, and you can get some food. The gas station's pizza will give you the shits before you make it to the state line."

"Fuck's sake, Austen," Wilder said. "No one makes it that far."

Cody briefly closed his eyes like he was willing them to grow up when they were already adults. "Lawson, I'm sure Aggie appreciates you stopping by—"

"Aggie can speak for herself," I said.

Everyone's focus turned to me, and I met every pair of eyes one by one. Aggie's expression was torn between knowing they cared about her and being fed up with the way they railroaded her. Time for the train to stop.

"Thank you, Ansen." Aggie slipped her hand through mine. "I do appreciate the gesture, Lawson, but after our last conversation, you can see why I'm wondering why you're really here."

Lawson's gaze landed on our linked hands, then how closely Aggie was standing next to me. His focus stroked over her face. Did he realize her still pink cheeks were from an orgasm—one *I* gave her? "I was concerned about you."

"How's my job?" she asked abruptly, the resentment growing in her eyes the longer she had to look at him. "The one you got promoted to after we broke up because coworkers weren't supposed to date? Yet you complained about how uncomfortable it was until I was asked to move, and you got the promotion."

"That's a dick move," I said in case he thought it was only Aggie who saw his motivations for what they were.

Lawson glared at me. "And who are you?"

"He was paid to marry Aggie years ago," Eliot answered a little too readily, "but she was pissed about it and broke up with him. Very coldly. And emotionlessly."

There'd been nothing emotionless about that day.

Cody stroked his freshly shaved jaw. "Don't suppose you know Aggie's going to be a rich woman after the will is handled, do you, Lawson?"

Aggie shook her head. "What a coincidence *Yellowstone* is your favorite show. You love Beth Dutton's character and maybe my frank tone and ranch upbringing was what had attracted you initially, but you couldn't handle a fraction of the attitude I had in real life." She tapped her chin like she was deep in thought. "Yet you watched enough to understand that when the patriarch dies, there can be plenty left behind to dole out." She narrowed her eyes. "I've moved on, Lawson. Thank you for coming, but you need to go."

With all the brothers focused on him, Lawson squirmed. Well, if that wasn't telling. "This isn't TV. I'm not in a Western."

I crossed my arms, ready to enforce her wishes if Lawson insisted on staying. She seemed to want this confrontation over with and to move on. Aggie wasn't one to dwell on drama, and I was glad to be on her side for this one.

"Okay. All right, then." Lawson smacked his lips, anger turning his gaze into a blue flame drifting between her and me. "I can see why he's gotta get paid before he settles for you."

Cody and Wilder flanked Lawson, but I got to him first, gripping his coat and spinning him. No one made her feel like shit and got away with it. Fucking no one.

"You get the hell outa here." I reached around her ex and whipped the door open, nearly taking out his nose. "You ever talk to her like that again, I'll shove my boot so far up your ass you're going to be tasting leather for eternity."

I pushed Lawson out the door and followed him out to make sure he got in his car and didn't tap the brake until he hit the hiding place he called a home.

"Fuck," Wilder muttered behind me. I glanced over my

shoulder. Cody, Eliot, and Austen were on Wilder's heels. I couldn't see Aggie behind them, but I knew she was there. She didn't hide like this pest.

Snowflakes swirled at my feet, but I barely noticed the bitter wind while I prowled in front of Lawson's Lexus. I kept at it until he backed out and spit gravel as he peeled away.

"Motherfucker," I growled. "I'm going to chase him out of the state with my truck."

"I'd be willing to give you a police escort." Wilder shook himself like he'd gotten caught supporting someone he was supposed to hate, but I appreciated the moment of comradery. It was a start. Too bad it had to come from Lawson insulting Aggie.

I marched toward Aggie, shouldering her brothers, but they gave way. Maybe they would finally consider that I was serious about their sister, but that wasn't my main concern at the moment. "He's an asshole. You know that, right? It's obvious he's a pussy."

"He is a pussy, thank you." She shivered. From the cold and maybe from the residual hurt of her ex's comments. I could do something about the cold at least. I crowded her inside.

Her brothers filed in behind us.

Eliot passed both of us. "You put on a good show," he said to me. "I can say that."

"Say it all you want—don't make it true." I draped an arm around her shoulders. A possessive move, but once they accepted she was mine, the easier the idea that she was it for me would be for them to swallow. "I'll sit out the funeral to keep talk from spreading like wildfire, but I'm staying one more night. I don't want Aggie alone tonight."

"She's not alone, dickweed," Eliot said.

"I'll be staying in the house," Austen added. "She won't

be alone." When I glared at him, he raised his hands. "I'm not saying you have to go. This isn't my house."

"We don't even know whose it is until the will reading tonight." Cody shoved a finger toward me. "I want you there. I'll be watching your reaction when Lorenzo reads off what she gets."

I sighed over this argument that I was here for the money. All of this was my fault. I took Barns's deal and let everyone think that was the only reason I was into Aggie. She was amazing, sexy, and if I could go back, I'd do it all differently. But I couldn't turn back time. I could only show them I was here for her now. I gave her shoulder a squeeze. "I'll be there—for Aggie."

"Sure," Wilder said, his tone bored and unbelieving.

Cody checked his fancy watch. "We've gotta get to the church." He gave me a pointed look. "We'll pick this up later."

Like hell we would. I said everything I needed to say. "Aggie and I aren't your business."

"Not how it works, man. She's our little sister." Austen clapped me on the back and wandered down the hallway toward the wing of bedrooms. "I'd better not hear anything cringey from you two tonight," he called over his shoulder.

"Because of that, I'm going to be louder!" Aggie shouted back, and I had to hold back my chortle.

Wilder made a disgusted noise as he walked out of the house.

Cody glanced at Eliot. "Are you driving separate?"

"Nah, I'll wait for Aggie and Austen," Eliot replied and turned a militant look toward me. "I don't want Ansen here alone while we're gone."

Aggie tensed. "Eliot—"

"Fair enough." I pressed a kiss in her hair and steered her toward her old bedroom. Her brothers didn't trust me, but I could make concessions to help grease the process when I could. "I'll drive around, maybe run to Miles City and grab some supplies."

Inside, she tipped her face up to me. "Sorry about all that."

I let a smug grin show. "Can't say I minded telling off your dick of an ex, knowing my cum is fresh inside you."

She made a strangled sound, caught between a laugh and a gasp. The flush returned to her cheeks, just like I wanted. I meant what I said.

I placed another kiss on her forehead. "Message when you think you'll be home, and I'll meet you here."

As much as I wanted to hold her at the funeral, my presence would bother her brothers, and the town would get to talking. I didn't care, but she did and so did the rest of her family. If I had a clear future in front of me, maybe I'd muscle next to her in the front-row pew in the church. But I didn't, so I'd roam eastern Montana until it was time to find out how much consoling Aggie needed tonight.

∩∩

Ansen

Cars were already lining the drive when I pulled in. Except for the snow and wind, the view was reminiscent of my non-wedding day. It'd been the only time the Knights had company that was more than one or two vehicles. As much as Barns had loved this place and the ranch, bursting with pride over what he'd built and the reputations he'd earned, he was as tight-fisted with sharing the views as he was the money.

I drove through the cars and parked by the garage where

I'd been last night. Eliot had moved snow all around the place to make room for parking for the will and trust meeting. I got out, looking forward to seeing Aggie again but dreading the whole ordeal. Barns had been a personality to be reckoned with, and I didn't anticipate this to be different. It was his chance for everyone to hear his voice from the other side one last time. Going into the house through the garage, I hoped for Aggie's sake that her daddy treated her right, at least in this.

After what her brothers said about me and the way Lawson showed up and the shit that came out of his mouth, she didn't need to feel like Barns didn't love her as much as her brothers—Barns could love more than this ranch and his oil well business.

Aggie wasn't in her bedroom. Voices filtered down the hallway from Cody's office. I had a strong aversion to going in there. Too much like returning to the scene of the crime. The devastation on Aggie's face. That betrayal in her eyes had been the first time I'd really questioned what I'd done. Otherwise, I'd been taking money from a bastard to live a damn good life. Aggie had become one of my favorite people —no harm, no foul. Until that second when understanding blazed across her face. My chest ached at the memory of the hurt and how I hadn't been able to comfort her afterward. Instead, I'd thrown it all in her face. Basically told her she was being unreasonable.

When I reached the living room, I found her staring out the giant picture window, her arms crossed in front of her like a hug. Her reddish-gold hair puffed around her head. In the glass's reflection, I could see she'd tucked some strands behind her ear. The outline of her body was one I knew well, but I took a moment to appreciate her figure. The way her back tapered in before flaring out. Her feet were crossed at the ankles.

She caught sight of me in the window, and her smile was relieved. "Ready?"

No. "Yes." I came up behind her and put my hands on her shoulders, looking out to see what she was seeing. Dark rolling hills, lit by yard lights and the moon. Clouds drifted through the dark sky, letting the brightest of stars peek out. I couldn't see the horses in the distance or the cows dotting the pastures. Could this be an omen? A peaceful night meant a mellow reading of the will and trust? "Everyone else here?"

"More than I expected." She glanced toward the office and leaned into me to speak quieter. "Some of the women Daddy dated, including a couple of his home health nurses, are here. Though, what nursing qualifications they have should've been questioned."

From what she'd said, Barns hadn't been concerned with their lack of nursing skills.

"I guess," she sighed. "Let's get this over with."

∩∩

Aggie

Ten years ago, I fled Ansen and my family down this long hallway, but tonight I walked with Ansen back to Cody's office. Were my brothers dreading this as much as I was? I wasn't confident Daddy wouldn't aim one final strike at Mama by shunning me. Time to find out.

We walked to the office side by side. A crush of faces turned our way when we entered. My brothers. Sutton sat next to Wilder, and I exchanged a small smile with her. Four women I knew from around town clocked my entrance.

Daddy's nursing help and a couple he'd dated. Two men whose land bordered ours.

Daddy hadn't been friendly with the neighbors any more than he had been with anyone else in town, but at times they'd had to work together, like when cattle got out, or storms came through and damaged structures and fencing. Was Daddy doing a plot twist and showing everyone who played a role in his life that he appreciated them?

Two chairs were empty in front of the desk closest to the door. I took the seat by Wilder, still in uniform. Ansen sat in the chair on the edge of everything as if he could fade into the wall and people would quit staring at him. His visit would get out after this, and my gut twisted at what everyone would think. They'd assume what Eliot had, that he'd showed up like Lawson, hoping to get rich through me.

I'd almost forgotten about Lawson's visit after I'd hopped into the pickup with my brothers for the funeral. If Ansen hadn't been here, Lawson's words would've gotten to me. But with a simple kiss on my forehead, he'd soothed away any damage done.

Cody was behind the desk, his ankle kicked over a knee and his fingers steepled in front of his mouth. The expensive watch Meg had given him was visible over his cuff, as if she was here with him, supporting him. The permanent furrow he was developing across his brow was in full force as he gazed at the bare top of his desk. His laptop was closed and pushed to the side, and only a notepad and pen sat in front of him. "We can begin, Lorenzo."

My insides somersaulted. Would Lawson's insults be the most minor of my hurt feelings today?

The stern salt-and-pepper-haired lawyer stood next to him, papers in hand. Lorenzo Ruiz and his law office had handled all of Daddy's business. Mama had used a lawyer from Billings when she'd divorced Daddy. Lorenzo ran his fingers over his black-and-white-striped tie. Other than Cody, he was the only other guy in a suit. Cody's was black. Lorenzo's was gray with a vest.

He cleared his throat and dug a pair of readers out of his breast pocket. "All right. Welcome, everyone. As many of you know, Barnaby Knight formed a living trust that's been in effect for years. He left a few final notes he wished to be read." Just like Daddy, Lorenzo got right to the point. Probably why they had worked well together—that and all the money Daddy had paid Ruiz Law over the years. A smart businessman would make sure to work well with someone like Daddy, who'd always have legal issues because of his ambition or actions. "A final word from Barnaby Knight to Frank Bull and Darren Mapmaker." The neighbors. They owned the cattle ranches that flanked either side of Knight land. "You've made a lot of damn money off Knight's bulls; you'd better not give my kids a lick of trouble. If you do, my lawyer will pursue compensation for the bull seed you've stolen letting your goddamn heifers into the bull pasture."

I held in a groan. Dammit, Daddy.

A gruff grumble came from behind me. "Keep your goddamn fences fixed, then."

Eliot briefly closed his eyes, then held his hands up. "S'okay, Frank. I know how it goes."

Lorenzo glanced around like he was waiting for more reactions. When there were none, he continued, "To Cindy Cullen, Kimber Lang, Karen Polski, and Tori Garza, you, uh . . ." He took a deep breath like he was steeling himself for what he said next. "Barnaby wanted you all to know he knew you were sleeping with him to get money, so he wanted you all here to make sure you knew you don't get, and I quote, 'Not a damn cent. No sex is that good.'"

I couldn't stop my quiet groan and rolled my gaze to the ceiling. Was this how the rest of the night would go? Should

I grab Ansen's hand, tell Cody to catch me up later, and leave?

Startled gasps sounded from behind me. No doubt from Cindy, Kimber, Karen, and Tori. Cody dropped his forehead to his fingertips and sighed. Sutton and Wilder exchanged perplexed looks. Austen smothered his mouth with his hand, probably holding a cackle in, and Eliot glowered at the floor for a moment before he stood and turned toward the women.

Cindy was standing, her dangly earrings swinging from the way she was punching her finger toward Lorenzo. "I didn't want a single dime from that man."

Eliot held his hands up. For a guy who seemed permanently grumpy, he was very calming. "I understand, Cindy. You provided excellent care."

Tori muttered, "Especially from between the sheets."

Cindy's golden eyes blazed. "Don't you dare cast stones, hussy. We all know you were trying to put a ring on it from the moment Birdie left."

I flinched at Mom's name, but I doubted Cindy was wrong.

Kimber snorted and flipped her dyed-red hair over her shoulders. "And when she died, you were right there to console his dick."

I squeezed my eyes shut. Yuck. But hearing they were like vultures after Mama's death inspired both sadness and anger. Yet I didn't know what really went on. The statements were nothing but accusations about relationships I knew nothing about, and I'd had enough of those today.

Anger was carved into Eliot's jaw. "Enough about Mama and Barns. Take the fight somewhere else—we're grieving."

Karen rolled her eyes and ran her tongue across her teeth, her lips pinched. "Are you really? Can anyone grieve that man? We all knew he cared more about the business than his family, and the smart ones read the writing on the wall before they slept with him."

"Enough," Eliot said, more resigned than upset. "None of you need to deal with this. You shouldn't have been dragged in, but he was our father and you need to leave now. I'll walk you all out. Frank. Darren. Mind giving us some privacy?"

Tonight, I was grateful for Eliot taking charge. I brimmed with pride for the way he handled the conflict, which helped with the simmering humiliation from the spectacle this will reading was turning out to be. He herded the ladies and the neighbors—who didn't look like they were done with the show—out the door. I exchanged "What the hell?" looks with my remaining brothers and gave Ansen's hand a pump. The hard part was coming. Would Daddy strike at us from the grave like he had the only other people who'd been somewhat close to him?

Eliot was back in minutes. He slumped in his chair and gazed at Lorenzo. "Please tell me it doesn't get worse."

The lawyer's expression wasn't promising. *Shit.* "Barnaby took great care in setting up his living trust. Know that these are his wishes. He's split everything equally and payments will be made in distributions as long as certain parameters are met."

"Fuck's sake," Wilder groaned.

"And if these parameters aren't met?" Austen sounded bored and not at all surprised.

"The money in the trust will divert to Knight's Arabians and Cattle Company."

"What about KOW?" Cody asked. If Barns had realized his moneymaker would've been shortened to sound like cow, he probably wouldn't have named it Knight's Oil Wells.

"KOW falls under Knight's Arabians and Cattle Company," Lorenzo said, not elaborating. Also, meaning that Cody was still a sort of peon as the CEO, not the owner.

It all went together. One tight company to be better controlled. I mentally repeated Wilder's sentiments. *Fuck's sake.*

Lorenzo nervously licked his lips and continued. "First, the house will be the property of Knight's Arabians and Cattle Company. The manager may reside here."

Eliot cocked his head like he heard what wasn't being said, and my stomach bottomed out. The house belonged to the ranch manager. Not necessarily Eliot. My brother had dedicated his life to this ranch, and he wouldn't technically own the house?

"Cody," Lorenzo continued, "as long as you maintain your position as CEO, you will receive one installment each year for the next twenty-five years."

Cody's jaw tensed, and his eyelids slid shut for a heartbeat. The man had just been told the sum of money that was probably large enough to retire on would only be his if he kept working until he could collect social security.

Lorenzo flipped to another sheet. "Wilder, you must take a position at Knight's Arabians and Cattle Company in order to collect your annual sum . . . for the next twenty-seven years."

Sutton's mouth was clenched so hard she could spit out the diamonds that used to be her teeth. She was staring at the floor, not meeting my concerned gaze or looking at her husband.

Wilder tipped his head back. "He's going to tie all of us to this damn place."

I nodded. Daddy was tightening the knots on all the ties between us and the ranch. Anxiety cinched around my throat. What would happen to me? Did Daddy think I should give up my home and job to come work the ranch? He hadn't seemed to care if I had duties around here before.

Would I move? Would I walk away from whatever Daddy wanted to offer me to keep what I had?

I wouldn't be able to answer until I heard what Lorenzo had to read off.

The lawyer peered through his glasses, his eyes shining large behind the lenses. "Austen, you won't receive an annual distribution as long as you are enlisted in the military. If you insist on staying in until you retire from the army, you will receive a ten percent distribution if you are not working for Knight's Arabians and Cattle Company." Lorenzo licked his lips. "Barnaby wanted to show his thanks for your service, but he commented that your place is at home."

"Fuck you, Barns," Austen muttered.

"Eliot . . . " The lines in Lorenzo's face deepened. "Nothing's really changed other than you will also receive an annual allotment of your trust as long as you continue as the ranch manager."

"For how fucking long, Lorenzo?" Eliot snapped.

"Thirty-two years."

I couldn't imagine knowing I was stuck as ranch manager for three more decades. Eliot had been working since he could walk, took the manager position shortly after I left, and now it was more of the same. Barnaby hadn't signed shit over to him.

"Who owns the company?" Cody asked Lorenzo.

"The trust, which is managed by Ruiz Law."

A tendon popped in Cody's jaw.

"I think we're all seeing the trend in stipulations," Eliot said grimly. He turned an apprehensive gaze to me. "And her? Is she going to have to sell her house and move home to get money that should belong to the entire family since the oil was found on family land that we've worked our entire lives?"

Ansen rested his hand on top of mine. Would Daddy try to manipulate me too? I had worked the ranch my entire life. Had he thought I was out playing and it was time to come home?

Lorenzo's brown skin paled. "Um . . . the final recipient is free of the stipulations and will receive a lump sum distribution."

"Thank fuck," Cody growled, and I nearly sagged. I didn't care about the money. I just wanted Daddy to show me in some way that I had meant something to him.

"Barnaby wanted to provide a similar opportunity for someone like he had received. Someone who reminded him of himself, a kindred spirit, if you will. Someone with similar ambitions, someone who had the same upbringing. Someone he came to see as another son. Ansen Barron."

Eighteen

ANSEN

Eliot jumped to his feet. "What?"

Swearing echoed through the room. Ringing in my ears muffled the shouting. I was in the will? Why? Final recipient? That meant . . . *Sonofabitch*. I looked at Aggie, but she was wan, her eyes squeezed shut, tears sneaking out to wet her light lashes.

"Hey," I said softly, ignoring her brothers glaring at me. Twisting in my seat to face her, I cupped her chin and turned her face toward me. "Are you okay?"

She inhaled a shaky breath. Her "no" was barely perceptible. She wiped her eyes with the back of her hand.

I'd never hated Barns, not even after I'd been busted— that had been all on me, but hate was the strongest emotion I was feeling toward him now. How could he do this to her? Why would he cut her out and treat her as if she never meant anything?

She had left the ranch. It was as simple as that in Barns's mind.

But so had I.

A kindred spirit.

Goddammit, I had my own dad. My own family.

And now I was . . . I didn't know. A millionaire? Barns had told me once what his net worth was thanks to the oil and investing. How he'd scraped together enough to buy a defunct well. Then another. Unused wells the bigger companies had wanted to ditch once fracking came about. Then another oil boom happened. His bottom line had soared. All because Birdie Knight hadn't wanted a thing to do with the land or the company when they'd divorced. He'd given her money, and she'd had the freedom to leave. He hadn't done the same for his daughter.

Aggie's shoulders shook. I gathered her to me and rose. She stood with me, surprisingly, and let me lead her to the door. I had to be the last person any Knight wanted to see right now.

"Where the hell are you going?" Wilder asked. Chair legs shuffled on the floor like he was shoving them out of his way.

I ignored him. Heavy steps behind me were likely all of Aggie's brothers, but I didn't care.

"Barron," Cody barked.

They would crowd after us, demanding answers I didn't have and digging away at the edges of Aggie's emotional wounds. Sighing, I stopped and immediately regretted doing so.

Aggie pulled away and mumbled, "I'm going to my room."

I grabbed her hand. "Ags."

She blinked at me with red-rimmed eyes and a pale face. "I can't do this right now."

I'd deal with her brothers, convince them to give her a few moments, but—*goddammit*—I didn't want to leave her side to do it. Hurt rippled from her, the waves growing larger from where the blow had landed. "Promise me you're not leaving."

She glanced around her at her brothers, then toward the living room. "I don't want to stay. There's nothing for me here. There never was."

It was late, dark out, and the middle of winter. She could be home by midnight, but we drove separately, and I didn't want her to be alone right now. She already felt like the dad who should've held her above everything and treasured her hadn't ever cared about her a day in his life. "We'll take my truck. Your brothers can get yours to Crocus Valley later, or we can come back and grab it. Fuck, we'll figure it out."

Her expression was bleak as she nodded. "I want to go home. I want to be with Tex." Her face crumpled. "He's never let me down."

I couldn't live up to a dog.

"No one's leaving until we talk this out," Cody said, pushing past his siblings. They formed a wall in the hallway, and Lorenzo was probably hiding in the office until the hubbub died down. Cody's gaze turned supportive when he looked at Aggie. "Come on, Aggie. You know what he was like. He couldn't control you with money or land. That's all this trust is about."

"Except he's making Ansen a millionaire, no strings attached," Eliot said hotly.

I held my hands up. The money was my last priority. And there were always strings. "I didn't ask for it."

"What did you do for it?" It was the most serious I'd ever seen Austen.

"Nothing, dammit. I'm not after your money." As soon as the words left my mouth, I knew I screwed up.

They exploded in a litany of accusations about the last time Barns paid me. I clamped an arm around a tense Aggie, spun on my boot heel, turning her with me, and marched us to her room. Kicking the door shut behind us and locking it in case the guys wanted to continue a pointless argument, I ground my teeth together.

"Aggie . . . "

She heaved out a breath and unzipped her short boots. She flung them off her feet and trudged to the bed. Guess we were staying. "He never loved me."

"He did, Aggie." I wasn't sure he loved anyone, but she didn't need to hear that.

She gave me a flat but dubious look. "He never called me after I left. Not once. I was the one to reach out."

I recalled my conversations with Barns. He'd bitched about her exes and complained his boys didn't want to work as hard as he'd had to growing up and then there was his toxic, late ex, Birdie. He'd never gushed about Aggie's college graduation, just grumbled that she didn't need it. He hadn't said he was worried about her or that he was proud of a damn thing she did. But I couldn't comprehend a parent not loving a daughter like Aggie.

"He loved you as much as he could love anyone," I amended.

"He was pretty fond of you." There was only a note of accusation in her tone.

Christ, she had to be hurting. What could I do to make it better? I loosely propped my hands on my hips, still standing by the door. "I don't know. I don't know what that was about. I just talked to him. He never mentioned including me in his will. I mean *never*. But then I never knew what game he was playing."

"No one did." With another heavy exhale, she swung her legs into bed. "It's the perfect way to fuck with me and my brothers." She sank deep into the covers, still dressed in the clothes she wore to the funeral.

"Can I lie with you?"

"I'm not kicking you out," she said wearily.

Not the resounding yes I'd hoped for, but it didn't matter. I had her permission to stay with her, to comfort her. I eased behind her under the covers. She was stiff when I pulled her close to my chest.

"I feel like I'm being a selfish brat," she said in a small voice. "Like I'm just pissed about the money."

"Everyone knows you're not like that."

"I never asked him for a thing." She adjusted her position, molding herself to me better. A good sign she wasn't dumping the blame and running. "Other than the normal kid stuff, you know? After he berated me for suggesting he waste one cent for my college when Mama left so much, I knew I was on my own."

I flattened my hand on her abdomen and circled my thumb. I'd rather be touching bare skin, but she was vulnerable.

"Mama's money is probably why he left me out—and dammit, it's not about the money, but I'm scared to think that even if I had stayed, or if Mama's life insurance hadn't been paid to me, nothing would be different. That in the end, I was nothing to him, no matter what. He couldn't take his pain out on Mama, so he inflicted it on me."

What she said made sense. Aggie had been an obligation to him, one he didn't see the need to care for during life or after death. She was too much like her mother, and it was the one area he let his fractured, blackened heart take the lead.

"You're rich now," she said, barely above a whisper.

Her words were sandpaper against my brain. "I don't have any money yet, Ags."

"But you will. And you'll be able to do anything you want. Wherever you want." Tension radiated through her body like a live cable tucked next to me.

I didn't dare let myself entertain the thought of how much Barnaby had left me. What would I think when it all dropped in my account—if it did? Would it feel like dirty money? Would I dare spend a dime?

It didn't matter. I'd dabbled with millions before, and nothing came of it but regrets. "Like I said, my account is as empty as it was yesterday, and I'm sure Cody and your brothers are going to work with Lorenzo to fight it."

"Daddy always said people thought he looked like a dumb cowboy, and he made millions off their arrogant assumptions. There'll be very few if any, legal loopholes my brothers can maneuver through."

"Your brothers are all Barnaby Knight's kids. If there's a way, they'll find it."

Her breathing was steady. I was content to hold her, yet I wouldn't fault her if she told me to leave. Somehow, the blame was at home on my shoulders.

"You're going to leave," she said. "You don't like it in Crocus Valley."

I was in Crocus Valley for her. "I'm not going anywhere yet."

"There it is. You said it again."

Weary of this whole fucking argument, I shook my head. "What again?"

She rolled to face me. "Whatever you might think, you speak like it's temporary. You're not leaving *right now*. You're not going anywhere *yet*."

"I've never known where I was going to be a year from any moment since I left home. I haven't had a place that felt like a home since my mama died." The trailer, Aggie's house, they weren't filled with my things. They weren't mine. Just like the money wasn't mine yet. I wasn't planning my future with words said by a lawyer I'd only met when Barns made me sign the contract to take payments with the final and biggest installment after I married Aggie. "I'm talking like I always talk."

"You'll have so many options when that money goes through—and it will. Daddy would've made sure of it."

In her words, she was saying she was afraid I would leave her. Her vulnerability was an arrow straight through my heart. She wasn't asking for me to stay. She wouldn't beg. Not Agatha Knight. But she assumed I wouldn't choose her.

"Aggie. I'm right here. With you. I don't have to be, but I am because you are where I want to be." I drifted my hands up her shirt, finally touching warm satin skin. I didn't have anything to offer her—and when I did, it'd be her family's money. A windfall that should've gone to her and her brothers. For now, I didn't have anything to give her but myself.

Laying my lips on hers, I tested her responsiveness. I'd back off if she wasn't into it, but she melted against me like she needed reassurance that I wasn't going anywhere.

I didn't know until this moment how much I meant what I said. I was with her because I wanted to be. No other reason. There'd always been reasons for my relationships in the past. They'd been more like strategy, no matter how much I told myself differently.

"I'd like to be inside you," I said against her lips, giving her the time to tell me no, this was inappropriate. But I had to show her I was choosing her. I could've left that day I arrived at her house on Crocus Lane, but I didn't. Because of her.

I felt her nod at the same time she tugged my shirt from my pants. We were a frenzy of movement, stripping each other under the blankets. I didn't toss the covers off. They added to the sense of privacy. Only us, in the dark, together.

Finally, we were both naked, and I was positioned between her legs, my erection prodding against her wet pussy. Undressing was enough to get her ready for me, and that was heady knowledge. I pushed inside of her slowly.

She groaned, then muffled her mouth against my shoulder. I didn't care if she was loud, but she did. I didn't need her family to know I was banging their sister after she was distraught.

This was straight fucking. No, there was no foreplay, we were doing plain old missionary, but nothing was between us. We were together, and that was what I wanted to tell her.

I rocked my hips slowly, loving the way she gripped me, the building demand in the answering roll of her body.

"I'm not going anywhere," I said, placing a kiss next to her mouth. "Okay?"

"Okay," she echoed, lacking conviction.

"This means something." I punched my pelvis forward. "You *mean* something to me. You haven't been a way to pass time while I'm down on my luck."

I hitched one of her legs up to hit the place guaranteed to make her feel *good*. She moaned and stuffed her hands into my hair, bringing my head down to smash her mouth against mine. She swept her tongue inside, meeting mine in a frenzy. I picked up the pace to match, catching her needy pants in my mouth.

I kicked a knee to the side, widening her legs even more, knowing the friction of her clit against my body would help her hit her peak. Her mouth dropped open, and I nibbled on her lower lip.

"You're mine, Agatha Knight. This pussy is mine, and I'm not going anywhere."

With a gasp, she hit her climax. I swallowed all the sound I could as she shook through her orgasm.

"Fuck, Aggie," I hissed. My strokes grew erratic, lightning building in my cock until I blew. I curled around her, smothering my groans and grunts with her hair. Her heels were planted into my hips as she ground against me.

The need to be quiet only amped up the intensity, like something inside me got off on trying not to be caught, while at the same time, I wished her brothers trusted how much their sister meant to me.

I didn't ease out of her right away. I planted lazy kisses on her, letting the aftershocks of her body roll over my spent hard-on. This was just for us. A way for us to communicate what we were afraid to say. What I was afraid to admit to myself.

She meant a lot to me. I had nothing to give her, but at the same time, I'd have to give up everything to be with her.

Nineteen

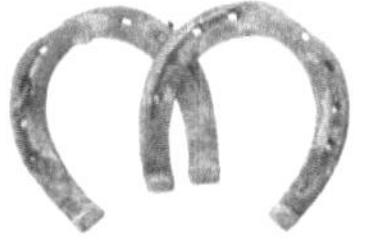

AGGIE

I got home from work, put on my long johns and some jeans, and went outside with Tex. Daddy's funeral had been a month ago. Ansen and I had snuck out of the house early in the morning before my brothers had roused. I messaged Sutton I was leaving to avoid more confrontations, and we'd driven home.

Ansen said he didn't mind leaving when I did, but he was willing to face my brothers.

I hadn't been.

I found him leaning by the door of the older barn. We'd worked to make it a temporary enclosure for the hopefully temporary ducks. The ability to close the crooked barn door at night made it the best option to keep foxes and coyotes from making a meal out of my rescues. I'd need an outside dog, and the way I was collecting rescues, I'd have one in no time.

The barn itself wasn't dead yet, but it needed some

structural care and TLC. I wouldn't want anyone in there for long periods of time or during bad weather, but Ansen had insisted on putting it to use. The ducks had been left after a family moved and were skating on their frozen water, hadn't had a food source, had few warm areas to bed down on, and two had already succumbed to the elements during the brutally cold stretch we had after the new year.

Ansen had built a quick and dirty separation so the six ducks didn't use the entire interior of the brown barn and so we didn't have to mess with much of the inside. He'd had to purchase more straw for them to bed down, and we got creative with the water for them during the winter using storage buckets and straw. For now, Ansen hauled fresh water every day.

Preparing for the new arrivals had been a welcome distraction for both of us. I woke each morning wondering if Ansen would find his bank account bursting and be gone.

Tex ran to Ansen's side and shoved his head under his hand. Ansen's deep chuckle reached me, warming me on the already unseasonably warm February day, hovering right at freezing. For whatever reason, he hadn't left yet. He'd told me in words I meant something to him, but I inspected every action to make sure.

He grinned at me. "Did you look in your fridge?"

"I just got home. Why?"

His smile widened. "I found eggs."

"Seriously?" I peered over the haphazard chicken wire fence enclosure he'd dug into the snow. Something more permanent could be built later—if we still had the ducks. "Should we have duck eggs for supper?"

"Let's do it."

I watched two white ducks waddle around, pecking at the mix of grains and cracked corn Ansen spread out for them. Four of the ducks were white and two were a dappled gray. If they had names, we didn't know them.

They had personalities, though. The white ducks ruled the roost. One of the dappled gray ducks was a goof and somehow had straw sticking out of its feathers in random places. Another would get a case of the zoomies at least once during chores like our activity excited her.

The sun was dipping on the other side of the barn, and the chill crowded back in. I warded off a shiver that didn't have to do with the temperature. "I put an ad out for Gingerbread."

Ansen jerked his head up from scratching Tex. "I'm not done with him."

"You've rehabilitated him, and he's healthy."

"He's also smart and strong. Look at the engine on him."

Gingerbread was in one of the smaller corrals by the barn, watching us. We'd discussed him last week. Ansen wanted more time to train him, said he could be an excellent roping horse, but that was the thing. I wasn't in the business of training roping horses. "We rescued him, Ansen. That's what AKA is. Now that the weather's nicer, Dr. Jake messaged me again about that draft horse he mentioned on New Year's Eve."

A muscle jumped in the corner of his jaw. We'd had Shelby and the four she came with for months, but their health had been worse. The pinto had needed rehab to correct postural and mobility issues that had been trained into him. Ansen worked on his behavioral problems from the abuse, but Gingerbread hadn't faced the health issues the others did. Selling our first rescue horse wasn't turning out to be easy when we were both horse people who could see potential in the animals and wanted to keep working with them. Yet I had a business to run and limited funds. I needed a sale before we accepted the draft horse. I needed it for the bottom line, and I needed it as a businessperson whose doors weren't anchored open.

"He's a good horse," I said. "He's had training, and it'll be easy to find him a home with people who know what they're doing."

"Why now?" Ansen crossed his arms and faced me. The shadow of the barn added edges to his face.

"The temperature the next two weeks looks seasonal with no storms. It'd be a good time to transport the retired draft horse, and I need the revenue to buy feed and provide vet care for him. He has arthritis, and former drafts often need several chiropractor visits for their chronic pain."

He wasn't fazed by my litany. "Just like it's time to sell Skinny instead of looking to purchase another Mangalitsa and breed her yourself? Their meat is like the Wagyu of pork. You could make a lot of money breeding her."

"I already work full-time." Since Ansen never made resounding statements about making Crocus Valley his home, I had to plan for being the only one to care for these animals. He told me I was his, but he also didn't have options at the time. He'd have millions soon.

He ignored my answer. "You sold Shrek two days after Dr. Jake cleared him."

"Time is money on a rescue, Ansen. I'm not the one getting millions in my account," I snapped. Shit. I hadn't meant to go there. Yet his windfall sawed through my mind. It wasn't that he was the target of Daddy's admiration—though that still hurt. Ansen would get the money, and he'd realize the world was wide open to him.

His lips were set in an *I knew it* pattern. "I'm not either. It could take months to get the payout—and that doesn't mean I'm leaving."

It didn't mean he was staying.

Cody had blown up my phone for two days after I'd returned home, and I firmly told him I was staying out of it. Daddy hadn't wanted me involved, or I would've been factored into his last thoughts.

Austen had gone back to California and sent me a funny meme once a week. He must be worried about me. Wilder asked Sutton about me based on her messages.

Sutton: Wilder wants to know if "that jackass" has left town yet.

Sutton: Wilder wants to know if Ansen's bought a new truck yet—that was the first sign last time.

Sutton: Wilder wants to make sure you're doing okay because he knows I won't tell him.

It would almost be sweet if Wilder wasn't nudging against my real fears.

Eliot spaced me out like usual. He was probably working with Cody to get the money free of the trust's constraints and Ansen.

"Months, huh?" I aimed for light, but my tone matched the shadows we stood in. I wandered to the edge of the fenced enclosure where the sun's rays still touched.

"Maybe sooner since Barnaby had his shit together."

I stuffed my hands in the pockets of the old coat I'd grabbed from the ranch. It was heavy, well-used, and warmer than any I owned. I wanted to be prepared to work in the cold. I'd also packed all my old boots, hats, and other coats. The rest of the clothing I'd either thrown out or donated. When I'd gotten out to my pickup, I found Eliot had already loaded all the tack I had used as a kid. I hadn't seen him before I left, but I knew it was his way to take some control over his circumstances. Whatever wasn't in the will, Eliot would damn well make the decisions for.

Selling Shrek had helped me purchase the extra supplies needed to house and feed the ducks without dipping into the reserves I had set aside. Business was happening on the rescue, but until I sold Skinny or Gingerbread, I couldn't take any more.

Ansen crossed to me and put his hands on my shoulders. "Aggie, I thought we talked about this."

"We did, and you still haven't said what you'll do."

"Because I'm not countin' my chickens before they're hatched. You've heard of that, right?"

"Everyone has," I said, cranky. Upset that he couldn't or wouldn't answer. "You won't even play the what-if game. What am I supposed to think?"

"That I'm not a douchebag who'll run out on you as soon as I get some cash in hand."

I gave him a steady look. It was more than some cash, and he knew it. He'd said it last time. Life-changing money.

And again, my life wasn't changing.

His breath gusted out of him on a cloud. "Maybe I'll buy the half section across from you and open my training business."

A tiny tendril of hope curled around my heart. "You hate the winter." All the places he'd worked had milder winters than Montana and North Dakota.

"I don't *like* it. Does anyone?"

The hope incinerated. "I love it here, and this is my home." There. I said it. We'd danced around this topic, and while I thought he knew my stance, I hadn't said it out loud since he hadn't been talking. "I built this place to be my forever home. And you've been dreaming of returning to Texas since you left. Admit it."

His brows drew together, and I finally had to confess to myself he'd been right all those years ago. He didn't lie to me. He wouldn't speak if what the other person wanted to hear was a lie. "I can't deny that I want to go home. My dad's there, and it'd be a perfect place to set up shop with the rodeo culture there." He peered into my eyes. "And you're telling me you won't leave Crocus Valley—for any reason?"

Drawing in a breath grew difficult. I knew it. He'd been wondering—because he didn't want to make his home here. I'd been willing to leave with him before. Just like I'd been willing to stick around the ranch for no other reason than Daddy wanted me there. "My home is here." Everything I have and had worked for was here.

His gaze shuttered, and he dropped his hold on me. "Is this your way of leaving without going anywhere?"

"What?"

"Like our wedding. Instead of talking through everything, you left. Only now you can't leave, so you're trying to get me to."

"How can you throw it at me that I left? After what you and Daddy did—"

"We had something real. Maybe the wedding was rushed because of Barns, but we had something real, and you walked away like it meant nothing." He shook his head when I opened my mouth to tell him he hadn't followed me to prove otherwise. "Never mind. We're beyond that. I'm focused on the now, Aggie, and I feel like you're trying to push a future you assume is destined to fail. I enjoy being with you. I work for you. I don't have the money. Can't we just . . . be?"

I recoiled. He was telling me to leave it because he didn't know what he wanted to do. My heart was out of my chest and pumping between us, open and vulnerable, his for the taking, but as long as it stayed in Crocus Valley, he didn't know if he wanted it.

Can't we just . . . be?

I didn't want him to go. I wanted him to stay forever. I wanted him to tell me he loved me and I was all he needed. But that wasn't what he'd said. *Can't we just . . . be?*

So, yeah. I guess, for now, I'd have to let it be. When I was the one standing in his taillights, I'd deal with it then.

Ansen

My phone was vibrating against the nightstand. Fancy mewed at my feet and adjusted her position. My room was bathed in shadows, but the rumble of a truck passed on the highway. Usually I couldn't hear the traffic that clearly. Right. I was in the fucking trailer, giving Aggie some room after our argument.

The time was after two in the morning, and I'd been sleeping like shit after talking with Aggie earlier.

She was putting space between us that had no right being there.

When she'd told me, with the finality I recognized to be an undying trait of hers, that she was never leaving Crocus Valley, I shouldn't have been surprised. Her admission finally revealed the fear she was hiding. She didn't believe what was growing between us was real or that it'd matter to me.

I had a decision to make. I was within months, or even weeks, of getting everything I wanted. The dreams I'd given up on had been handed back to me by a cantankerous old man who didn't love or respect his family like he should.

But those dreams were down south. My childhood home. Even my dad was there. If I stayed, I'd be living in

Aggie's house, helping with her business. I'd be a millionaire and still living off someone. Didn't feel like success.

If I stayed, bought the land across from her place, erected a shop, stables, and a riding ring, would Aggie resent me? Could I use her family's money right in front of her? Didn't feel right. Neither did leaving her. I just wanted time to think. I didn't give myself that before. I'd reacted—to Barns's offer, to her breaking it off with me, and getting told to leave Montana. I couldn't screw this up and lose her again.

My phone buzzed again. The screen lit up with Archer's name. Groggy, I sat up. Alarm gathered in my brain as the fog cleared. Archer was calling me at two in the morning. Something was wrong. I answered with a rushed, "Yeah?"

"Ansen, it's Dad. He's in the hospital."

Too late. That was all I could think. I'd spent too long avoiding Dad, being ashamed of myself, and now I was too late. He was going to be gone before I had the means to take care of him. Before he saw me achieve a single goal. "What the fuck happened?"

"He got rammed by a cow this afternoon. Broke some ribs. Contusions. I don't know what else. He was pretty groggy, but he refused to have anyone call us until he could talk to us himself. I told him I'd tell you so he could rest. I'm taking a flight right away in the morning."

"I'll head out in ten." I could be there by tomorrow evening. I was already rolling out of bed.

"I can give you my flight details."

"I'll drive. He's going to need help, and you have work and a family."

There was a pause. "Thanks. Drive safe."

He disconnected.

He wasn't used to me being around or available, but

then nothing like this had happened. Dad was always there, toiling away in a job he'd done most of his life and enjoying the ten acres he'd finally been able to buy for himself during his nonworking hours.

I tossed on the clothes I'd been wearing the day before. Then I dumped all my belongings on the bed, making Fancy let out a disgruntled snort, and dug out my suitcase. I stuffed everything into my luggage. It took only a pitiful few moments to pack everything I owned that was in the trailer house.

The dishes weren't mine. None of the furniture. Without Aggie's books, I didn't even need much extra space for the winter gear I'd purchased. What didn't fit would get tossed in the back seat.

I'd need my tack. I'd fill in for Dad while he recovered, and his place and animals would need care.

I squatted at the corner of the bed and scratched along Fancy's jaw. She'd been with me every night I wasn't staying at Aggie's, and over the last month, I'd been more thankful for her presence.

Did I bring her along? Ask Aggie to care for her? I hated to leave her alone in the house when I might be gone for weeks, but it didn't seem fair to leave Aggie with a new cat in her house while she also had to take over rescue duties.

I hauled my baggage to the pickup first. Once I was back inside, I found Fancy's carrier and loaded her up. She'd been abandoned once, and while I knew Aggie would make sure she was taken care of, even give her a place in the house, I couldn't abandon her. I couldn't leave one more place and everything behind and assume everyone else would pick up after me.

She meowed on the way out to the pickup. I tucked her into the passenger seat and even buckled the carrier in. My first stop was the big barn to grab my tack. Reflective eyes stared at me from the dark depths of the barn. I was never here this late at night, and the kittens didn't know what to make of it. I pushed all my stuff into the bed of the pickup and hopped back in.

The pickup was still cold by the time I pulled into Aggie's driveway. I pounded on her front door and rang the doorbell. Tex's answering bark gave me hope she wouldn't sleep through the assault on her door.

"Aggie, it's me," I called.

The entry light flipped on and the door opened. A groggy but cute Aggie blinked at me, her hair a mess and her freckle-covered nose scrunched against the light. "What's going on?"

"I have to go." The sleep wiped from her eyes, and I continued. "Dad got hurt."

"Oh my god. Is he okay?"

"He's in the hospital, and it sounds like he'll need help and time to recover." I couldn't bring myself to tell her I was leaving, just like she suspected. I was going, but I'd be back.

"You're going to Texas?"

I nodded, stepping inside and shutting the door behind me. "I'm bringing Fancy with me, so you don't have to worry about her on top of all the others."

Her jaw worked, but she didn't reply.

The resignation deep in her eyes gutted me. "Aggie, I'm coming back."

She peered up at me like she was studying every twitch in my face. "Are you?"

It'd be the only way to earn her trust for good. "Once it's all figured out."

She inhaled like she was going to say something, then deflated. "I hope your dad's okay."

"Aggie, I'm coming back."

She gave me a small smile. "Don't give me false hope."

"Dammit." I pulled her into my arms, and she came easily. Her unbound breasts pushed against my coat, and damn, if I only had some extra time. "I told you once this wasn't over between us, and I still mean it."

"But you have to go, and you might not want to come back."

"If you're here, I'll want to come back. Aggie . . . " I loosened my hold and tipped her chin up. The words piled on the end of my tongue, but I couldn't say the phrase I'd only said a handful of times in my life, and I didn't know why. "You mean the world to me. I'm coming back. I promise. Just promise me you'll be here."

"Ansen . . . " She sounded so resigned, my heart fractured, but then her eyes filled with resolve. She patted my chest. "Don't worry about me. I'm not going anywhere. Take care of what you need to and tell me what you decide, okay?"

"I mean it. This isn't over between us."

"Not yet."

I held that militant chin between my thumb and forefinger. "Never." Her eyes flared at my vehemence. "We'll figure this out. I'm not letting money come between us one more time. I know it looks bad that I'm jetting town while I'm on the brink of winning your inheritance lottery, but you have to trust me. Okay?"

"I just don't think . . . " She shook her head. "Never mind."

"Just don't think what, Ags?"

She licked her lips, and I wished I would've gotten over myself and gone to bed with her last night, but she'd been pushing me away and I was tired of it.

"Nothing," she said. "I don't want to keep you."

"Aggie."

"Ansen, you have to get going. It's a long drive, and I

know you're worried about your dad. Take care of yourself and Fancy."

She had something on her mind, and she wasn't going to share.

Shit, I had to go. The drive with bathroom breaks and at least one stop for food would take almost twenty hours. Add more time if I ran into snow or ice, or goddammit, even tornadoes, the farther south I went.

I pulled her to me again and planted a kiss on her mouth. I could sink in, get lost forever. Tell her I had so many regrets about everyone I'd left hanging in my life who happened to be the most important people to me, but I needed to get to Dad in case he was getting worse as I stood in Aggie's entry.

I pulled back just as quickly. She blinked like she was stunned.

"Call me with any questions. I have my gear so I can help Dad keep his job while he's mending."

"Oh." Dismay played over her features before she squashed it. "Right. Of course."

Fuck, it looked bad. "I'll be back."

Wearily, she pushed me toward the door. "Get to your dad."

"He only has me and Archer."

She nodded and rubbed my back. "I know. Go."

It was too cold for her to follow me outside in bare feet. The door clicked softly behind me, and I looked around. My truck was running in the driveway, looking like it belonged there. The house was just like the one Aggie and I had dreamed about building. And the land . . . called to me. The animals. They weren't my job. They'd become my passion.

Like the fucking ducks. I had looked forward to learning more about them. They were fun to watch peck around the enclosure. Would they be here by the time I got back?

I told her I'd return. I'd left Buffalo Gully the first time and never looked back. The same for every job after. This time felt different. Aggie wasn't going anywhere. So there was someone left behind I wanted to get back to.

<h1 style="text-align:center">Twenty</h1>

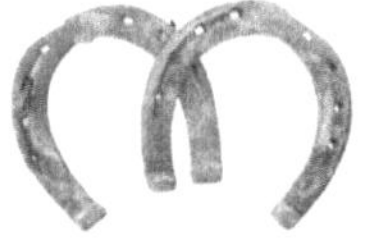

AGGIE

"He's got the money." Cody had a pair of mirrored shades on, facing the tract of land across from my property. "And it's been a month since he left."

I leaned my elbows on the porch fence. My niece and nephew were playing with Tex. For an early March day, the sun was out, the wind was down, and spring was undeniably on its way. "We've been keeping in touch."

A know-it-all brow arched under his sunglasses.

I bristled, hating I had to justify why Ansen was still gone. We had been in touch. A few general messages a week. How was his dad? How were the animals? Archer was there. Archer was back in North Dakota. "His dad is on the mend. Ansen's been working in his place so he doesn't get fired."

Cody made a disbelieving grunt. "His old ranch is for sale."

Shock hit my chest, and my heart skipped a beat. Ansen

didn't mention his old home was up for grabs. I pushed off the railing. "What are you saying?"

"I'm saying I'm worried you're waiting on heartbreak." He turned his back to the kids like he didn't want them to hear. "He championed you when the will was read, and I mean, none of us missed that. But according to Lorenzo, now he's a millionaire."

Another palpitation thumped in my chest. Ansen hadn't told me he'd gotten the money either. "Don't you think I've been worried about that?" I whispered. "I don't need you reminding me every time you text or stop in."

He dropped his chin. "I don't mean to pester you."

"Yes, you do. You always mean to pester me. Just when I think we can be adult siblings, you treat me like I'm going to swim in the water tank again."

"It wasn't fresh water."

"I found out after I climbed in," I snapped, then laughed. Who was acting like the kid now? "I had to ride it out, or it'd look even worse for me."

"Damn, Aggie. That's such a Knight thing to do."

Grayson ran up to us. "Dad, look what I can do!" He wrapped his arms around Tex's neck and swung a leg over the dog's back.

"G, that dog is too old to be playing horse," Cody said in the "Dad" tone I was glad was aimed at someone else. "Get off him."

My little nephew's shoulders slumped, but then he whacked his seven-year-old sister's shoulder. "You're it."

Ivy giggled and ran after him. Grayson's plain black snow boots slipped in the melting slush. The temperature was over forty degrees, and being outside was like a day at the beach—the gravel driveway was our sand and the snowmelt was the water source.

I soaked up the scene in front of me, but a pensive

atmosphere surrounded Cody. "How's it going with the in-laws?"

He grunted, but a line formed across his brow. "They're, uh, looking at schools. For the fall."

"What?" Cody couldn't give up the kids. They couldn't move across Montana and away from all the rest of their family. How many days like this would we get?

"School in Buffalo Gully has been . . . " He pushed his sunglasses up and rubbed at his eyes. "Grayson's been having outbursts, and I think the change might be good for him."

"But you work from home." He had often gone to the office at the ranch to work, but since Meg died, he'd stayed at home. "Can't you at least go with them?"

His gaze was steady on the kids. Grayson tripped and fell, runoff from a nearby snowbank splashing in his face. Ivy tagged him and was streaking across the lawn when Grayson rolled up and shrieked.

I jumped, the shrill sound startling me. I pushed off the railing to run to him.

"I got him," Cody said and strode across the driveway. "Hey, buddy. What's hurt?"

He got Grayson to his feet, and my nephew pointed accusingly to his sister, who ignored him and frolicked with Tex. I couldn't make out what Cody was saying over Grayson's shouts. Several minutes went by before Grayson quieted and my brother straightened. Grayson trudged off to sit on the cold concrete of my driveway.

Cody's jaw was tight when he returned to stand next to me. He put his hands on the railing and dropped his head. "So, yeah," he said only loud enough for me to hear. "That's what's been going on, and his teacher has lost her patience."

"He'll have a new one." But it was a small town.

"He's already been labeled." Cody said exactly what I

was thinking. "He's always been a more emotional kid than others, but I think getting out of Buffalo Gully would help him, and I have to be closer to the ranch than Helena." He glanced from Ivy and Tex to where Grayson morosely traced a finger over the concrete. "You know how often I think Meg would rather her parents raise the kids than me all by myself?"

We weren't a touchy-feely family, but I laid my hand on his arm. "It's not Meg's decision. You're their dad. You practically raised us."

Instead of easing his conscience, he nodded as if I had confirmed his decision. "You guys weren't like them."

"We were kind of assholes."

His smile was quick and gone in a flash. He faced the house and leaned against the railing again. "Did you know Sutton was going to file for divorce?"

There was no censure in his question. Like he respected I would've kept Sutton's confidence. I'd been on the phone late several nights with her. She served Wilder papers last Monday. "Yes. I wish they could've worked it out."

"Well, Wilder didn't make it easy."

Surprised, I stared at him. I didn't think he critiqued my brothers' lives like he had mine.

He shrugged. "I tried to warn him, but he hides behind that damn badge. And he thought working both that job and at the ranch to get a few years of distributions would be fine, but . . . "

"But Sutton's in her thirties and wants a family."

"He'd give her that."

"She'd be a married, single mom."

"I'm not saying I don't get it." His mouth flattened. "Wilder's not happy with you."

"Why?" I'd been a sounding board for Sutton. She was in love with her husband, but she needed to feel loved in return. Wilder was my brother. I wouldn't campaign for his heartbreak, but I'd support her finding her happiness.

"He's angry at the world right now, and since you're her friend, you'll get to be the brunt of it. He's like Barns in that sense."

"You saw it too? With Daddy?"

"From the beginning. It's probably why we buffered you from everything. Didn't want to give him a reason to finally blow," Cody grunted. "Maybe he should've. Anyway, Wilder thinks you encouraged her to divorce." He cleared his throat. "Since you were closer to Mama."

"Oh." I frowned. Wilder's assumptions hurt, and I'd have to call him about it. "What Mama did affected me too. And yeah, her words stayed with me, and when I left before the wedding, I thought she'd be proud of me. But since being with Ansen again, I've been angry with her." Cody's silence encouraged me to keep going. "She left. Daddy didn't care. And I didn't give Ansen a chance to leave me first. What if he would've stayed?"

"You think he would've stayed?" His question was filled with genuine curiosity.

"I don't know. I don't know if he knows either, maybe for a little while. Maybe he would've rejected the money and married me anyway. Maybe Daddy would've blown then. Maybe Ansen and I were too immature to make anything work anyway." So many scenarios. I had quit wondering for the most part. It was done. "I mean, I was willing to do whatever he wanted, to give up my dreams."

"What were your dreams?"

"To be needed." The answer left before I thought about it. Cody set a hand on the railing and hooked the fingers of his other hand through a belt loop of his gray slacks. Now that I had his attention, I wanted to hide. How did I explain something I'd only just had the epiphany about? "If I had to pick a career back then, it would've been ranching. I really love working with animals, yet training horses wasn't exactly my dream. Living around them, yes."

"You want to do exactly what you're doing here?"

"Yes. I can make it work without Ansen. On a smaller scale." The back of my throat burned. I hated to think of life without him when I'd gotten a taste of it.

"You think he's not coming back?"

Wasn't that the question every damn day? My tenuous trust was growing weaker with each passing of the sun. Cody's news that Ansen's old ranch was for sale was like a pair of shiny silver scissors poised, waiting to sever it completely. "I don't know." My reply was ragged.

Cody studied me. "I have to admit . . . I thought he was full of shit when he showed up on your doorstep."

"He didn't just show up."

"He's proven to grab opportunities when he sees them." He held up a hand before I could interject. "But I didn't get the impression he was acting after the will reading. His only concern seemed to be you. I hope he returns for you. That being said, I gotta ask—why won't you move?"

Familiar defensiveness rose. "I worked really hard for all this, and I have an amazing job. If I leave, everything will be his." He gave another arrogant cock of his brow. "I know, I know. I can sell the house and the property. But the job . . . "

"You have experience with finance in the oil industry. You basically grew up oil-industry adjacent. Ansen's in *Texas*. There are a lot of oil and animals in Texas."

I scowled. Could I have a conversation with my oldest brother that didn't devolve into him talking to me like I couldn't do anything? "Are you trying to get me to move? You don't think I can work and run the rescue by myself?"

"Aggie," he said in his frustratingly calm boardroom voice, "I'm not questioning whether you can do it. I'm asking you why you want to do it by yourself when you could have it all with a guy you're clearly in love with."

"Oh." Tears stung the backs of my eyes. Between Cody's confidence that I could do it by myself and calling me out about how madly in love I was with a new millionaire who could have any woman with a crook of his finger, I wanted to run inside and slam the door. Cody's vulnerability with me earlier was the only reason I spoke my biggest fear out loud. "What if he doesn't love me?"

"Well . . . you said you regretted leaving last time. Maybe this time, you give him the chance to reject you first. Either way, it's going to hurt. Pick your pain." He propped his elbows on the railing again, staring at his kids. "But there's also a chance it'll all work out this time."

∩∩

Ansen

I gazed at a home that was smaller and more run down than I remembered. During one of the many long hours I'd been by Dad's side in the hospital, he'd mentioned our old place was for sale. The urge to rush here hadn't been as strong as I would've thought. I'd scrolled through the details, noted the price, and then concentrated on Dad.

I hadn't been back since I'd graduated. The town was about the same. Small and dusty. Happily country. I didn't care to roam around and see if I recognized anyone or if they remembered me. None of them had cared when I lived here.

Dad stood stiffly next to me. His shoulders were rigid, thanks to the minimal pain meds he used. He claimed the pain was almost gone, but this was the first trip we'd taken since he'd been discharged. The last several weeks had been me making him stay put at his house while I took care of everything.

Archer made a trip out every weekend. Dad hated the attention, but every time both Archer and I were in the same room with him, he practically floated off the couch.

Dad had moved across the county after I left, and for the first time, I realized how much he'd endured to give us as stable a home as possible. He'd stayed in a crap job, getting treated like dirt and being paid less, because he didn't dare uproot us to find out a new situation was worse. And Archer and I had blamed him in our cocky, unknowing way.

"You did a lot for us," I said gruffly.

He glanced at me, surprised. The cuts on his face had healed in the six weeks since the accident. We'd teased him that it was lucky the mama cow hadn't branded him with a hoofprint in the middle of his forehead.

His gaze turned back to the squat home that used to be majestic in my mind. A divot formed between his brows. "It wasn't near enough. If I'd been better with money . . ."

"How many people can say that, though? It's not like any of us are taught what to do with a sudden load of cash." I scuffed a boot in the dirt. I was rich. The money had come through quicker than expected, but that was "thy Knight's will" being done. I hadn't told Aggie yet. I needed to make sure I had clear, concise answers for her after the way we parted. She would lose all trust in me otherwise. "I had a perfectly good pickup, and the first thing I did when Barnaby gave me some money after I started dating Aggie was buy a brand-new one."

He chuckled and wrapped an arm around himself. The trip was knocking the wind out of him. Bumping around in the pickup, climbing in and out, stretched muscles and limbs that'd had a limited range of motion for weeks. "I hope you've learned a few lessons from that and from me."

"I could buy this place right now." One call. I had enough to purchase it over asking price. I had enough to motivate the closing and get the old owners the hell off the property. Like they'd booted Mama and Dad out of the house when Dad had been forced to sell. Only they had already moved to Phoenix to live next to a golf course.

Dad jerked his head to look at me and winced. He still moved gingerly. "Why would you want to do that?"

Shocked, I stared at him. Wasn't it obvious? "This was our home."

He frowned, his gaze sweeping across the empty house and the expanse of shops, barns, and dilapidated fence line around it. Greenish-brown shrubs and brush scattered the flat acres behind it. Some rolling hills broke up the view in the distance and behind them, the cabin we'd relocated to after losing the place, which had blown down in a storm.

What was he seeing? I'd been able to live in a lot of beautiful places, but as I stared at the scenery that was achingly familiar, I wondered how gorgeous those white rolling hills around Crocus Valley would be once the spring thaw passed and they turned green.

"It was our home a long time ago," Dad agreed, his tone solemn. "Are you thinking of moving here?"

"I don't know." I'd been pushing off decisions until I had money, and now that I had money and this place was for sale, I knew what I wanted. Disappointing Dad wasn't it, and I might end up doing just that.

"I'm . . . " The furrow in his brow deepened. "I've been thinking of moving."

"Out of Texas?" It was Dad's day to surprise me.

His smile was understanding. "There's no one here for me anymore. Hasn't been for a while. Archer's brought it up a few times, moving closer to him and the kids, but I never thought it was an option."

"Then you returned and talked to your siblings?"

"Yeah." He said it on a long drawl. "I thought, hell, if Cameron can change, damn near anyone can become a different person. Besides, I'm not as young as I used to be, and these long days are . . . long." He gave a soft chuckle. "And I miss them kids."

I laughed, but my mind spun with the fracturing of my plans and assumptions. "You don't want this old place back? A way to reclaim what was once yours?"

His eyes crinkled at the corners, looking like an older version of my brother. "Ansen, it's not the place—or the land—or the house. It's the people who make a home. That was my biggest failure, you know. Not making a good home for you boys after your mama died. I didn't know how to be warm. How to be understanding. All I knew to do was work."

"And work was what we did." My tone came out teasing, prompting us both to laugh. His words rang in my head. I'd been afraid to give up the one unattainable goal that had suddenly become attainable when I didn't want it. "I thought I could make it all right again. I thought I could work hard and earn enough and when this was for sale again, I'd buy it. And we'd all have our home back. And now it's no longer what I want to do, and I'm afraid of letting you down yet again."

"Ansen." He placed a hand on my shoulder, a sign what he was saying would be important. "I want you to be happy. If buying our old home does it, so be it. If walking away and never looking back is what you need, I support you."

"I want to be with Aggie." It was what I always wanted. A big part of me had hoped I could have both her and this place. Like I could hold on to her and to this old dream and have it all. My tight hold would cost me her if I wasn't as clear as a summer morning.

"She must be a special lady," he said warmly.

"She is. But she's set to stay in Crocus Valley, working for Uncle Cameron."

"And it's hard to let go of an idea you've held on to so tightly for so long."

It seemed silly when he said it. An idea. A plan. And I had let it rule so much of my life. "I want to be with Aggie." I took my hat off and pushed a hand through my hair. A hunk fell on my forehead, and I crushed my hat back on over it. "I promised I'd be back, but in a way, I feel like she has one foot out the door. She doesn't completely trust me, and standing here, I can't help but wonder if she's right not to. Was I planning to leave an out, just in case this all worked out?" It was fucked up. I wanted to be with Aggie more than anything. My feelings shouldn't be terrifying, but those I cared about tended to disappear from my world.

"You know why I purchased this property after I met your mother?"

Grateful to be yanked out of the traffic circle my thoughts were stuck in, I answered. "She said you drove north until you found paradise."

He scoffed, but fondness was in his gaze. "She made it sound so romantic. I guess that's what we did. Mostly, we found out she was pregnant and needed to put down roots somewhere. It could've been Oklahoma or Nebraska. I probably would've stopped before we hit North Dakota, but that was only because of my stubborn pride. We both wanted a place away from our families, and it happened to be here."

Just like that. They'd needed to stop and raise a kid. There was nothing else about this land or house that called to them. They'd just put in a stake and made a home. Aggie wasn't afraid to let her roots run deep, but I'd done nothing to show her my roots went further than scratching at the dirt.

"I stayed with Stephanie because I didn't think I deserved any better." I didn't have one lick of faith in myself. But for some reason, Barnaby Knight had put twenty percent of his poker chips on me.

I wouldn't do what he did when he got Birdie's land and money. I wouldn't use it to control people, especially those I loved. He wanted to keep the cycle going for his kids, but I could stop it with his daughter.

She had given me a second chance when she should've forgotten me. "I don't deserve her."

Dad sucked his lips against his teeth. "We're often the worst judges of what we deserve. Only those who love us the most understand we deserve the best."

I thought Aggie was pushing me away, and she was, but only because she wanted me to have my dreams. "I'm an idiot."

"Better to figure that out sooner than later." He slapped my back and winced, gently rotating his shoulder. "And you're not an idiot. You're sensitive. You feel deeply. Had I recognized it or grown up in a family that acknowledged feelings, I would've handled you and Archer better. It was easier to kick you boys outside and ignore your emotions. Hindsight makes things perfectly clear."

"What if I ruined it?"

"Aren't you still talking to her? I assume she's why you're looking at your phone a hundred times an hour."

My communication with Aggie had been brief and polite. I'd tried to call before bed, but the conversations ended stilted instead of sexy. When I tried to warm up our talks, the words fell flat and cold between us. She was waiting for me to sever the tie and I . . .

I was at my old home, the place she knew I dreamed

about, when nothing mattered but her. "I'm checking my phone a hundred times because she hasn't responded."

She sold Gingerbread to a family with a budding roper. She'd sent a picture of them standing around Gingerbread and said the mom in the family had experience working with project horses. Aggie had found the perfect fucking family for a horse I'd wanted to see hit his potential. I'd sent her pictures of Dad's place and his horse, Buckstop, and I'd gotten a simple reply. **Nice**.

I took out my phone—still no missed calls or messages—and snapped a few pictures of the house and the area around it. The corrals where we used to work cattle were a speck in the background. But it was enough. Seeing them as tiny grains on the screen rammed home that there was nothing here for me. Everything I wanted was on forty acres in Crocus Valley.

I almost turned to Dad and said I had to get going, I needed to get back to Aggie, but seeing him with an arm wrapped around his middle slapped my lips shut. He might be healing well, but he was over sixty and recovering from getting rammed by an angry mama cow. He wasn't swinging into a saddle anytime soon, and his job didn't exactly cover much for benefits.

If he was moving to a different state, he'd need me and Archer to help. He'd refused any money from me as soon as I'd told him the story. *Don't think you're going to treat me like a charity. I didn't know Barnaby Knight, and I'm not taking his money.*

I knew Barnaby, and I hadn't had a choice—this time.

"I need to call Aggie when we get back."

"I reckon we should get going." I opened the door for him, and he scowled at me as he climbed in, muttering, "I ain't gettin' that old."

Grinning, I jogged around to the driver's side. Once we

were on the highway driving to the other side of Guthrie, I relaxed, but only slightly. The worry of how badly I'd fucked up but wasn't in a position to fix my mess raced back and forth along my shoulders. I was antsy but also hopeful. Scared my stubborn Aggie had decided not to trust me with her heart after all.

"Need anything from town?" I asked as we drove through to take a smaller highway north.

He grunted, his eyelids dropping. "My bed's calling my name. I've never taken so many goddamn naps."

He was growing more disgruntled by the day. A good sign. But I didn't cherish the looming argument that he needed to take more time to recover and should sit his ass back down.

Archer was visiting again this weekend. We could both talk to him.

When I pulled into the drive, a nice dust cloud kicked up behind us, and a familiar red pickup was sitting in front of the detached garage. A girl sauntering from the house to the parked truck ground my world to a welcomed halt.

Aggie was wearing the Wranglers that were getting nice and worn from doing chores while I'd been gone. Her blue-and-gold hoodie from her university days was in better shape than the beat-up sweaters she used to wear when we'd first met. The straw hat she had always worn when I first met her was planted on her head, and she was squinting at our approach.

"We've got a guest?" Dad asked.

I would've slammed to a stop, but I couldn't propel Dad into his seat belt. "It's Aggie." I sounded like Christmas had come early.

I pulled behind her pickup like I was intentionally blocking her in, and maybe I was. She regarded me warily, like she wasn't sure I wanted her there. I hopped out, my long strides eating up the distance between us. Yanking her into my arms, I lifted her and spun her around, burying my nose in her neck and inhaling that familiar and very missed coconut-beach scent.

"Hot damn, I missed you." I stopped twirling us.

Her hat had fallen off, and her arms were anchored tightly around my neck. "Does that mean you don't mind I showed up without calling?"

"It means I've been a dumbass." I set her down and grabbed her hat. I dusted it off and plunked it on her head. "Do you know my old home is for sale?"

Worry clouded her eyes, and she nodded. "Cody told me."

"He's a nosy fucker."

She huffed out a laugh. "He's also one of the reasons why I'm here."

"Why are you here? Is everything okay?" Boots crunched on dirt, and she finally noticed Dad. "Hi. Sorry I crashed your place while you're recovering."

Dad's friendly expression was suppressing his thrill, but the shine of it was in his eyes. He enjoyed seeing me crazy about someone. "You're welcome anytime." He stuck his hand out. "Allan Barron. I've heard a lot about you."

Aggie's eyes flickered, happy and surprised. She shook his hand. "Nice to finally meet you."

Dad stepped back. "I hate to admit I need to rest my eyes. I'll let you two catch up."

"You and Archer look like him," she murmured as Dad walked away.

"A little taller and darker hair. Otherwise, Mama said it was like we were stamped from him."

"I wish I could've met her."

"She'd have loved you and Laney. She'd have been thrilled neither of you put up with our shit."

Her smile was faint. "You've put up with plenty of mine."

I hooked my hands around her waist. "I'd like to put up with more, but first—why are you here?" I didn't want there to be a problem. I wanted her to tell me she couldn't go one more day without me, and even though it was my fault I wasn't with her, she crossed the country just to hang out for a while.

"I've been thinking." She chewed the inside of her cheek. "About what I really want."

Icicles formed in my veins. Please be me. "What do you really want, Aggie?"

"You. I can sell my place and get a job out here. You'll have to help me haul the horses because I can't bring myself to think about selling Shelby and the rest. Then there's Tex. I didn't want to bring him in case . . ."

"There is no 'in case.'" I'd been afraid to bring my two dreams together and watch them shatter each other, but Aggie once again proved she was way too good for me. She was willing to sell all her hard work to follow me to a plot of dust a thousand miles away? This woman was fucking amazing. She gave me herself, a cat, five horses, and even Tex, and I didn't care if he was technically mine first. It was time to show her how important she was to me—and how much I wanted her to have her dreams. "I'm going back to you— once Dad is cleared to work again, and he's probably moving too."

She blinked. "You're coming back?"

"I told you I would."

"Not for, like, good."

"Agatha Christie Knight—"

"I told you not to use my full name."

"—I happen to love you."

She snapped her mouth shut, and her eyes grew luminous. "You do?" she asked like she was afraid I'd say no.

So I'd have to tell her a million times a year for the rest of my life. "Yes. I loved you then and was too scared to admit it. But what I feel now blows what I felt then out of the water. I love you, Aggie. And it's terrifying to admit when everyone I loved left me. Mama. Archer. Dad in his own way. You."

"Oh, Ansen. I love you too." Her fingers danced over my jawline. "I've been waiting so long to hear you say that."

"I love you. I love you. I love you. I have a lot of damn time to make up for." And I'd never tire of hearing the phrase slip off her tongue. "You wanted me to say it before I left, didn't you?"

I should've. I should've gone with my instinct, but maybe a small part of me had worried the money would change me. That I would become a millionaire and turn into the guy Aggie and her brothers thought I was back then—a guy out for himself. Or I thought my dream of buying out my old home would override what was in my heart. I'd been as scared of getting the cash as everyone else was of me getting it. Aggie was the most important thing in my life, and money had fucked it up once.

"I just thought . . . " Her pink tongue darted out to lick her lips. "If you said the words, then you were really coming back."

Even a fucking jackass would've picked up on that. "I felt it, Aggie. It's important to me to prove it, and you being down here, ready to come after my stupid ass? It means the world. You mean the world. I love you." I planted my mouth on hers, then pulled away. "I have a brother again. My dad. You. I'd be a fool to give you up, and I'm going to spend my life proving I'm not a fool."

"Your home—"

"Is wherever you are. Not where my memories are. I'm

not buying the ranch I grew up on." My calloused fingers bumped over her smooth skin. "You are my home."

The brown in her eyes went liquid, but worry sparked in the green flecks. "But what will you do?"

The answer popped into my head instantly. If it hadn't been for my single-minded obsession about getting back what I had when I was younger, I'd have seen the answer before. Laughter spilled out of me. Her brows drew together, and I kissed the crease they made. "I'm going to give Lorenzo a call."

Epilogue

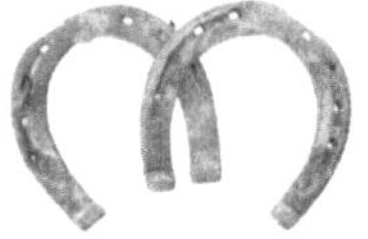

AGGIE

Nerves fluttered through my stomach. I hitched up the hem of my gauzy white skirt and admired my boots, remembering when I did this once long ago. This time, I was in a different state. Different house. Different room. Different dress. Same boots. My dress was a wispy, western-style wedding gown. Loose and casual. Me.

Tex was chewing on a rib bone in the corner, more mellow than he was then.

I had picked the same date. No more getting lost in movies and ice cream on June the second.

Sutton was with me again, but I'd told her to wear whatever was comfortable. She was in a yellow sundress with daisies, her hair in a braid circling her head. Her pacing around my bedroom was different than last time, but the divorce between her and Wilder wasn't complete, and this would be the first time they were together since she'd served him papers.

She was already living in Crocus Valley and starting her own vet practice. Dr. Jake had tried to talk her into joining him, probably in more than one way, but she'd declined, at least with the business—I didn't want to know about the rest. She claimed Knight's Arabians and Cattle Company had dictated her career for too long for her to sign any power over to someone else.

Wilder was talking to me again, as much as he was talking to anyone. After I'd called him, told him the divorce sucked, and while I was Sutton's friend, I was his sister and would never want to see him hurting, he'd grudgingly admitted he wondered if I encouraged her. If he needed to be angry at someone, he should look in the mirror. I hadn't said that. Maybe I should've.

Meg was gone, but I had another sister-in-law supporting me, and she supported *me*, not who she thought I should be. Laney was reclining on the made bed—Ansen's doing—also in a yellow sundress with daisies. She and Sutton had come up with the cohesive look despite my "whatever." Her feet hung off the end and her sandals dangled from her feet, chill. No nerves, which Sutton and I needed.

I'd gotten to know Laney more over the last few months. She was refreshingly down to earth with a blunt edge I appreciated. I would always miss Meg, but Laney's refreshing acceptance of me, however I came, was welcome.

Vienne poked her head in. "Just letting you know every-thing's set, and the kids are good." She gave us an excited thumbs-up before scurrying away.

Laney smirked. "I can't believe she offered to watch the kids so I could stand up for you." Archer was the best man. "Can you have another wedding tomorrow?"

"It's already my second," I joked.

"Technically, the first one didn't happen," Sutton pointed out.

"This one's already better." I searched for my phone to check the time.

"Twenty minutes," Sutton answered for me and pointed to my phone on the dresser behind me. In plain sight.

I was a little nervous. Residual trauma didn't just vanish.

Shaking my hands, I tried to rid myself of my anxiety. I was ecstatic to be marrying the man of my dreams, but I'd be relieved when this day ended drama-free with a set of "I dos."

The delighted screeches of the nieces and nephews drifted in from outside. With Ansen's family, there were as many people as the last time we were going to get married, but this time the guests weren't only my family members or nosy townsfolk. The only people at today's event were family and friends. I didn't need to show off to anyone.

"I can't tell you how proud Allan is to be standing up for Ansen with Archer." Laney grinned. "I told Archer we need to renew our vows so he can be a part of our wedding." She grimaced, looking sheepish. "And Ansen. And the rest of our families. That's what we get for eloping."

"I'm so glad Allan moved to North Dakota." Ansen would've lived with me anyway, but his dad would've weighed on his mind, and our visits to Texas would've always felt too short and infrequent. Ansen's dad lived in the trailer, at first insisting he'd find his own place, but we told him I'd have to sell it and have it hauled out if someone wasn't living there. I didn't need a trailer-house-sized mouse nest on my property.

"He's having such a good time," Laney said. "Archer and I are both so glad he moved. My parents aren't warm and fuzzy, so the kids get a grandparent who can't seem to be around them enough."

I chuckled. Seeing Ansen's dad with the kids made me excited to see him with ours. Allan was like another, slightly more responsible, kid. He'd relocated shortly after Ansen and I returned to Crocus Valley. Archer had helped him sell his home and land, refusing to accept any commission. Working cattle was no longer a job when he got to help Archer—refusing payment. He spent his off time bullshitting with locals, guys he'd grown up with and his siblings at Coal Haven's diner, and getting to know his nieces and nephews and their kids. He adored spoiling his grandkids.

He also spent a ton of time at the rescue. I'd hired him part time—refusing to accept his offer to work for free. The guy was an animal magnet like his son. Horses loved him. The chickens laid more eggs when he was around. Laney bought the ducks to add to her egg business. And he got a kick out of the pigs.

Truth be told, Allan had filled a father figure role for me in the short time he'd been here. He loved listening to my plans, constantly gushing about the house I'd built and what I was doing with the rescue. He told everyone about how he raised two sons and now he gets to have two daughters.

Sutton finally perched on the end of the bed. She waved her finger from my boots to my dress. "Something old, something new. Do you have your something borrowed, something blue?"

"The hair clip is Laney's." My twist was loose and simple, letting several curly strands frame my face. I snapped my fingers, letting the hem of the dress drop. "Oh—the blue bandanna is in the living room." Ansen and I had a little blindfolded fun the other night with my makeshift garter.

Heat swamped my body. We'd have even more fun tonight.

"I can grab it," she offered, but fear was written over her

features. The thought of an awkward run-in with Wilder kept her in place.

Laney was about to get up, but I waved them off. "I got it."

I walked on the balls of my feet to keep from thunking down the hall. As I approached my office, I heard men's voices.

Cody's drifted out. "What you did with the money . . . "

An old chill rushed down my spine, but I slapped it away. No one who wasn't the official presiding over the wedding was getting paid to marry anyone today. We were finally getting the day we should've had back then.

"It's nothing," Ansen said gruffly. "Like you, I didn't want Barns bossing me around after he was gone."

Cody made an agreeing grunt. "Still, donating it to the rescue was something none of us saw coming."

"Because you thought I'd be gone." There was no animosity in Ansen's tone. We'd talked it out, and he'd done the same with my brothers when they learned he planned to donate the entire sum to AKA Rescue.

He'd suggested turning it over to me, insisting what was his was ours, but it didn't feel right when my brothers had to each prance like a show horse for their inheritance. The money was his. Daddy had wanted him to have it. What everyone else thought didn't matter. I had insisted Ansen keep the money. I encouraged him to buy his former home in Texas and hire a manager or even purchase the property across from this place. He'd have land and could start his training business.

He didn't take any of my suggestions. AKA got a giant donation.

I'd been able to quit my job and become the full-time rescue manager. The rescue had millions invested, save for what Ansen kept out to start training horses. This summer and fall, we would fix up the barns and riding rings, and he could take clients. We would delay the honeymoon, but not for the work. Ansen wanted to take me to a beach in the middle of the North Dakota winter.

I turned into the doorway of the office. My brother and Ansen were standing by the desk. A bookshelf with all the books Ansen had repaired was behind them. He'd pieced me back together just like those books.

Cody lifted a brow. "Thought you weren't supposed to see the groom before the wedding."

"We've been through enough bad luck," I said.

Ansen's hot gaze swept down my body, taking in my dress, until he landed on my boots and promise filled his eyes. He'd told me that he'd entertained several fantasies about these boots wrapped around his hips. Naked chores were still a thing.

I was going to make his dreams of the boots a reality tonight. Maybe sooner, in the barn, when we could sneak away.

Instead of the tux he'd worn last time, he was in a crisp white shirt and new black jeans. He was holding his freshly cleaned cowboy hat at his side. The man I was marrying was the Ansen I had first fallen in love with—and the Ansen I'd fallen even harder for.

My brothers weren't dressed much differently, except for Cody in black slacks instead of black denim. Even Wilder looked like the brother I'd grown up with. He was outside with Austen and Eliot, meeting all of Ansen's family.

"I wanted to make sure there were no hard feelings with your future husband," Cody said, smoothing his hand down his shirt. "Since the kids and I are going to be around all summer."

He was convinced the kids would be better off with his in-laws, but I had the idea he could stay in Crocus Valley for the summer to get away from it all for a while. Even if his mind was made up, perhaps they all could use time away while being together. He could work from anywhere, and Buffalo Gully was a short trip away when he needed to return. He was renting a house in town, but the tension across his shoulders was hard enough to stack bricks on. I hoped the experience was a good one and he'd change his mind.

"Naw, man," Ansen said. "We're fine as long as Aggie's good."

Cody lifted his chin toward the door. "You'd better get out there, Barron. I have a bride to escort your way."

Ansen walked out, stopping to drop a quick kiss and a lingering touch on my arm that convinced me I'd find myself wrapped around him in the barn not long after we said our vows. "See you in a few, Aggie baby."

The nerves were gone, replaced only by excitement. I grinned at Cody. He chuckled and shook his head. "I'm proud of you, Aggie. Not because you're marrying some guy." He flashed another quick smile. "I thought Austen was brave when he joined the army, but then you left."

I basked in his pride, but confusion set in. "Mama's money made that possible."

"You would've figured it out. Worked three jobs, financed college, something. You would've left and not come back no matter what."

"I probably would've." Knowing the only option had been to go back to Daddy and get treated like nothing would've kept me away.

"I should've moved somewhere else with Meg, but I wanted to keep the legacy going. For all of us."

Sympathy streamed through me. "Daddy tied your hands with that."

"He did what he did best." The corner of his mouth

tipped up. "Anyway, not to be maudlin, as Meg would say, but I wanted to say I'm proud of you. You got balls, kid."

"I hope you and the others can figure out how to untangle yourselves from the trust without getting cut off."

He shrugged like it wasn't my worry, and in a way, it wasn't.

Sutton and Laney stopped in the hallway. Cody and I followed them out. Archer and Allan were waiting by the sliding door. Two tall, handsome men. Allan grinned, his eyes glistening when he took in his family. Laney took her husband's arm. Archer gave her the same heated look Ansen had given me. Sutton was my matron of honor, but I wanted the married couple to enjoy this together. So they'd walk down together. Allan would be a sturdy support when he led her past Wilder's watchful gaze.

Cody waited next to me until the others marched past the tables and chairs to stand by a tall Ansen. I let my gaze wander over the attendees. A mix of friendly faces smiled back at me.

I couldn't believe we had to come this far and wait this long to get the wedding we wanted.

"I should tell you," Cody murmured under his breath, "this wedding is the talk of the fucking town. They're pretty damn impressed you landed a millionaire, and he gave you all the money."

My grin took over my face. The details were a little inaccurate, but I didn't care. The guy they thought couldn't possibly be into me loved me and treated me better than anyone in my life.

The music started from a Bluetooth speaker, thanks to Vienne and the kids. Grayson waved and grinned at his dad. Cody led me through the guests. Ansen's throat worked as he watched me approach.

My belly fluttered in all the best ways. My dream wedding with my dream man at our home.

When he took my hands, he leaned to whisper into my ear, "Goddamn, you're beautiful."

"You're not so bad yourself, slick."

The rest of the night was a whirl. Well-wishes, a celebratory Fireball shot with Sutton and lawn games. Hours later, I was wrapped in Ansen's arms around a raging firepit with some of the guests. Allan was helping his grandkids roast marshmallows. Laney was cuddled into Archer's lap, much like I was with my new husband. Tex slept on the porch.

The ring that glinted on my finger was the one Ansen had originally proposed to me with. I held my hand out. The flames danced in the simple diamond. "I can't believe you kept our rings."

"Part of me always hoped I could turn back time and make it all right. You made me an honest man, Agatha Christie Barron."

"The change in last name doesn't help."

He chuckled. "So what theme are we going to name our kids after?"

I tipped my face to the side. The planes of his face flickered in the fire. "We need to stay away from the beginning of the alphabet. There are too many *A*s around."

He smiled, his thumb absentmindedly stroking a circle under my sternum. "Maybe my real question is, how soon do we start having kids?"

"If our little tryst in the barn didn't do it?"

His laughter rumbled through my back. "Don't remind me, or we're going right back there, and it won't be so discreet this time."

It hadn't been discreet before. Half the guests had seen us sneaking away, and Vienne and her daughter had kept the kids busy and away from the barn.

I laid my head on his shoulder. "Consider the birth control gone."

His satisfied grunt was only loud enough for me. "Good. We wasted enough time. I want to see you with our kid, Aggie. I want us to give them the life we should've had growing up."

"We will." I tangled my fingers in his. "We have a new future to prepare for."

———

Thanks for reading!

Cody and the kids move to Crocus Valley for the summer, but he might end up needing a little help. Hiring a nanny could be the best thing he's ever done, or he might fall too hard for a woman who's intent on ditching town as soon as the summer's over in A Tarnished Memory.

To get a glimpse of Aggie and Ansen as parents, get a bonus epilogue when you sign up for my newsletter at mariejohn stonwriter.com.

Marie Johnston writes paranormal and contemporary romance and has collected several awards in both genres. Before she was a writer, she was a microbiologist. Depending on the situation, she can be oddly unconcerned about germs or weirdly phobic. She's also a licensed medical technician and has worked as a public health microbiologist and as a lab tech in hospital and clinic labs. Marie's been a volunteer EMT, a college instructor, a security guard, a phlebotomist, a hotel clerk, and a coffee pourer in a bingo hall. All fodder for a writer!! She has four kids, cats, and a half blind Corgie.

mariejohnstonwriter.com

Follow me:

www.ingramcontent.com/pod-product-compliance
Lightning Source LLC
Chambersburg PA
CBHW031325210726

48287CB00005B/1688